Past Lives, Future Lives Revealed

Dr. Bruce Goldberg

New Page Books
A division of The Career Press, Inc.
Franklin Lakes, NJ

PAST LIVES, FUTURE LIVES REVEALED

Cover design by Cheryl Cohan Finbow

Printed in the U.S.A. by Book-mart Press

To order this title, please call toll-free 1-800-CAREER-1 (NJ and Canada: 201-848-0310) to order using VISA or MasterCard, or for further information on books from Career Press.

The Career Press, Inc., 3 Tice Road, PO Box 687,
Franklin Lakes, NJ 07417

www.careerpress.com
www.newpagebooks.com

Goldberg, Bruce, 1948-

Past lives, future lives revealed / by Dr. Bruce Goldberg

p. cm.

Includes bibliographical references and index.

ISBN 1-56414-739-8 (pbk.)

1. Reincarnation therapy. 2. Reincarnation therapy—Case studies.

3. Autogenic training. I. Title.

RC489.R43G643 2004
616.89'14—dc22

2003070221

Dedication

This book is dedicated to my thousands of patients who have been kind enough to share their past and future lives with me, without which this book would not have been possible. In addition, I dedicate this book to the Universal Laws, which, when followed, allow us all to grow and eventually ascend.

Acknowledgments

I would like to thank Michael Lewis, Acquisitions Editor of New Page Books, for his interest and assistance in bringing this book to the public. In addition, my heartfelt gratitude goes out to my editor, Nicole DeFelice. Without her experience and detailed supervision, this book's final form would be quite different. Finally, I cannot express enough appreciation to my typist, Marianne Colasanti, for her tireless efforts and spiritual support.

Contents

Introduction

Throughout this book, I will present cases of my patients who have seen their past and future lives. For those of you who assume a belief in reincarnation places you in the minority, think again. A recent Gallup poll showed that 58 percent of Americans accept the concept of reincarnation.[1]

We will also explore the concept of future lives and detail time travelers from our future who come back in time and interact with us. The concept of fragments of our own soul from past lives (subpersonalities) will be presented along with case histories.

In order for you to experience these fascinating time excursions, I present several hypnotic exercises to guide you backward and forward through time.

There are many patterns we exhibit today that can easily be traced back to prior lifetimes. Obesity is often related to starvation in past lives. Desertion of a family member in centuries past can lead to an overprotective parent today. A fear of water today can result from a past life drowning. In addition, Egyptians cherish cats; a child killed by a bomb in World War II fears loud noises today; a man who was a celibate priest who always prayed for resistance to sexual urges during the Middle Ages is impotent today; and a woman who saw her children die of scarlet fever in the 19th century and swore she would never have another child is barren in the 21st century.

Those examples illustrate some of the principles of karma (cause and effect) and reincarnation. Let us explore this theory in detail with a case of male homosexuality I treated utilizing past life regression through hypnosis.

A male homosexual came to my office with the desire to eliminate his previous sexual behavioral patterns. During a past life in ancient Rome as a female prostitute, he (as a she) very much enjoyed the work of sexually satisfying men.

In another past life in England during the early 1800s, this male patient was again a female. His life was that of a shopkeeper's wife. This was a hard life, as her husband was a cruel man who was selfish in bed and physically abused his wife. Having sex with him was more of "doing her duty." The only solace she had in life was a lesbian relationship with a neighbor. In this life, she learned the pleasures of homosexual love, whereas her heterosexual relationship was completely unsatisfying.

Within two months following therapy, this male patient broke up with his male lover and has since become engaged to a woman. Two years after this case was completed, a follow-up conversation with this patient revealed that he is very happy with his heterosexual relationship, and has had no relapses.

This case is a wonderful example of past life therapy's potential to resolve conflicts about sexuality. It is important to recognize that I did not advocate that this male patient should abandon being a practicing homosexual; the patient's own desire was to alter his sexual behavior patterns.

By exploring two of his past lives as a woman, my patient likely gained several valuable insights about himself with regard to his feelings toward both men and women. But even beyond the issue of sexual preference and gender identity, I believe this case has much to say to us about a soul's desire to experience and advance through various social structures, which was an unspoken subtext to this man's story.

I think we can safely assume that the prostitute's ability to satisfy men sexually, while psychologically empowering to her, was associated with belonging to a taboo social class. By contrast, the English shopkeeper's wife, while likely enjoying the comforts and stature of belonging to a social class of greater prestige, was psychologically powerless in an unhappy marriage to an abusive man. To meet her sexual needs, she became engaged in a lesbian affair, embracing another kind of social taboo.

It would appear that this soul had become well-skilled in the use of sex as the currency of relationships, along with gaining an understanding that women in any social class, be they prostitutes or housewives, are historically less powerful than men. By taking on a male body, this soul may have reasonably expected to continue climbing the ladder of social status that being male guaranteed.

Because this soul had a pattern of living out sexual taboos, it is no surprise that he would, as a man, first adopt a homosexual lifestyle, for which men in our culture have historically suffered social discrimination. Given this soul's steady social progression from lower class (prostitute) to middle class (shopkeeper's wife), it is also logical that he would want to attain the more coveted, respected status of a male head-of-household, which, of course, required forming a heterosexual bond. Ironically, despite this soul's experiences that women have less power than men, only by winning the heart and hand of a woman in this life could he achieve the social bearing it would seem his soul desired. I believe the true test of growth for this transgender soul in his present lifetime is to become the kind of man with whom he, as a former she, may have loved to be in relationship! As a former prostitute and abused housewife, his soul surely knows which pitfalls to avoid.

When my first book *Past Lives—Future Lives* was released in 1982, it made quite an impression in the field, mostly because it was the first book ever written on future life progression. It has since been an international best-seller and published in 10 languages. This has resulted in my being interviewed on hundreds of television and radio stations, including NBC, CBS, CNN, and for *The Washington Post*, *TIME*, *Los Angeles Times*, and programs such as *Oprah*, *Coast to Coast with Art Bell*, and many others.

In 1994, CBS television aired a movie based on my second book, *The Search for Grace*, on which I was the consultant. Subsequently, I have been a consultant to television networks and screenwriters from all over the world.

Past Lives—Future Lives has become a classic book in the field and has led me to conduct more than 35,000 past life progressions and future life progressions on more than 14,000 individuals since 1974. This has resulted in an evolution of my work to include energy healing through a technique I developed known as *superconscience mind tap,* out-of-body experiences, working with UFO abductees, and most importantly, patients who communicate with time travelers from our future.

We will discuss each of these tools throughout this book by way of case histories and transcripts of the actual regressions and progressions involved. The technology of the future and its effects upon our spiritual growth will also be explored. Finally, the true purpose of our incarnation on this planet, namely ascension, will be presented.

The exercises included in this completely updated book will allow you to experience these fascinating techniques of time travel and out-of-body travel, all of which are perfectly safe and have been time-tested for 30 years.

Hypnosis is not a new discipline, and its use can be traced to ancient Egypt. Actually, hypnosis is present in our lives today in the form of advertising, teaching, sales, healthcare, and religion.

Hypnosis is a fascinating subject that has been unjustly surrounded by myths and distortions such as connotations of magic, the supernatural, and the occult. Many movies and novels have contributed to these misconceptions. Since World War II, experimentation and practice have led to rapid advances in our knowledge and techniques spurred on by its widespread acceptance, in 1958, by the American Medical Association.

Hypnosis is being taught to doctors, police officers, lawyers, clergymen, salesmen, athletes, executives, students, and many others who have found it beneficial to their professions. All hypnosis is really self-hypnosis—a state that the subject produces himself with the hypnotist serving only as the guide or the teacher. Anyone who is willing to apply himself can learn this technique.

Hypnosis is a natural and relaxing state of mind that we all enter into for seven hours every day. Daydreams and dreams during our sleep are examples of this phenomenon. Everyone can be hypnotized to some extent. People will, however, vary as to the depth acquired and the length of time required for conditioning. All one needs to experience self-hypnosis is a desire and the application of simple techniques.

Hypnosis is not a medicine or cure. It is a powerful tool that may be used in therapy to assist people in such goals as developing self-confidence, controlling habits, overcoming shyness, relieving insomnia, developing hidden talents, improving memory and concentration, and putting order into your life.

Here is a list of some of the goals that hypnosis can assist you in achieving:

1. Eliminating insomnia.
2. Increasing relaxation and eliminating tension.
3. Increasing and focusing concentration.
4. Improving memory (hypernesia).
5. Improving reflexes.
6. Increasing self-confidence.
7. Controlling pain.
8. Improving sex life.
9. Increasing organization and efficiency.
10. Increasing motivation.
11. Improving interpersonal relationships.
12. Slowing the aging process.

13. Facilitating a better career path.
14. Eliminating anxiety and depression.
15. Overcoming bereavement.
16. Eliminating headaches, including migraines.
17. Eliminating allergies and skin disorders.
18. Strengthening one's immune system to resist diseases.
19. Eliminating habits, phobias, and other negative tendencies (self-defeating sequences).
20. Improving decisiveness.
21. Improving the quality of people, and circumstances in general, that you attract into your life.
22. Increasing your ability to earn and hold onto money.
23. Overcoming obsessive-compulsive behavior.
24. Improving the overall quality of your life.
25. Improving psychic awareness—ESP, meditation, astral projection (out-of-body experience), telepathy, superconscious mind taps, and so on.
26. Eliminating the fear of death by viewing one's past and future lives.
27. Attracting a soul mate into your life.
28. Establishing and maintaining harmony of body, mind, and spirit.

In summarizing hypnosis, we can state:

1. You cannot be hypnotized against your will, and even after a hypnotic state is achieved, you will be able to hear, talk, think, act, or open your eyes at any time.

2. Even a directly proposed hypnotic suggestion cannot make you do anything against your morals, religion, or self-preservation. If such a suggestion were given, you would either refuse to comply or would come out of the trance.
3. The ego cannot be detached in hypnosis, so secrets will not come out while in a trance, and you won't do anything you wouldn't normally do if you felt relaxed about the situation.
4. The best hypnotic subjects are not unintelligent people. The more strong-willed, intelligent, and imaginative you are, the better subject you will probably be.

Most people who inquire about hypnosis are interested in one of the following:

1. Overcoming a problem.
2. Accomplishing an objective.
3. Having an experience.

Hypnosis is certainly no magic wand, but when used correctly, it can give you an edge. It can provide you with a running start and help you open all the necessary doors as you proceed towards achieving your goals.

Note to the Reader

This book is the result of the professional experiences accumulated by the author since 1974, working individually with more than 14,000 patients. The material included herein is intended to complement, not replace, the advice of your own physician, psychotherapist, or other healthcare professional, whom you should always consult about your circumstances before starting or stopping any medication or any other course of treatment, exercise regimen, or diet.

At times, the masculine pronoun has been used as a convenience. It is intended to indicate both male and female genders where this is applicable. All names and identifying references, except those of celebrities, have been altered to protect the privacy of my patients. All other facts are accurate and have not been altered.

—Dr. Bruce Goldberg
Woodland Hills, California

Chapter 1

My Mission

I can trace the origin of my mission to train others in spiritual growth, or as I like to refer to it, psychic empowerment, back to February, 1969. Up until that time (I was 20 years old), I had never had a brush with death.

I was a junior at Southern Connecticut State College in New Haven, Connecticut, majoring in biology with a minor in chemistry. My goal was to enter dental school in the fall of 1970; I had no metaphysical aspirations whatsoever. As my semester break ended, I began to drive back to New Haven from my parents' home in East Meadow, Long Island.

As fate would have it, a severe snowstorm ensued. Being excited about starting a new semester, I ignored my parents' insistence that I postpone my departure until the weather subsided. The storm worsened as I approached the Bronx. My car simply drifted into a pile of snow and I was stranded.

There were no cars on the highway and I knew I had to seek shelter. As I got out of the car, I tried unsuccessfully to free my car from the snow and drive to some safety. My gloves, pants, and jacket became wet and I began to experience severe chills.

I wandered across the highway and noticed absolutely no cars (police, taxis, etc.) out. It is impossible for me to estimate how long I traveled, but I knew I was in trouble and would die of exposure if I didn't find shelter soon.

Suddenly, a woman's soft voice entered my mind and instructed me to walk at a 45-degree angle from my current path. I did so and soon came upon a neon sign that read "Tardis" (not the well-known New York restaurant Sardis).

This Tardis establishment was a catering company and the only open building in sight. I entered the building and my life was literally saved by that alluring female voice. The Tardis employee allowed me to warm up for a few hours, provided me coffee, and one of their employees drove me to a subway station, as the snowstorm had eased. I then obtained a motel room for the night and took a train to New Haven the following day. My parents returned my car to me a week or so later.

The next phase of my mission occurred in 1972 during the summer following my sophomore year in dental school at the University of Maryland. Up until that time, I still had no metaphysical aspirations or interest. My life was dedicated to studying dentistry and not much else, as I had little money and had to work my way through school.

One Saturday afternoon, I heard that same voice I encountered in 1969 and was instructed to go to a local bookstore in downtown Baltimore. At first I rejected the idea, but decided I had little to lose. This bookstore was a New Age one, and shortly after I entered it, a tall, young beautiful woman with long blond hair and piercing blue eyes approached me.

As she spoke to me, I instantly recognized her voice as the one I heard a just few minutes before. She was dressed in a white gown and appeared as a Greek goddess. The only thing she said to me was, "I think you will find this book both interesting and profound to your life's work." After handing me a book, she dematerialized right before my very eyes!

The book that she gave me was Morey Bernstein's *The Search for Bridey Murphy.*[1] This nonfiction book described a documented case of reincarnation that resulted from Morey Bernstein's (a Colorado businessman) hypnotic regression of a housewife named Virginia Tighe into a 19th century past life in Cork, Ireland as one Bridey Murphy.

This book stimulated me to delve more into metaphysics and parapsychology. I immediately began reading books on astrology, numerology, tarot, reincarnation, and the like. It was at this time that I decided to learn hypnosis and use it in my future career for pain control and dental fears, which I did throughout my 13 years of dental practice.

I also decided to experiment with hypnotic past life regression and see if I could elicit past lives from people. By 1974, I had established a part-time hypnotherapy practice and began doing past life regressions. Later that year, following my graduation from dental school, I moved to Florida to begin a general practice residency.

It was in Tallahassee that my professional life took a fortuitous change. One of my patients regressed into several lives and reported many verifiable details. That wasn't as significant as the fact that she overcame two habits (bulimia and smoking) and a water phobia as a result of these sessions. At no time did I give her therapeutic suggestions to do anything but explore a past life. This demonstrated to me the unlimited potential of past life therapy.

By 1976, I had moved back to Baltimore to begin my practice of dentistry (full time) and past life regression hypnotherapy (part time). One fateful day in 1977, I asked a patient to go *to* the origin of her problem, not back to the cause. Instead of regressing to a prior life, she moved *forward* (progressed) to the 23rd century! This was the beginning of my discovery and development of future life progression hypnotherapy, which is documented in my first book *Past Lives—Future Lives*,[2] and is the first book ever written on future life progression.

Experimentation with more than 500 patients established that it was not the data from past or future lives that resulted in *permanent* changes in people's lives, but rather communication with their Higher Self or superconscious mind (the perfect component of our subconscious mind or soul that originally came from the God energy complex).

This led me to develop my now famous superconscious mind tap technique (or cleansing), which consists of introducing the patient's subconscious mind (soul) to its Higher Self. The Higher Self can now train the individual to allow the perfect energy of the Higher Self to effect a raising of the quality of the soul's energy (frequency vibrational rate) during the dream (REM) cycle. We are all out of the body and have access to our Higher Self without the distraction of our defense mechanisms (rationalization, intellectualization, displacement, sublimation, etc.) during our dream state.

The discovery of the superconscious mind tap truly revolutionized my practice and hopefully the entire field. By 1978, my dental practice became my part-time profession, and hypnotherapy was my full-time calling.

Throughout the years, I have had dreams and other manifestations of this woman, whom I assume was a spirit guide. I relocated my hypnotherapy office to Los Angeles and retired from dentistry in 1989. In July of 1999, I finally discovered who this entity is. Her name is Nemil and she is a time traveler ("chrononaut") from the 35th century when teleportation is mastered for time traveling back and forward through time.

Time travelers use names that represent their missions. Nemil is an acronym made from "millennium" and her mission is to assist those individuals who will assist the spiritual growth of our planet. I am only one of many people she works with.

Nemil knows Traksa, the time traveler from the 36th century that is pictured in my book *Time Travelers from Our Future*[3] and on my Website. I have had much communication with him. There is most definitely a consciousness shift coming and these chrononauts are here to guide us through it to a more positive future.

Superconscious Mind Tap

A superconscious mind tap is the process through which I as a hypnotherapist introduce the patient's subconscious mind to its superconscious or Higher Self. This superconscious mind level is perfect and thus, accessing or tapping into this level results in a raising of the energy level of the patient's subconscious mind. Therapy is accomplished through tapping into this superconscious mind. Another term for a superconscious mind tap is *cleansing*.

The first step in hypnotherapy is to improve this self-image. If you build a house on quicksand, it won't be around to benefit from appreciation. I highly recommend the use of cassette tapes to help establish a sound and strong psychological foundation from which patients can more fully understand their karmic purpose and make strides toward fulfilling their karma.

Most of a patient's therapy will take effect during the dream level at night. Recent medical research establishes that we enter REM (rapid eye movement), a characteristic of the dream state, for three hours each night. Because our defense mechanisms (willpower or analytical mind) cannot function once we enter the sleep cycle, this is a most efficient cleansing opportunity.[4] Our brain waves now appears as alpha waves. During this dream state, the emotional cleansing necessary for our survival occurs, but deeper energy cleansing is not part of this survival function. It will not occur unless we are trained for it. If we are properly trained, we will use approximately one hour of the REM cycle to cleanse our alpha level. Because each minute in hypnosis is equivalent to three of our earth minutes, three to four hours of therapeutic energy cleansing is actually experienced by the patient. It is no wonder that this therapy is so short, successful, and popular. The patient is trained in relatively few sessions to be totally independent of the therapist and to attain any goal that is humanly possible. The patient uses superconscious mind cassette tapes to assist in this goal.

There are three levels of manifestation of an issue. First, there is the physical level. Using depression as an example, the associated lack of energy and malaise are examples of the physical level. Next is the emotional level. In this example, unexplained crying would be a symptom of this level. The last and most important level is the energy level. This level is the actual frequency vibrational rate of the patient's alpha level or subconscious mind. In other words, this is the level of spiritual growth or karmic status of the individual. The energy level controls the emotional level, which in turn influences the physical level. Thus, the only level I am concerned with when I conduct a hypnotherapy session is the energy level. Once we raise the patient's frequency vibrational rate to a new threshold—a major breakthrough—this new level or rate is established and irreversible. The patient may plateau for a while, but this new rate cannot be lowered. Thus, the emotional and physical symptoms, as well as the causes, are resolved by treating the ultimate cause, which is the patient's energy level or frequency vibrational rate.

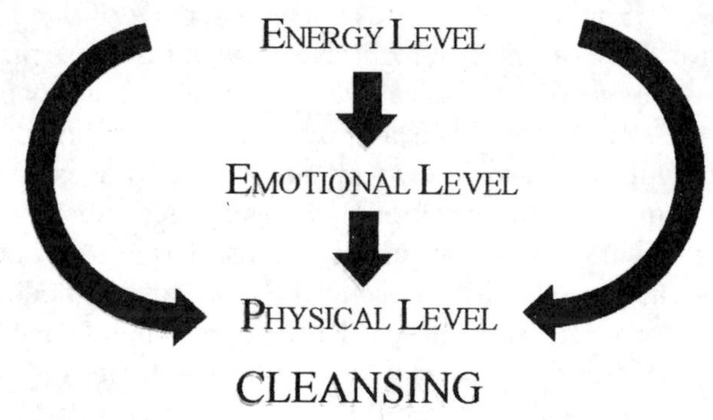

Figure 1

You will note that the arrows always flow down from the energy level to the physical, but not in reverse; also observe that the energy level can change the physical level directly without having to use the emotional level as an intermediary. An example of this latter phenomenon would be the removal of psychosomatic pain or a headache.

How does past life regression, age progression, or future life progression fit into this approach? The answer is simple. These techniques are used as stepping stones to reach the superconscious mind and to satisfy the patient's curiosity.

These techniques, taken together, account for approximately 5 percent of the therapy; 95 percent of any therapeutic result will come from cleansing at the superconscious level.

This cleansing will also greatly reduce the time and number of sessions required to train patients to resolve their conflicts and maximize their potential. Thus, it is not necessary to explore past or future lives for this therapy to work. Because this is not cognitive or analytical therapy, I am not particularly interested in the intellectual "cause" of the issue. In this type of therapy, process is everything. The whys are not important. All that is necessary is that the patient must be motivated to attain a goal, that goal must be possible to attain, and the patient must trust the therapist. As long as these three conditions are met, any goal is achievable.

Throughout the therapeutic process, a patient will experience good days and bad days. The bad days are actually more therapeutic, because during these days, the energy needed by the conscious mind in order to interfere with the therapy is drained, so the defense mechanism is disengaged. The purpose of our defense mechanisms (rationalization, intellectualization, displacement, etc.) is to keep our behavior the same. To this end, they will do anything to disrupt change. Fortunately, the defense mechanisms' energy supply is limited. Every time they exert themselves, they are literally burning themselves out. Good days do not result in a direct drain to the defense mechanisms, but do indirectly sap their energy. By raising one's energy level (frequency vibrational rate), as a result of these good days, the defense mechanisms must expend even more energy in their attempt to reverse this therapeutic progress. Because our subconscious mind has an unlimited energy supply (by accessing the superconscious mind), it will always win in the end.

Chapter 2

The Big Picture

So you say you don't believe you have lived in a past life? Well, lie back, get comfortable and close your eyes while I count slowly from 10...9...8...7....

Just mention hypnosis and most people have visions of falling into deep trance that leave them completely helpless. Of course, they are in the hands of a hypnotist who wields total control and can make them do *anything* he wants them to.

If that is what you think hypnosis is, you're about to be enlightened.

Actually, you hypnotize yourself every day. The average person slips into an alpha trance or hypnotic state from three to six hours a day. You probably call it a daydream, lost in your thoughts, or becoming engrossed in a television show or movie. Another name for hypnosis is deep relaxation, which is all that this process entails. While in hypnosis, you are aware of all that is happening around you and won't or can't be forced to do anything you don't want to do.

All you are doing is bypassing your conscious mind and allowing your subconscious to come through. Your subconscious is a vast storehouse of information and abilities and is supposed to include details about your present, past, and future life experiences.

To get an idea of how regression works, sit back for a moment and reflect back on your childhood. Like most people, your mind will skip from significant event to significant event. You're regressing. While it is not as accurate or deep as hypnotic regression, it's basically the same idea.

Your future lives are not necessarily better than the one you're living now. The pathway to perfection is full of ruts and holes, it seems. Many people think they spent their past lives as kings, queens, and clerics. Fact is, the average person has had 1,000 or more lives and they can be, to put it kindly, *varied*. You would probably find that you've been a little bit of everything you wanted, or didn't want to be.

I believe we are basically energy, tuned to a particular wavelength, so to speak. That energy, or the soul, leaves the body at the point of death and goes on to what we'll call the soul plane. It is there that you evaluate your life and become acclimated to your new existence with the help of spirit guides and our Higher Self (the perfect component of our soul).

On this "other side," there is no time or space. This is where you choose your next life, including where, when, and how you will be born, who your parents, relatives, and friends will be, and the major events in your life.

All of this is designed for you to learn lessons or to change your karmic cycle, which simply means, "what you sow, ye shall reap." The positive and negative things you do in this life will be carried over and karmic debts paid or received according to your own plan.

Because there is no time or space on the other side, it is possible to incarnate at different times in our sense of history past, present, or future. The objective of reincarnation is simply to learn in this school called Earth. And you choose the time and place to best learn your lessons.

Our Earthly series of lifetimes is certainly not the ultimate reality, but one of several possibilities. It is our mind, or consciousness, that continues through each one of our incarnations. It contains the memories of all of our past, present, and future lifetimes, through accessing something known as the Akashic records. These records are fifth dimensional charts on our reincarnation or karmic cycle. We are in reality, energy. As such, we cannot be destroyed. We cannot die. We simply appear to change bodies every 75 years or so.

Skeptics, especially those who pride themselves on their rationalism, must come to terms with the fact that quantum physics and superstring theory are now accepted scientific paradigms. Concepts formerly ridiculed as "metaphysical"—multidimensionality, simultaneity, even reincarnation and karma—now have a scientific foundation.

Karma

The basic law of karma has come to mean action and reaction, or cause and effect. Any action that is considered harmful or evil to the well-being of another is recompensed exactly in proportion to the harm done. The reverse also applies.

One of the basic principles of karma is that every soul (entity) has free will. There is always freedom of choice. Each soul is drawn to parents who can provide the biological heredity and physical environment needed to learn karmic lessons. Psychic genetics is more important than biological genetics in determining the character of our lives. In addition, all lessons and deeds are recorded in the entity's Akashic records, which are used to determine each new lifetime. These records, as I previously stated, are the sum total of our past, present, and future lives, and are accessible through our superconscious mind (Higher Self).

If you are unhappy about your life, your financial situation, your relationships, or your health, for example, then you must realize that a cause exists. These causes can be traced back to past lives. Your subconscious mind retains all of these causes because it has a perfect memory bank. The subconscious mind also survives death, so that a new life means merely exchanging one body for another. You have the same subconscious, only now it has learned some lessons, and hopefully, grown spiritually.

All of the things you have or have not done in this and all of your past lives will generate certain effects in this life as well as in future lifetimes. The laws of karma are perfectly just. The soul always has free will. Karma can bring you happiness or sadness, depending on the effects you have earned and the paths you have chosen to take. It is not the purpose of karma to reward or punish. Its purpose is to educate the subconscious, and to purify it. Once the subconscious is purified, it no longer needs karma, or the "karmic cycle," as we refer to it. The result is ascension and a return to God.

If, however, we react to certain tests in our lives negatively (with hatred, revenge, jealousy, pettiness, or some other negative emotion), then we have not learned our lesson, but have failed the test and will have to retake it in either this or a future lifetime.

Free Will

Because the soul always has free will, it is our decision to be born at a certain time and place. It is our decision to choose our parents, friends, lovers, and enemies. We cannot blame other people or a bad childhood or marriage for our present problems. We are directly responsible for our lives because we have chosen the environment.

The Next 1,000 Years

The information presented here is the result of several thousand hypnotic future life progressions conducted on individual patients since I discovered this technique in 1977. What I am about to report represents only one frequency, or parallel universe. This means that you may not actually experience this future if you are on a different frequency. I refer you to my books *Time Travelers from Our Future* and *Custom Design Your Own Destiny* for an in-depth discussion of these parallel universes.

No significant earthquakes causing massive loss of life will occur until the year 2050. In that year Los Angeles, San Francisco, and New York will suffer devastating property damage mostly, with few people dying as a result. Absolutely no nuclear wars will take place until the 24th century.

During the 21st century, world peace will finally become a reality. Peace lasts for 300 years. The Earth will undergo geographic changes; scientific progress will be most evident. Hunger, greed, jealousy, prejudice, and other negative aspects of society seem to have been almost entirely eliminated by the end of the 21st century.

Solar power will be incorporated into everyday life in the 22nd century. The lifespan of the average adult will be increased to more than 90 years. Cancer and AIDS are finally cured.

The 23rd century will be characterized by noiseless and efficient transportation. Nuclear power is used extensively and is safe and clean. Experiments in weather control are a top priority. The average lifespan is now more than 110 years. Politically, the Earth is democratic with two major groups. One is called the Western Federation of Nations and is composed of North America, South America, Europe, Africa, and the Middle East. The Eastern Alliance is the other group, and is made up of Russia, China, India, Japan, Southeast Asia, New Zealand, and Australia.

A small-scale nuclear war occurs in the 24th century. Further geographic changes take place on the Earth's surface, and the League of One is the democratic form of government for the entire planet, replacing the Western Federation and the Eastern Alliance. Cold fusion and other free energy sources are now in use.

It is during the 25th century that we finally control the weather. Androids are used to perform all menial tasks.

Underwater cities, genetic engineering, and interplanetary travel dominate the 26th century. We will have regular contact with extraterrestrials. Information pills will keep citizens well informed. The lifespan is increased to more than 215 years. Sickness and disease are almost unknown.

During the 28th century, the League of One is replaced by the Atlantic and Pacific Federations. These groups are also democratic, and are composed of the same nations that were a part of the old Western Federation and Eastern Alliance. There are no wars.

This paradigm remains relatively stable through the beginning of the 31st century, when we finally master time travel. At this time, time travelers from our future begin to go back in time to not only the 20th century, but all the way back to millions of years into prehistory to supervise both our evolution and spiritual growth.

Some examples of the technology of the next 1,000 years are:

- Anti-gravity amusement parks (like Disneyland) that float several thousand feet above the Earth. A force field protects people from falling off the edge.
- A food simulator that creates any meal you desire from your thoughts alone.
- An *alpha syncolarium* device that looks like an isolation tank. By sending energy signals through the body, along with sounds, the body is distressed and our DHEA production by the adrenal glands and gonads are accelerated so that our life spans may be increased to 900 years.
- Holographic relaxation centers equivalent to the *holodeck* in *Star Trek*.
- Virtual reality techniques are applied to a small room to make it appear vast in size.
- Objects can be shrunk in size for storage and later enlarged back to their original configuration.

- Each home and office contains a teleportation station so there is no need for vehicles of any kind for short trips.
- Ships are still used to transport large groups of people for long distances, but these vehicles are piloted by thought.

Chapter 3

A Past Life in the Amazon

Before I begin depicting past and future lives of some of my patients, a discussion of how they receive this data is important. Very few people receive visual images accompanied by a tremendous amount of data or emotions. Most people receive information followed by a cloudy impression or sense of an environment.

In my book *Past Lives—Future Lives*[1], I described the five ways of receiving past life data.

Many people are curious about what they will experience in a past life regression. There are many possible experiences.

1. You may see a scene and at the same time. Be aware of information related to this scene. I refer to this as both an audio and visual experience and it results in excellent data. It's as if you are watching a movie or television show.
2. You may see cloudy or quick impressions that tend to disappear just as you are about to understand them.
3. You may appear to "know"or be aware of the environment without actually seeing or hearing anything.
4. You may feel as if someone is whispering in your ear.

5. Reading words that appear before your inner eyes is a very rare type of experience, although this may be how some people know what the data is or what country they are living in.

Ann was a 40-year-old divorced nurse when she came to my Los Angeles office in 1997. Her problem was sexual dysfunction and it began during her 12-year marriage to her now ex-husband, Fred. Fred was a former professional football player and was not very tender in bed. He was generally cruel and vulgar to Ann.

Her recent relationships had been sexually frustrating and all ended prematurely, mostly due to this unresolved issue. Ann wanted help and was curious to see how a former life might fit into her current problem.

We begin Ann's past life exploration with this most interesting and relevant life in the Amazon.

Dr. G.: Where do you find yourself?

Ann: I am by a river, a very long river.

Dr. G.: Are you a male or female?

Ann: I am a young girl.

Dr. G.: What is your name?

Ann: Fawa. My name is Fawa.

Fawa was a young teenage girl living in Brazil near the Amazon River. She described her people as a tribe that spent most of their time in the jungle hunting and gathering. This jungle girl lived with her parents and was an only child. Their village was very small and was lead by their Chief, Sagu.

Dr. G.: Tell me about your Chief.

Ann: He is a tall and strong man, but I am afraid of him.

Dr. G.: What is it about him that you fear?

Ann.: He is very mean and when he makes a bad decision he takes it out on others, including my father.

Dr. G.: Is Sagu mean to you?

Ann: No. He is nice to women. He has many women.

Sagu was quite a character. According to Fawa, he was a poor Chief who often made improper tribal decisions. Might was more important than intelligence or good judgment in Fawa's tribe. Sagu obtained his position as Chief by successfully challenging and killing his predecessor. One of his many fringe benefits as Chief was a pick of any woman in the tribe at any time.

It didn't matter if they were married or very young; he could do whatever he wanted. The only way to change the leader was by death, either natural, accidental, or as a result of a successful challenge by one of the men.

Sagu was the biggest and strongest, so he didn't have much to worry about. However, he was quite insecure and paranoid and had to constantly justify his actions and blame all of his errors on others or the Gods.

Dr. G.: Fawa, has Sagu forced himself on you sexually? Is that why he frightens you?

Ann: No, he hasn't done that to me. He thinks I'm too ugly. He is just so mean to the men that I feel very uncomfortable in his presence.

Fawa did her best to keep away from Sagu. She did her chores, helped prepare the food, and assisted with the caring of the younger children. There was plenty of food, but the one persistent problem they faced was attacks by neighboring tribes. Apparently, there was no comraderie between the various tribes, and these attacks were common.

Fawa's father was not a fan of Sagu. For one thing, he didn't like the fact that the Chief slept with his wife whenever he chose. For another, he disagreed with most of Sagu's decisions. It seemed that Sagu just wasn't very bright, but all the men were afraid of him because of his size.

Dr. G.: Is Sagu that much larger than the other men?

Ann: It's not that he is that much larger, it's more like he is more savage. He is stronger than the others but he just likes to hurt people and killing gives him pleasure.

Fawa went on to describe how Sagu took particular pleasure in killing an invading warrior. It was as if he just couldn't wait for a fight so he could kill someone. Sagu did not believe in taking prisoners. He did believe in killing.

The Chief had never been wounded in battle. He was a skillful warrior and, although hated by his people, they needed him for protection.

Such was the environment Fawa found herself in as I questioned her further.

Dr. G.: Fawa, do you have a boy that you like?

Ann: Yes, I like Moke.

Dr. G.: What does Moke think of the Chief?

Ann: Like everyone else, he hates Sagu. Sagu killed Moke's father when his father challenged Sagu for leadership.

Moke thus had a special axe to grind with Sagu. Any man at any time could challenge Sagu for the privilege of leading the tribe. The only problem was that it consisted of a fight to the death and Sagu was by far the most skillful fighter in the tribe.

I progressed Fawa forward to a significant event in her life. She is now 18 and some things have changed.

Dr. G.: What is going on at this time Fawa?

Ann: It's Sagu. Yesterday I was summoned to his hut. He took me.

Dr. G.: Do you mean he had sex with you?

Ann: Yes, and he was not gentle. He hurt me and laughed at me.

Dr. G.: I'm sorry to hear that. Didn't you say he always thought that you were ugly?

Ann: That was before. I've grown now and Moke tells me I'm beautiful. Sagu thought so too. He is an animal.

Dr. G.: What can you do about that?

Ann: My father is very angry. He never liked Sagu being with my mother, but now that he has had his way with me, I'm afraid.

Dr. G.: What is your father going to do?

Ann: He is going to challenge Sagu to a fight to the death. I know my father loves me but he cannot win. Sagu will kill him.

The challenge was made official. Fawa's father prepared himself for the battle as best he could. He was a fine warrior, but Sagu was the best. Fawa's father fought bravely, but Sagu bested him and slit his throat.

Dr. G.: What is happening now?

Ann: I can't look. My father is dead. I hate Sagu. I wish I were a man so I could challenge him.

Moke consoled Fawa while this happened. He was very supportive and loved her dearly.

Dr. G.: What did Sagu do after his victory?

Ann: He had my mother killed. Just like that he performed a ceremony in which poisonous snakes were placed by my mother. They bit her and she died a horrible death.

Dr. G.: How can he do that?

Ann: Sagu can do anything he wants. When a Chief successfully defeats a challenger, he can celebrate anyway he can. I'm lucky he didn't have me killed.

Dr. G.: Why did he spare you?

Ann: He wants me physically again. He is an animal and I don't know what I'm going to do. If it weren't for Moke, I think I would drown myself in the big river.

Fawa was in a precarious situation. Moke was, indeed, her only saving grace. I learned from Fawa that Moke was a bright native. He was not quite fully grown, but was a natural warrior. Moke shared Fawa's disdain for Sagu but there wasn't much he could do about it at the time.

Dr. G.: Do you and Moke plan to wed?

Ann: Yes. I love him and we will wed soon. I am worried.

Dr. G.: About what?

Ann: Moke hates Sagu almost as much as I do. He tells me that someday he will challenge him and I know he will be killed by Sagu if he does.

Dr. G.: How does Sagu feel about Moke?

Ann: Sagu tries to make fun of Moke any chance he gets.

It seemed Sagu was jealous of Moke's intelligence. Sagu was all brute strength. He made poor decisions and noted how bright and quick Moke was. Moke was popular with the tribe and helped plan certain strategies that greatly benefited Fawa's people.

Sagu couldn't just throw Moke out of the tribe without causing many problems. He could, however, embarrass Moke at any chance he got, which was often.

As time passed, Fawa and Moke were wed. Sagu appeared to lose interest in Fawa and entertained himself with the other women in the tribe.

Dr. G.: How is married life treating you?

Ann: It's wonderful. Moke is a good provider and always so considerate to my needs.

Dr. G.: And the tribe?

Ann: Well, Moke has designed some new weapons that allow the men to hunt better. Moke is always thinking about ways to improve our life.

Dr. G.: How do the others respond to his efforts?

Ann: Oh, everybody likes him. They are amazed at his ability to do things.

Dr. G.: And Sagu?

Ann: Well, that's another matter. Sagu is threatened by anyone who can do things he can't, like think. He has little choice but to accept Moke's inventions only because they work and everyone in the tribe realizes their usefulness.

Dr. G.: Please continue.

Ann: Sagu takes every opportunity he can to put Moke down. There is nobody else in the tribe that does the things my Moke can do.

It became obvious that a dangerous pattern was emerging. Moke was a bright and inventive young adult. His ideas were popular with the rest of his people. In fact, Moke himself was very well liked.

If circumstances were different Moke would easily have been elected tribal Chief. Even though he was young, he was far superior to everyone else in the tribe.

Sagu's insecurity and jealousy of Moke made the Chief even more neurotic. He couldn't just kill or ostracize Moke without initiating a rebellion among his people. This tribe was small, but there were enough men present to remove Sagu if he was foolish enough to attempt such an act.

Fawa understood this situation all too well. She supported Moke in his actions and noted the conflict between Sagu's totalitarian rule and the will of the people.

Dr. G.: Do the other men in the tribe share your feelings about Moke being the new Chief?

Ann: Yes, they do. The problem is, even Moke with all his cunning just could never beat Sagu in a challenge. There is no exception to the rule of challenge. For Moke to be our Chief, he must kill Sagu in a battle.

Dr. G.: What does Moke say about this?

Ann: My Moke is very wise for his years. He tries not to get emotional about his problem, but he does want to challenge Sagu.

Dr. G.: How do you feel about this?

Ann: I don't want him to die. My feelings are known to him and he assures me he will do nothing about it now, but will wait for the proper time.

Dr. G.: How can he possibly beat Sagu?

Ann: Moke is working it out. He is strong and spends some extra time every day adding to his strength. He is a planner and I know if anyone can do it, he can.

Fawa had complete confidence in Moke. She knew it was a nearly impossible task. What is interesting to note about Moke's extra preparation was that it was similar to a 20th-century boxer working out—running, exercising—to get into condition for a big fight.

It was impossible to establish a date for this life, but it was most definitely a primitive one. There were no technologically advanced civilizations here.

I progressed Fawa forward to an important event in her life.

Dr. G.: What has happened since I last spoke to you?

Ann: I'm with child and I am so happy.

Dr. G.: I'm happy for you too, Fawa. How does Moke feel about your pregnancy?

Ann: Moke is wonderful. He is looking forward to the baby and wants to have more children.

Dr. G.: I know this is a difficult and delicate matter, but what about Sagu? Has he been with you since the time you told me about?

Ann: No.

I moved Fawa ahead in time.

Dr. G.: What is happening at this time?

Ann: I'm so angry.

Dr. G.: What is it?

Ann: It's Sagu. He almost got us all killed with his latest decision.

Dr. G.: What was that?

Ann: Most of the men are in the jungle hunting. One of the scouts saw a tribe moving very far away from them. This was a tribe that we have faced before in battle. They are mean and like to fight.

Dr. G.: Please continue.

Ann: Sagu could easily have ignored them because they were too far away and didn't notice our people.

Dr. G.: What did Sagu do?

Ann: He decided he wanted to fight. It has been a while since he was in battle so he decided to do some killing.

Dr. G.: What happened next?

Ann: Sagu and the other warriors then followed this tribe of men and they started fighting.

Dr. G.: Please continue.

Ann: We were outnumbered. Sagu didn't think that was important. Some our best men were killed in this battle.

Dr. G.: What about Moke?

Ann: Moke survived. He was wounded, but he will be all right.

Dr. G.: And Sagu?

Ann: Our Chief escaped this battle without so much as a cut. He killed a number of their men and was the main reason they ran away.

So Sagu did his thing again. He did not carefully weigh the situation but ordered this attack just to satisfy his own selfish needs.

Moke's wound healed, and a number of months later, Fawa gave birth to a son.

Dr. G.: How is your baby?

Ann: He is fine. I can tell he will be smart just like his father.

Dr. G.: How is Moke doing?

Ann: He is doing well. His pride of our son is known to all. Moke will make a good father.

Dr. G.: How did Moke feel about that last encounter in the jungle with the war-like tribe?

Ann: That is something else. Ever since that time, he has been trying to devise a plan that would allow him to beat Sagu.

Dr. G.: Does he talk to you about it?

Ann: Yes, very much. I try to talk him out of this idea, but it's no use. He says he wants to raise our son in a better way than following the ways of Sagu.

Dr. G.: How can he beat Sagu?

Ann: That's just it. I don't know. He is giving it a lot of thought and I know he will come up with something. I just pray to our Gods that it will work. I just don't know what I would do if I lost him. We need him. I need him.

Moke went off into the jungle every now and then by himself. This was not unusual, so it did not attract suspicion. The only person Moke had to worry about was Sagu. Even if his neighbors knew what he was up to, they would never tell Sagu.

Fawa was the only person Moke told about his plan.

Dr. G.: What is this plan?

Ann: Moke is so smart. When he goes into the jungle he stays in one spot for hours. What he is doing is setting a trap for Sagu.

Dr. G.: What exactly is this trap?

Ann: I don't know all the details but he is digging a hole and putting wooden stakes that are very sharp at the bottom of this hole. He wants to make it so Sagu will fall into this trap.

Dr. G.: But how does he know that Sagu will agree to fight him in this spot?

Ann: That's easy. The one who challenges the Chief chooses where the fight will take place.

Dr. G.: But how does he know that he could position Sagu to fall into this trap? If he can't, won't he be killed in battle?

Ann: Yes. I do not know the answer to that. He won't even tell me those details.

So the plan was being finalized. Moke met secretly with some of the other men to work out the details. Sagu had no loyal subjects. He had no spies. The other men hated him, but were deathly afraid of him also. There was no way this plan was going to find its way back to Sagu.

While all of this was going on, Sagu is enjoying himself. He sleeps with the wives and daughters of his fellow tribesmen and acts in his usual arrogant way.

Moke and his friends were ready, so the next step was to formally make the challenge.

Dr. G.: What happened next?

Ann: Moke challenged Sagu and the Chief just laughed at him.

Dr. G.: Did Sagu accept this challenge?

Ann: Yes, he had to.

Dr. G.: How do you feel about what Moke is about to do?

Ann: I don't like it. Of course, I am worried about him but something tells me that it's going to work out. I will pray to the Gods for Moke's victory.

A few days later, the battle of his life and death began. Because Moke was the challenger, he chose the weapons. Sagu was surprised the only weapon allowed was a long pole. This was definitely not Sagu's style, but he didn't care.

Sagu tried to unnerve Moke on this fateful morning by bragging how fast he would disarm him and then beat him to death. The problem that worried everyone was just that. Moke didn't stand a chance with besting Sagu by hand-to-hand combat. His plan had to work.

When they began, everyone in the tribe relocated to the clearing in the jungle that Moke chose.

Dr. G.: Was Sagu suspicious of the spot selected?

Ann: No. He was just ready to kill my Moke.

Dr. G.: Tell me what happened next?

Ann: They stood facing each other in the clearing. Moke positioned himself in a certain spot and two men brought the poles for each of them.

Dr. G.: Go on.

Ann: When they were ready, a strange sound, like a large animal was heard. Moke looked in that direction and he froze.

Dr. G.: Please continue.

Ann: The other men looked in the same direction and as soon as Sagu (whose back was to the sound) turned to see what the source of the sound was, Moke picked up the pole and lunged forward. Sagu fell back a few steps and the grass opened up and all I heard was a horrible scream.

Moke constructed some kind of horn and when used in a certain way it made an animal sound that was quite loud. One of the men in the tribe made this sound when Moke gave him a certain signal.

That momentary distraction as Sagu turned around was all that Moke needed to execute his plan. When Sagu fell into the pit he was instantly killed by the wooden stakes. Moke became Chief and Fawa had a happy ending to their past life.

From the superconscious, I discovered that Moke is a man named Paul, who Ann wasn't aware of when this regression was conducted. Sagu was Fred, as I suspected. The superconscious mind is the perfect part of our soul's energy. By accessing the superconscious, a patient can find out if an individual from a past life is someone the patient knows, or has known. I call this *karmic scripting*. It can also allude to future relationships.

Within four months after this regression, Ann met a man named Paul and began a rather fulfilling relationship with him. Her sexual dysfunction disappeared and never returned. She described him as brilliant and classy.

Another aspect of Ann's past life as Fawa that impressed me was the ingenuity of Moke (Paul). He was smart enough to overcome tremendous odds to defeat Sagu and assist his tribe in their future endeavors with competent leadership.

One final point to mention deals with the violence and sexual components of Fawa's life. When a patient explores the origin of a difficulty or past life ties with someone who mistreated them, such negative scenarios are to be expected. We will see this pattern repeated several times throughout this book.

Chapter 4

A Documented Case of Reincarnation

My second book, *The Search for Grace*[1], deals with a documented case of reincarnation. It traces the past life relationship a woman had with a man who murdered her in 20 of 46 past lives that we explored! *The Search for Grace* (1994) has also been featured as the "CBS Movie of the Week." I had the pleasure of being the consultant on this film.

The Search for Grace illustrates some of the many therapeutic benefits of past life hypnotherapy through one particular patient, Ivy.

Ivy was a trained scientist and a very intelligent woman. The idea that she had lived before fascinated her. She showed no interest in either age progression or future life progression. She had no prior interest in history, but to return to a point in history and have historical support that she was there made the idea of regression very exciting to her.

All of the instructions to Ivy prior to regressing her were designed to have her choose a past life that would explain and remove the difficulties surrounding her current relationships: her relationship with John, a man who had literally tried to kill Ivy on three previous occasions; and Dave, a man whose company she enjoyed, and with whom she wanted to continue her relationship.

In this chapter, we will explore one of Ivy's past lives with John that was not depicted in my book. Fortunately, she was able to overcome her obsession with John and resolved this issue.

Ivy did relate her last life to me as a 1920s Buffalo, New York housewife named Grace Doze who was murdered on May 17, 1927 by her bootlegger lover (the past life of John) named Jake. She provided me with two dozen verifiable facts. CBS television hired a researcher to check out the facts Ivy gave me and aired this case as a television movie on May 17, 1994 (exactly 67 years to the hour from Grace Doze's murder!).

Of the facts Ivy gave, 22 of 24 checked out with newspaper reports. The only two errors were her age and the name of her son. Grace Doze was consistently reported as being 30 years old when she was murdered and her son's name was stated as Chester, Jr. Ivy informed me, speaking as Grace Doze, that she was 32 years old, and her son's name was Cliff. I asked the researcher to obtain Grace's death certificate and her son's birth certificate. As it turned out, Ivy was correct. In order to obtain these records, one must be a family member or have permission from the Governor's office, proving that Ivy could not have obtained these records on her own.

In either case, a paper trail would exist. Nobody requested these records from 1927 to 1992 (CBS's researcher represented the 1992 request), so this case stands out as a very well documented case of reincarnation. My appearance on the 11 p.m. news nationwide following the airing of this film further added to its message of psychic empowerment.

In this particular past life, we find Ivy living as a woman in Denmark in 1061. During this particular regression, as well as many others, Ivy experienced changes in the depth and tone of her voice. When you regress the same person into 46 different past lives as I did with Ivy, a wide range of experiences and changes in personality traits are observed.

Dr. G.: Where are you at this time?

Ivy: I'm in a large dining room.

Dr. G.: Are you alone?

Ivy: No, there are two adults present. I think they are my mother and father.

Dr. G.: What is this occasion?

Ivy: It's not a special day. We are just having dinner. This is a rather large dining room table for just the three of us.

Ivy's family was rather wealthy. She was an only child and approximately 16 years old. She was an attractive teenager and she had an easy life.

Dr. G.: What does your father do?

Ivy: He works for the King in some capacity. I think he is an advisor.

Dr. G.: Do you enjoy your life?

Ivy: Oh, yes. I get to go to parties and the men always treat me like a lady.

Dr. G.: Do you wish you had brothers and sisters?

Ivy: No, no I don't. I like the attention I receive as being an only child. Father's friends often bring me gifts when they come over the house.

Dr. G.: Do you have a suitor?

Ivy: Well, there is a boy who likes me and I see him once in a while.

Dr. G.: Do you want to see him more often?

Ivy: It doesn't really matter. I like him, but not so much as other people in my life.

I was trying to find out if this suitor represented someone of significance to Ivy. All of my instructions to Ivy prior to regressing her were designed to have her choose a past life that would be significant in explaining and removing the difficulties surrounding her current relationships with John and Dave.

This particular boyfriend was not that important to Ivy, but she still enjoyed his company and wanted to continue seeing him. Ivy's name was Rachael and her life was very much occupied with social activities. Because her father was an advisor to the King, their attendance at social functions was mandatory.

Dr. G.: Can you tell me about your father's work?

Ivy: I don't know much about what he does.

Dr. G.: Doesn't he ever discuss it?

Ivy: All I know is that he deals with things that are supposed to be secret. I think it has to do with the Army and protecting the King.

Dr. G.: Does your father enjoy what he does?

Ivy: Sometimes he is very excited, even though he can't tell us [her mother and herself] what is going on.

Dr. G.: And other times?

Ivy: He gets very sad and worried. I can tell when something is wrong.

Dr. G.: Does this worry you?

Ivy: A little, but there is just nothing I can do about it, so I try not to worry.

At first, I thought that Rachael was just a frivolous girl, but the more I conversed with her, the more I realized that she was a realist. Being a woman in the 11th century means having no control over your life. Rachael accepted this and merely dealt with life on the terms and conditions that were presented to her.

She was a bright, active, and strong woman from a powerful family heavily involved in politics during a very difficult time. She described many invasions and wars with neighboring countries. It was not a time of political stability. The King was very security conscious, almost to the extent of paranoia. Considering the many unexplained deaths among the nobility, this attitude was probably necessary for survival.

I progressed Rachael forward to a significant event in her life.

Dr. G.: What has happened since I last spoke to you?

Ivy: I am very upset with my father.

Dr. G.: Why?

Ivy.: He has been very moody with me lately. No matter what I do, it's just not right.

Dr. G.: Do you know what is troubling him?

Ivy: Yes, I think I do. The King has been worried about all of these wars and invasions. He has ordered more ships to be built than usual. I think our King is putting pressure on all of his advisors. Because my father advises him on military matters and security issues, father is under a lot of stress.

Dr. G.: How has he taken this out on you?

Ivy: He has forbid me to see my boyfriend. Just like that, he tells me I can't see him anymore.

Dr. G.: But I thought you told me that he wasn't that close a friend to you. So why does this make that much of a difference?

Ivy: I may not be in love with him, but I am a woman [she is now 19]. I don't like being told that I simply can't see someone.

Dr. G.: Did he tell you why he doesn't want you to see this man?

Ivy: Not really. I think it has to do with security or military matters. Nobody tells me anything.

It seems that Rachael's suitor was suspected of being a spy, possibly an assassin. Her father was ordered to keep his daughter away from that man because they feared he was trying to use Rachael to somehow get to the King. There apparently was some incriminating evidence to substantiate these allegations.

Dr. G.: Will you see this suitor anyway?

Ivy: Absolutely not. If father forbids me, then I will not see him again. I will not go against the wishes of my father, not for anyone.

Rachael accepted this situation with class. She didn't really miss seeing that man as much as she just didn't like being told what to do. Being the realist that she was meant going on with her life and maintaining loyalty to her family.

Dr. G.: Do you ever think about getting married?

Ivy: Not really. I don't have much of a say in it anyway. When my father thinks the time is right, he will arrange for my marriage.

Dr. G.: Is that acceptable to you?

Ivy: It's the way it is and I will do what is expected of me.

From that exchange, I learned to deal with other matters. Relationships with men just weren't that important to Rachael. Because I knew this life would somehow involve either John, Dave, or both, I continued.

Dr. G.: Is there anything special that you are looking forward to?

Ivy: Yes, there is. The King is having a large dinner party and he has invited us. I can't wait.

Dr. G.: What is special about this function?

Ivy: A lot of important people are going to be there. It won't be just the usual people, but nobility from all over the country.

Dr. G.: Do you know why these people have been invited here at this particular time?

Ivy: Well, it probably concerns the Army. Either we are going to war or peaceful negotiations are in progress. I try not to concern myself with these matters.

That is an interesting choice, indeed. Nothing else of significance seemed to be happening in Rachael's life so I next progressed her to the dinner itself.

Dr. G.: What is gong on now?

Ivy: Oh, it's really great. Everyone seems so relaxed now.

Dr. G.: What happened?

Ivy: For the past few days, there have been all kinds of meetings. Father has been working day and night. He hasn't slept well and is always worried.

Dr. G.: So why have this party now?

Ivy: They always celebrate after these kinds of discussions.

Dr. G.: But you said that everyone seems so relaxed. What has happened to change the previously tense situation?

Ivy: It seems that the threats to our nation have been dealt with. Apparently, some sort of peace treaty was signed or some agreement was reached. This was the result of the work of the King's advisors and emissaries.

Dr. G.: And your father?

Ivy: Yes, that is the best part of it. Because of Father's work, he is being rewarded. The King is giving him more land and power.

Dr. G.: I can see why he is so relaxed.

Ivy: I do worry so when he works like this. But now things are safe and he is in great favor with our King.

Dr. G.: This sounds very important.

Ivy: The opinion of the King is everything to my people.

The King can have anyone he wants killed or imprisoned or forced out of the country.

Dr. G.: Is anything else going on that you are excited about?

Ivy: The King wants to come to my home for dinner. Can you imagine that? It is a great honor for our family. I can't wait.

The party went on for quite a while. Eventually Rachael and her parents returned to their home. Rachael and her mother were in charge of making the necessary preparations for the King's visit. Their servants were busy preparing the house and Rachael became more and more excited as the special day drew near. The only person more important to Rachael than her father was the King. Rachael was most definitely a loyal subject. We shall shortly see an ironic twist of fate in relationship to this loyalty.

Having a King over to your house is no simple matter. Security preparations had to be taken, even when he dined with a trusted advisor. Rachael didn't mind all of the extra people around. She was so honored to be part of a family hosting a visit from the King that any minor inconvenience could be forgiven.

I progressed Rachael to the actual dinner with the King.

Dr. G.: How are things going?

Ivy: All right, I guess.

Dr. G.: You don't sound particularly happy.

Ivy: Well, it's just that there are so many strange people around in the kitchen and other places. I feel like a stranger in my own home.

Dr. G.: I thought you were excited about the King's visit?

Ivy: Yes, I am. It's just that there are so many details to attend to that it's hard to find time to relax.

Eventually, things settled down and Rachael and her parents dined with the King and his men. The meal was large with many courses. Because Rachael's father was such a trusted advisor, the King did not bring his food taster.

Dr. G.: How are things now?

Ivy: Much better. The meal is excellent and everyone seems to be enjoying themself.

Dr. G.: And your father?

Ivy: He looks relaxed and very proud of Mother and me.

I then progressed Rachael to a significant event, if any, in relationship to this dinner.

Dr. G.: What is happening at this time?

Ivy: I don't know, but I'm frightened.

Dr. G.: Slowly, tell me what is bothering you.

Ivy: It's the King. He looks ill. Everyone thinks it must be the food. They think he's been poisoned.

Dr. G.: Is anyone else sick?

Ivy: No, that's just it. It's only the King who looks as if he is ill.

Dr. G.: Isn't that unusual?

Ivy: It means that if it is food poisoning then only the King's meal was poisoned. That means someone in our house is responsible and we will all be in great danger. I am really scared.

I progressed Rachael forward to the final outcome of the King's illness.

Dr. G.: What has happened, Rachael?

Ivy: Oh, it's terrible. We all seem to be under some sort of house arrest. The King is in my parents' bedroom with his people. He looks bad I'm told and everyone thinks he is going to die. Even if he doesn't die, this will mean a lot of problems for my father and my family.

Dr. G.: Move to the resolution of the King's condition.

Ivy: He died. Oh my lord, the King is dead and he died in my family's house.

Dr. G.: Now please stay calm, Rachael, and tell me what his security people found out, if anything, about who did this?

Ivy: It took a long time, many hours anyway. Everyone was searched and the kitchen was almost taken apart.

Dr. G.: What did they find?

Ivy: They finally caught the murderer. You are not going to believe who it was.

Dr. G.: Who is it?

Ivy: It's my former suitor. Do you remember the man I used to see sometimes?

Dr. G.: Yes, please go on.

Ivy: Well the reason my father forbade me to see him was that this man was suspected of being a spy. They knew he was involved with the King's enemies and plotted to kill our leader.

Dr. G.: Why didn't your father tell you this?

Ivy: He was ordered not to. He also didn't want to frighten me. The King and his other advisors didn't want to let their enemies know they were on to them.

Dr. G.: Then why this visit? I would think that the King would consider this outing particularly dangerous.

Ivy: I'm told that he would, except that when this peace treaty was signed or whatever they did to come to an agreement, they felt the assassination plot was dropped.

Dr. G.: It looks as if they miscalculated. So what will happen to your father?

Ivy: We are all under arrest and will be taken to the castle in the morning.

The next day, Rachael and her family, along with the murder and others who came with the King, were taken to the castle. The murderer was executed immediately and Rachael and her parents were placed in the dungeon. The murderer could not say who put him up to it and was killed before he could clear her family. The cook was killed and an investigation with a type of hearing was held to determine what to do about Rachael and her family.

Rachael's parents were placed in different cells so that Rachael was alone and frightened.

Dr. G.: How are you being treated?

Ivy: It's terrible. I'm so scared. There are two guards and I'm confused.

Dr. G.: About what?

Ivy: One of the guards (Lars) is very nice to me. He brings me extra food and talks to me in a very respectful manner.

Dr. G.: And the other guard?

Ivy: Erik is the other one. He is tall and mean. I am really afraid of him. He hits me for no reason and threatens me often.

Dr. G.: Can Lars help you out?

Ivy: I told Lars about it and he is sympathetic. He tells me that Erik has a bad reputation. Erik likes to abuse the prisoners, especially the women. (Ivy blushed in her chair when she said this).

Dr. G.: You mean he rapes the women?

Ivy: Yes. He is also known to kill the women after he uses them. Nobody seems to mind because he does his job and the prisoners are all afraid of him so they don't cause many problems.

Dr. G.: But aren't things different with your family due to your father's status with the court?

Ivy: That's all changed now. My father, and my mother, and myself too, are accused of conspiring to murder the King. My relationship with the murderer is very serious evidence against us. It doesn't look good at all.

I next progressed Rachael to a significant event that occurred during her incarceration.

Dr. G.: What is happening now?

Ivy: Oh my God, I can't get out.

Dr. G.: What is going on?

Ivy: Erik is torturing me. I pass out a lot and I hurt all over.

Dr. G.: What does he do to you?

Ivy: It's hard to describe. I feel so drained. Now he ripped my clothes off and is going to rape me. No, no, keep away...

Rachael described a rather traumatic scene of being repeatedly raped by Erik. She was a virgin so this was even more traumatic for her. She described blood everywhere. She thought she would be killed but when she woke up Lars was in her cell.

Dr. G.: How does Lars treat you?

Ivy: He is wonderful. Lars tends to my wounds and talks to me. I can't move a muscle. Lars could do anything he wants to me but instead he is kind and almost loving.

Dr. G.: Does he tell you anything about your parents?

Ivy: They're both dead. Neither my father nor mother could take the torture. Erik killed them both and then he raped me.

Dr. G.: Why didn't Erik kill you too?

Ivy: They gave him some extra time to work on me, since I was the one socializing with the King's murderer. But Lars tells me that the real reason is probably that Erik just wants to rape me again.

Dr. G.: What can you do about this? Can Lars help?

Ivy: Not really. Lars is being wonderful, but Erik is his superior and nobody in the castle is willing to show me any mercy. There is no way I'm going to survive long.

Rachael was in deep trouble. Over the next week, Erik came into her cell and tortured her. He took great pleasure in giving her pain. After each encounter, he raped her, and rather brutally. Rachael conditioned herself to go unconscious and prayed for death. She knew that there was no way out of this. Erik would abuse her as long as he wished and then kill her when he became bored. He would then report that she confessed or whatever they wanted to hear.

Dr. G.: Rachael, what has happened since I last spoke to you?

Ivy: I just want to die. Erik is a disgusting animal. When he knows I'm awake he stands by my cell and mocks me. Then he teases me and tells me what he is going to do to me later.

Dr. G.: What about Lars?

Ivy: Lars is very supportive. He knows I don't have much time left. Lars tells me that it's up to Erik when I die and that will be probably in the next couple of days.

Dr. G.: What will you do?

Ivy: You know it's really strange. I should be scared to death but I spent most of my time thinking of Lars.

Dr. G.: Because he has been so kind to you?

Ivy: Yes, but it's more than that. I actually think Lars loves me in some strange way.

Dr. G.: And how do you feel about him?

Ivy: I have never felt this way for a man before, but I really care for him. It's not just because he is kind to me. I just like him. If only things were different.

The next 24 hours proved to be most unusual. Erik bragged to Lars that he was going to kill Rachael in two days. Lars not only told Rachael this, but suggested a plan that could save her. He told Rachael that he was going to help her escape. He didn't care what happened to him.

Rachael didn't know what to say. She readily agreed and tried not to get her hopes up too high.

Dr. G.: How are you going to escape?

Ivy: Lars is going to unlock the cell and have a horse waiting for me in the middle of the night. He has provided some food and water and instructed me where to go for safety.

Dr. G.: Please go on.

Ivy: I asked him if he would come with me but he said he couldn't. He told me he loves me but his traveling with me would make it impossible for me to reach the border.

Later that night, Lars executed his part of the escape perfectly. The problem was that Erik chose a most inopportune moment to pay a visit to Rachael's cell. When he discovered her gone, he went berserk. Erik knew that Lars had to be responsible, so he found him and beat him up terribly. Then when Lars was unconscious, Erik slit his throat. Lars died defending the woman he loved. Meanwhile, Rachael was able to escape from the castle and made it to the countryside.

Dr. G.: Where are you now?

Ivy: I'm lost. I have run out of food and water and don't know where the border is.

Dr. G.: Move to the resolution of this problem?

Ivy: I can't move. I'm so weak. All I want to do is sleep.

Rachael died of exposure on her way to the border. From the superconscious mind level, I discovered that her father in her life as Rachael was her current-life father. Erik is John and Lars is Dave in her life as Ivy. The murderer was a man at a former job she held who harassed her daily before she finally quit.

Thus ends this most unusual and different life from the ones we previously explored. The karmic triangle with John and Dave was becoming more and more evident with each past life regression I conducted.

Chapter 5

Roots, Caribbean Style

Out of the more than 35,000 past life regressions and future life progressions I have conducted on more than 14,000 individuals, soul mate cases are the most rewarding.

My research shows that there are three types of soul mates. The most desirable classification is called a *"twin flame"* or *true soul mate*. Both of these souls originated from the same oversoul, which split into two subsouls. Because they both have the same energy source, they are perfectly compatible.

The *boundary soul mate* represents the second category. This is a positive relationship with only minor problems and differences. You have only been with this person in a limited number of past lives, and they have all been rewarding experiences.

A *retribution soul mate* has shared many more lives with you and is the least attractive type. You feel irresistibly drawn to this person, but the results are commonly negative and long lasting.

Kim and Brett represented a truly loving couple from the Midwest, who had been married for seven years and in a blissful relationship. Kim was the only member of the couple to be regressed. She wanted to see if they were together in previous lives.

Frank was Kim's ex-husband, who stole several hundred thousand dollars from her and cheated on her constantly during their marriage. Fortunately, none of these traits were exhibited by Brett.

In some cases, a primitive past life can be contaminated by civilization when a more technologically advanced society encroaches on the former.

Kim's past life illustrates such a development.

Dr. G.: Where do you find yourself?

Kim: I am in a jungle.

Dr. G.: Where is this jungle?

Kim: Africa. I'm in an African jungle and I'm scared.

Kim described herself as a 5-year-old African female. She was on her way back to her village with her older brother. He decided to climb a tree to get some food, and Kim was frightened by an animal.

Shortly after this exchange, I progressed her to a time when she returned to her village.

Dr. G.: What is your name? (Kim hesitated before she answered. She needed some time to translate her name into something her 20th-century mind could relate).

Kim: Ruby. You can call me Ruby.

Dr. G.: Ruby, tell me a little about yourself.

Kim: I am just a child. I like to play, but nobody has any time for me.

Ruby was lonely. Her village was quite small and there were only a few children her age. The teenagers and adults spent most of their time hunting, gathering, and protecting themselves from the elements.

As I moved her forward, she was now about 13 years old.

Dr. G.: Ruby, what has happened since I last spoke to you?

Kim: My people died from a sickness. We have to move. I don't like to move around.

Ruby's village was almost wiped out by some sort of plague. She and her people constantly moved to different locations in search of food and to escape what was infecting them.

I would not use the term *adventurous* to describe her. Ruby liked to be secure and stay in one place. That was rather difficult in her African jungle environment. As far as I could determine, the year was about 1650.

I moved her forward again to follow her progress.

Dr. G.: Where are you now?

Kim: There is trouble. We must move again.

Dr. G.: What is it?

Kim: White people. They come from the water and have taken my people. Nobody is safe. We must go and hide.

Apparently some English slave traders have been active near Ruby's village. Those men kidnapped the local natives and shipped them off to the Caribbean islands and colonial America.

Ruby's people were in a bind. They had disease to fear. In addition, it was a constant struggle to get enough food and provide shelter. The last thing they needed was the threat of slave traders following them through the jungle with their nets and other weapons.

I moved Ruby ahead to a significant event.

Dr. G.: Where are you now?

Kim: I'm by a hut waiting for my family to return.

Ruby's family and the rest of the village were out scouting a new location. She didn't like to wander around with them so she stayed in the village by herself.

The next thing she reported was the most traumatic to her. The slave traders discovered her people and captured every one of them. Their next procedure was to look for signs of a village and remove anybody else they could find. When they came to Ruby's village, she was alone.

Dr. G.: Ruby, what are you going to do?

Kim: I, I don't know. There's no place to hide. I just don't know.

Ruby was almost motionless. She was frightened of the white men and just sat by her hut. They came and carried her away. She didn't make it any easier for them but was transported to their ship nevertheless.

She described the voyage as being most unpleasant. Because she was a skinny 12 year old, who looked even younger, she escaped the degradation of being raped. Her mother and some of the other women weren't so fortunate.

It seemed like an eternity, but eventually the ship docked at a Caribbean island. It was there she was separated from her family and sold to a white man who manufactured furniture.

Dr. G.: How are you being treated?

Kim: It's not that bad.

Dr. G.: Tell me about your life.

Kim: I am being trained to take care of this man's house.

Dr. G.: How many slaves does he have?

Kim: Just a few. They are nice to me, but I am lonely and miss my family.

During the next four or five years, Ruby was taught to speak English and trained to cook and clean the home of the man who owned her. His name was Edward and he was very strange. Ruby described him as being totally unpredictable. Some days he was nice and pleasant and others he was mean and arrogant.

His furniture business prospered on this island and he shipped most of his products to other lands. Edward paid little attention to Ruby. Sometimes he would yell at her, but he never physically abused her.

Dr. G.: Did you ever find out where your family was sent?

Kim: No. They were shipped off and I know I will never see them again.

Dr. G.: Tell me more about Edward.

Kim: He is a very strange man.

Dr. G.: Is he married?

Kim: No. He is middle aged and he never brings women to the house.

Dr. G.: Does he date?

Kim: He only goes with whores. He goes into the bad section of town and buys a woman for the night.

Edward was not a man of personality. In addition to his mood swings, he believed in buying people. He purchased his slaves and rented his evening's entertainment. In business, he was the same way. It was common practice for him to bribe officials and to make all sorts of underhanded deals to secure additional business.

His reputation was that of a man you dare not cross. Edward fully abided by the concept of vengeance. If any competitor or other contact of his wronged him in any way, Edward would find some way to enact his revenge.

Ruby was understandably frightened of him, but fortunately he left her alone. I progressed her forward to a significant event.

Dr. G.: What is going on at this time?

Kim: It's late at night and I'm frightened.

Dr. G.: What are you scared of?

Kim: It's him [Edward]. He came home drunk and started throwing things around. I've never seen him so mad.

Dr. G.: Do you know what caused this?

Kim: Yes, I heard he lost a shipment of furniture and he doesn't like losing money. I must attend to his needs.

It was one of her duties to make sure her drunken master got himself to bed in one piece. As she helped him to his room he became a little more sober.

Dr. G.: What happened next?

Kim: He, he is ripping my clothes off. No, please no, don't....

Ruby was raped by this drunken furniture maker. In his usual unpredictable personality, he just decided to rape her. This man had never so much as touched Ruby before.

Dr. G.: How are you doing now?

Kim: I'm okay. I guess. I feel so ashamed. What am I supposed to do?

Ruby was not the most decisive person. She knew there wasn't much she could do about her situation, so she continued with her duties.

I moved her forward by a few months to see how she was making out.

Dr. G.: Did Edward continue having sex with you?

Kim: No. I don't understand that man. That night he raped me, I saw a different side of him. I was so frightened that he would continue forcing himself on me.

Dr. G.: And he hasn't?

Kim: Not once since then. Thank God he seems to have returned to his usual routines and sees his whores just like before.

Edward was indeed a strange man. He never brought his prostitutes home with him. In fact, he kept a clean and respectable home. With the exception of the night he raped Ruby, nothing of a sinister nature occurred in Edward's personal residence.

One thing Ruby did describe that I found significant was Edward's aversion to children. He hated children. A year or two after she arrived at his home, one of the other slaves became pregnant by a native islander. Edward immediately sold her and lost his temper on a daily basis for weeks following that event.

I progressed her forward to a significant event.

Dr. G.: What is going on with you Ruby?

Kim: I'm in trouble.

Dr. G.: What is the matter?

Kim: I'm pregnant. He [Edward] is going to get rid of me.

Ruby was summoned into Edward's den one evening. He was sober and just looked at her with disgust. She was so frightened, she was shaking. He proceeded to beat her while repeating over and over again how she broke the rules.

Fortunately for Ruby, Edward stopped this beating before seriously hurting her. He sold her to a man who owned and ran a hotel in town.

Dr. G.: I know this has been a difficult time for you. What has happened since I last spoke to you?

Kim: I'm not pregnant.

Dr. G.: You mean you lost the baby?

Kim: No. I was never pregnant to begin with.

Ruby's luck was definitely improving. She did not like being Edward's slave one bit. This false pregnancy of hers was the only practical way she could have escaped this most uncomfortable life.

Dr. G.: Tell me about your new master?

Kim: His name is Roger and he runs a nice hotel.

Dr. G.: What are your duties?

Kim: I make the beds and clean the rooms. Master Roger is very kind to me.

This was most definitely a move up for Ruby. This was a good-size hotel, but there were other girls there to help her. Roger lived in a nice home not far from the hotel and her quarters were in his personal residence. This was a nice "job" for Ruby. Everyone seemed to get along with each other, and Ruby was happy for the first time in her young life.

Dr. G.: Ruby, does anything scare you these days?

Kim: No. I can't recall when I wasn't frightened of someone or something. I feel safe now.

As time went by, Ruby adjusted easily to this life. She forgot about Edward and worked very hard for Master Roger.

Dr. G.: Do you have a special man in your life?

Kim: Not really. I do get into town once in a while, and I go out with some of the men. But there's nobody special in my life.

Ruby's self image was improving. She found it easier to meet some of the male slaves and local laborers on her days off. She would socialize, and even become intimate with them, but there was no special person in her life, nor was she looking for a Mr. Right at this time.

Dr. G.: Do you want to get married some day?

Kim: No. I like my life right now just the way it is. I have everything I want and I'm satisfied.

Ruby's needs were simple. She had everything she wanted in life and a kind master.

Dr. G.: Tell me more about Master Roger.

Kim: He is a very kind man. Sometimes he gives me gifts of clothes that are fancy when he knows I have a new man in my life.

Dr. G.: Does he show a special personal interest in you?

Kim: He's not interested in me sexually, if that's what you mean. He just tolerates me and the others well.

Dr. G.: Does Master Roger have a family?

Kim: His wife died some years back and he has no children. He seems to be happy just taking care of his hotel and providing for our needs.

There didn't seem to be any immediate threat or causes of concern to Ruby. She had a safe and secure life and she became involved with men whenever she wanted without the obligations of a long-term relationship.

Dr. G.: Is there anything about your duties that you find unpleasant?

Kim: Yes. Sometimes a man stays in the hotel with a woman who is not his wife and this can become uncomfortable.

Dr. G.: How so?

Kim: Master Roger doesn't encourage that kind of behavior when it happens. Some of these whores act in a low class way. Master Roger nicely asks them to leave.

Dr. G.: Doesn't he know who these regulars are so he can just not give them a room?

Kim: It's not regulars. These are men who travel here on business, so Master Roger doesn't know who they are.

Dr. G.: What about the women?

Kim: There are so many new women coming and going to our island that it is impossible to keep track of them. I don't even know who is really a man's wife and who is just a whore.

Roger really did try to run a respectable hotel, but the transient nature of the island and the business of trading made it very difficult to enforce. Apparently, these incidents were few and far between, so Roger wasn't that concerned about them.

Ruby assimilated very well into this culture. She never seemed to miss her family or African heritage. Her life was simple, but relatively free from stress, and was fulfilling to her.

When I progressed Ruby forward, a most unusual event transpired.

Dr. G.: What is happening at this time, Ruby?

Kim: I was cleaning up a room when I heard a strange sound down the hall.

Dr. G.: What was it?

Kim: I thought I heard a scream, but it was more like a high-pitched sound.

Ruby went to investigate this situation and when she knocked on the door to the suspect room, a familiar face greeted her.

Dr. G.: Who is it?

Kim: It's him! It's Edward.

Dr. G.: What happened next?

Kim: He, he pulled me into the room and told me he wanted me in the bed with the other woman.

Edward was somewhat drunk. He brought a prostitute to Roger's hotel and spent the night with her. This was the first time he had gone to this hotel.

Ruby's former master now decided to expand his sexual interests. He, of course, recognized Ruby and demanded she join him and his rented escort for a threesome.

Dr. G.: What did you do?

Kim: I, I had no choice. I knew he would beat me if I objected.

Dr. G.: Why didn't you just scream for help?

Kim: He had a gun on a nightstand by the bed. I was afraid he would use it on me. He is out of control when he drinks.

Edward wasn't exactly predictable when he was sober. As sexually free and uninhibited as Ruby was with her various lovers, this was quite different. The thought of having sex with Edward was utterly repulsive to Ruby. However, the homosexual acts she was being forced to commit with Edward's prostitute disgusted her even further.

After it was over, Edward hit Ruby a few times for good measure, and she ran out of the room. Ruby went to her quarters in Roger's house and cried. She refused to leave her room.

Dr. G.: What did Roger do?

Kim: After he came home, he knocked on my door and we talked. He is such a good listener. I was afraid to tell him because he bought me from that man [Edward].

NOTE: Whenever Ruby described Edward, it was almost always "that man" or "him." She couldn't even bring herself to call him by name.

Dr. G.: Did Roger tell you how he was going to deal with this situation?

Kim: Roger said he was going to have a talk with him. Roger is not a violent man, so I didn't think he could do anything rash.

Dr. G.: What about Edward? Are you concerned he will do something violent?

Kim: I really don't know.

Nobody, not even Edward, knew what he was going to do next. This didn't sound good. Roger was a gentleman, and he was going to pay a call on a man who was armed and dangerous and has absolutely no respect for human life, especially that of a slave.

Roger decided the best place to discuss this delicate matter was Edward's home, rather than his place of business. That evening, Roger drove over to Edward's home.

Dr. G.: Ruby, what did you do while Roger was away?

Kim: I went with him.

Dr. G.: What? You mean Roger let you come along on a visit like this?

Kim: He didn't know it at the time, but I hid in the back of his wagon. It was a bumpy ride, but I got there all right.

As Roger pulled his wagon up to Edward's house, Ruby waited. Edward's servant let Roger in and Ruby went around to a window by the living room. She guessed correctly that this was where the discussion would take place.

She didn't hear anything, but she could see them. At first, the conversation seemed quite civil. Roger came to work this out and to make sure that Edward never harmed Ruby again. He also made it clear that Edward was never to come to his hotel again. Roger was calm and direct during this conversation.

Ruby was straining herself trying to hear what was going on, but she just couldn't. Using her knowledge of the house, she remembered that one of the windows could be opened from the outside, so she tried to do just that.

Dr. G.: What happened next?

Kim: I made a noise and both of them turned my way to see what caused it.

Dr. G.: Go on.

Kim: I felt embarrassed, but there was nothing else I could do.

Dr. G.: What did you do?

Kim: Roger motioned for me to come in and I went around to the front door and joined them.

This was a mistake because as soon as she entered the living room, Edward started yelling. He lost control and attacked Roger.

Dr. G.: What did Roger do?

Kim: He was taken by surprise. That man [Edward] started strangling my master, and I was frightened.

Dr. G.: Please continue, I know it's difficult.

Kim: Roger started to turn blue and his tongue was sticking out so I grabbed a vase and hit that man [Edward] with it.

Dr. G.: What happened next?

Kim: I grabbed a shotgun from the hunting rack and shot Edward three times. He died instantly.

Kim's superconscious mind tape informed me that Roger is Brett and Edward is Frank. What I like about this case is that a woman saved her male soul mate's life. Usually, the reverse occurs.

Today, Kim and Brett are as happy as ever. Whether they are boundary soul mates or twin flames, only time will tell.

Chapter 6

A Nymphomaniac's Past Life

I have always felt that some of the most significant experiences come from primitive lifetimes. Our highly technological society is quite stressful and confusing to most people. The more advanced the civilization is, the more detached we get from our basic being.

Consider those who involve themselves in spiritual development. Living in a monastery in the 21st century requires a return to a very simplistic life. Daily meditation would be far more common to those cultures today. Next, we can consider primitive societies that exist today in remote locations such as parts of South America, Africa, or Australia.

The Aborigines of Australia are an excellent example of how primitive people utilize these principles for survival. It is so hot in the Australian desert, that these people must sit motionless for hours at a time to preserve their energy.

Another benefit of exploring these primitive lifetimes is that they are pure experiences. These lives are less contaminated by artificial technological improvements. Basic emotions, basic drives, and more natural responses to the world around them are far more characteristic of these simple existences.

In 1996, a 31-year-old graphic artist named Fran called me to assist her in overcoming her problem with nymphomania. She simply could not refuse to sexually satisfy nearly every man she met. This compulsive behavior caused her difficulties both personally and professionally.

She recently met Allan and began dating him, but could not be faithful. Fran wanted to be rid of this compulsive behavior and move on with her life.

I have no idea where a patient is going to go when I begin a past life regression. Sometimes they have an idea if they have had a recent dream about a possible past life, or if they have responded well to my past life regression conditioning cassette. Fran's past life was most definitely related to her present nymphomania problem.

Dr. G.: Where do you find yourself?

Fran: I'm on an island. It's not a very large island.

Dr. G.: Are you male or female?

Fran: I'm a girl.

Dr. G.: What is your name?

Fran: [Fran couldn't answer this question immediately. She had to translate the name into something she could relate to me] Eva. I am called Eva.

Dr. G.: Tell me about your family.

Fran: I live with my parents and brother.

Dr. G.: Are you happy?

Fran: I can't really answer that. I have fun and play a lot, but I get into trouble also.

Fran described her life as a 10-year-old girl on a Polynesian island. She was a very rebellious child and her parents had to discipline her often. Her brother was the complete opposite. He loved to fish with her father and was a quiet and well behaved older brother.

Eva didn't resent her brother or her parents. She just wanted to do whatever she wanted to do and whenever she felt like it. This independent form of behavior was not acceptable to her tribe. Eva was also a loner. She did not relate well to others and spent a lot of time by herself.

Dr. G.: Eva, what have you been up to?

Fran: I went exploring.

Dr. G.: Where to?

Fran: I took one of the canoes and just went to sea.

Dr. G.: How long were you gone?

Fran: I don't know. It was a long time. My parents didn't like it.

Dr. G.: Were you punished?

Fran: Yes. My father was especially bothered by this because the chief held counsel with him.

Eva was an adventurous young island girl. The problem with the tribe was that she was setting a bad example, particularly for the girls. The chief of the tribe discussed this with Eva's father many times. This was embarrassing for her father, and didn't exactly please her mother. From what Eva described, her father was pretty easygoing, but her mother was much more of a disciplinarian.

Dr. G.: Did the chief speak to you directly about this?

Fran: No. That is not our way. It is the responsibility of the parents to guide their children.

Dr. G.: Are you purposely trying to humiliate your father?

Fran: No. I love my father. It's hard to describe. Sometimes I just get this feeling that makes me do something that I know is wrong.

Dr. G.: Are there any other reasons you do this?

Fran: Yes, it's fun. I am skillful at going to sea, and I like to go out farther and to different places each time.

Dr. G.: How do you know where to come back?

Fran: I don't know. I just use my instincts and I always come home safely. I never get lost. There is no need to worry about me.

Many parents of adolescents today could identify with this trait. Eva felt indestructible and her success at these tasks just added to her confidence. The one thing that bothered me about what she said was the "feeling" that made her do the wrong thing. I made a mental note to follow its path, if any.

Dr. G.: Eva, how do you get along with your brother?

Fran: Okay, I guess. He's not much fun. He's older and he works with my father. Sometimes he tells me I should be more like him.

I next progressed Eva forward in time to a significant event. She was about 16 years old.

Dr. G.: What has transpired since I last spoke to you?

Fran: There was an eruption on a nearby island.

Dr. G.: What kind of an eruption?

Fran: It's a volcanic eruption. Some of my people were visiting this island, and all of a sudden, it erupted. There was all this stuff coming out of the volcano. Many people were killed or hurt.

Dr. G.: What happened to the rest of them?

Fran: My people helped them leave and took them to another island.

Dr. G.: Are your people worried that the same thing might happen to your island?

Fran: They try not to think about it. There are volcanoes on most of the nearby islands and this is the first one to do this since I can remember.

Dr. G.: So, what does the chief do?

Fran: He held counsel with the elders and they decided that we should not concern ourselves with erupting volcanoes. Our island is good and there is plenty to eat. We will be all right.

Dr. G.: Tell me about yourself. Do you have a boyfriend? [When I asked her this Fran looked very shy and embarrassed. This was quite a change from the indestructible and unmovable Eva I have spoken to before.]

Fran: Well, there is a boy whom I like. He is a great fisherman and the son of an elder.

Dr. G.: What is his name?

Fran: Sim.

Dr. G.: Do you see him privately?

Fran: Well, not exactly. He knows my reputation as being a little difficult. Sim is very quiet and I think I frighten him.

Dr. G.: What are you going to do about this?

Fran: I help him with his other work and I think he is starting to like me more.

Dr. G.: What other work is that?

Fran: He makes the carvings on wood and sometimes stone. It takes a long time and I bring him things and talk to him to help pass the time.

Eva described Sim as being tall, light skinned, and black haired. He had an athletic physique and Eva really looked forward to spending time with him.

Dr. G.: What kind of carvings does Sim make?

Fran: He carves figures of the Gods.

Dr. G.: What does he do with them?

Fran: Most of them are used in our rituals and religious rites.

Dr. G.: How are things with your family?

Fran: My parents argue a lot, mostly over me. They think I'm too wild and should take a mate.

Dr. G.: Is that why you are interested in Sim?

Fran: I'm interested in Sim because I like him, not because my parents think it's the right thing.

Not long after this conversation a very unusual thing happened to Eva.

Dr. G.: What is going on now, Eva?

Fran: I have become a dancer during our rituals. It's a lot of fun.

Dr. G.: Is this part of your custom?

Fran: Yes. I asked to do this and the elders agreed. I guess they thought it would keep me out of trouble.

Dr. G.: How do your parents feel about your dancing?

Fran: My father doesn't object to it, but my mother doesn't like it at all. She says that it will be harder for me to find a mate.

Dr. G.: What does Sim say about this?

Fran: He has no control over me. We are just friends.

I next moved Eva forward to any significant event that would involve her dancing.

Dr. G.: Where are you now?

Fran: I'm dancing. It's night and I feel strange.

Dr. G.: How strange?

Fran: I don't know. It's like I can't control my body. Something is making me do things.

What occurred next was even stranger. Eva danced in a rather exotic and sensual fashion. She had no control over her action whatsoever. This was extreme even for her.

Dr. G.: Tell me what happened next.

Fran: I danced around the men and started taking my clothes off. I teased them and then I made love to them, most of them.

Dr. G.: What did your father do while this was going on?

Fran: He just watched. I know he didn't approve, but this is not against our ways.

Dr. G.: What about Sim?

Fran: I made love to him, too. I wasn't aware of him as Sim. I just did what the feeling made me do.

Dr. G.: Tell me more about this feeling.

Fran: It's very strange. I mean, one minute, I'm Eva dancing and having a good time. Then, all of a sudden, I don't know who I am. It's as if my body was being controlled by someone else.

Dr. G.: This feeling, is it anything like you described when you were younger? You know, the feeling that made you do things that you knew were wrong.

Fran: You know, you are right. I never thought of that. What I felt as a child was much weaker, but now that I think about it, it was similar.

I was now more concerned for Eva. She was no longer describing mere independence or teenage thoughts of immortality. She was describing possession. Her people didn't treat this possession as something evil or something to remove. These were primitive people who believed in many Gods. This was just an action by the Gods, so they included it in their rituals.

Dr. G.: How long does this feeling last?

Fran: A couple of hours, I guess.

Dr. G.: And when it disappears, how are you left?

Fran: Well, I feel cold when the feeling comes over me. When it leaves, I don't remember that much. I do recall what I did, but there are times that I just blank out.

These are classic characteristics of possession. It's too bad that she didn't practice spiritual protection techniques with white light and other means. This could have prevented this spell. We will deal with this issue in detail in Chapter 10.

Dr. G.: How does Sim respond to you after the ceremony?

Fran: The next day I saw him and he just wouldn't discuss it. He ignored it completely. I sure wasn't going to bring it up.

Eva became known for her dancing. The feeling came into her body just about every time she danced. It became expected and merely included as part of their rites.

Dr. G.: How did this role affect you?

Fran: I went on with my chores as usual. It was only during these rituals that I felt strange.

Dr. G.: Do you feel guilty about this?

Fran: No, I wouldn't say that.

Dr. G.: What about your relationship with Sim?

Fran: Sim and I are getting closer. I don't really think it has much to do with my duties as a dancer. We were getting closer before this started.

Dr. G.: Has anything else significant happened?

Fran: Well, I have become well-known as a dancer. I guess I'm the only one on my island and in the neighboring islands with this feeling.

Dr. G.: How does this affect you?

Fran: Men come from other islands to see me and to take part in the ceremony. I kind of like this attention.

Dr. G.: Does Sim like it?

Fran: As I said before, he is very quiet and shy. He doesn't come right out and say so, but I just know he doesn't like it.

Dr. G.: Have you thought of giving this up?

Fran: I have, but I can't just now. Sim is the son of one of our tribal elders. His father would not want his son to be the reason these rituals stopped. Also, the men who come from the other islands trade with us more regularly. So this is good for our people.

Dr. G.: And your parents?

Fran: My father doesn't object, but my mother does. Even though she knows Sim and I will wed, she gives me a hard time.

This went on for many months. Eva kept dancing and being the center of these orgies. People came from near and far to see her and take part in these ceremonies. The island prospered and Eva's relationship with Sim grew.

Dr. G.: What is going on at this time?

Fran: Sim and I are married. We are very happy and I think my mother finally approves of something I did.

Dr. G.: Are you still dancing?

Fran: Yes.

Dr. G.: Do you still get that feeling when you dance?

Fran: Yes.

Dr. G.: Does that feeling ever come over you at times other than when you are dancing?

Fran: Now that you mention it, no. It's only when I'm dancing that I notice this feeling. Isn't that strange?

I progressed her forward by a few years to a significant event.

Dr. G.: Tell me what you have been up to.

Fran: The feeling has almost left me since you last asked me about it.

Dr. G.: When did this happen?

Fran: Very recently. First I noticed it getting a little weaker each time I danced. Then it wouldn't be there at all. Now I haven't had the feeling in more than a month.

Dr. G.: Do you still dance?

Fran: Yes, but I don't engage in sex with the men.

Dr. G.: Isn't that part of the ritual?

Fran: Only if I want it to be. You see, if I don't experience the feeling, then I don't want to have sex with the men.

Dr. G.: What effect does this have on the tribe?

Fran: I'm not as special as I was. Because I just dance, it's not as exciting, so the men from the other island don't come here as often.

Dr. G.: What about the trade they engage in?

Fran: Oh, those people still come and our island has prospered much since I started dancing. It's just these other men don't come.

Dr. G.: So, does that mean that you haven't hurt the tribe by your change in dancing?

Fran: Yes, that's right. As a matter of fact, the Chief and the elders actually like me.

Shortly after this, Eva decided she didn't want to dance anymore. She was replaced by another girl who just did routine dancing, and Eva returned to a normal life.

Dr. G.: Do you miss the attention you received when you were dancing?

Fran: Not really. It was fun for a while, but now I keep myself busy and am very happy with Sim.

Dr. G.: Do you plan to have any children?

Fran: Yes. We are working on it, but the fertility Gods have not been kind to us.

Dr. G.: Is there something wrong?

Fran: I don't know. Maybe it's all the excitement and changes from the feeling.

Dr. G.: How does Sim respond to this?

Fran: He is very loving and supportive. My father is not taking it well.

Dr. G.: In what way?

Fran: It does not look good for me to not be with child. Sim is the son of an elder and this is a reflection on his manhood. It's embarrassing to everyone.

Dr. G.: What can you do about it?

Fran: My mother and I pray to the Gods, but there is nothing else I can do.

Dr. G.: Does this cause conflict between your parents?

Fran: Yes it does. My mother argues often about this with my father and this is not good. Just when they were feeling proud of me, this dancing and these child bearing issues crops up.

During the next few months, things began to settle down. Eva reported no other experiences with the feeling.

I progressed her to a significant event in her life.

Dr. G.: What is happening at this time?

Fran: It's that new man.

Dr. G.: Who's that?

Fran: There is a new man from a nearby island who used to come here when I was dancing. He stopped coming after I stopped dancing. Now he is back again.

Dr. G.: Is that unusual?

Fran: Yes it is. He is not a trader. He just came to see me dance and I don't know why he is here now.

Dr. G.: Are you attracted to him?

Fran: No, I am afraid of him. I try to keep away from him, but it's hard.

Dr. G.: What does he do when he comes to the island?

Fran: It's strange. He collects things. One time he asked me for a shell necklace I was wearing.

Dr. G.: Did you give it to him?

Fran: No. When I refused to give it to him he offered to trade a special carving knife for it.

Dr. G.: What did you do?

Fran: I knew that Sim would like the knife so I traded with him. The knife was worth much more than the necklace, so I just couldn't resist.

The mysterious islander's name was Mar. I didn't like the idea of him obtaining Eva's necklace. It could be a simple and harmless souvenir from Eva's former dancing days (equivalent to getting an autograph from a celebrity). On the other hand, it could be used in some magick ritual (love spell, etc.), which was not uncommon for these primitive people. Also, it could help explain the origin of the "feeling."

Dr. G. What happened next?

Fran: Everything went well. Sim loved the knife and was proud of me for the trade.

Dr. G.: Does he know of Mar's interest in you?

Fran: He doesn't think there is one.

As I moved Eva forward, I instructed her to move to any significant event involving Mar.

Dr. G.: What has happened since I last spoke to you?

Fran: It's back.

Dr. G.: What is?

Fran: The feeling. I'm getting the feeling again.

Dr. G.: How strong is it and what do you do when you get this feeling?

Fran: It's not as strong as it was when I was dancing but I feel tingly all over. I am drawn to Mar and I want to see him.

Dr. G.: Have you seen him?

Fran: Yes. We have been together a few times.

Dr. G.: This is important, Eva. When you are with Mar, is it always preceded by this feeling?

Fran: Yes.

Dr. G.: And do you feel powerless to stop when it is going on at that time?

Fran: Yes.

It was as I suspected. Eva was the victim of some magick ritual. For those readers who think voodoo is bunk, I would suggest reading my book *Protected by the Light*[1], which discusses many forms of psychic attacks.

Eva was powerless to resist Mar and began having an affair with him. She didn't find him particularly attractive and her relationship with Sim was good, but this didn't matter. Mar told Eva that if she pleased him, he would use a spell to eliminate her infertility problem. But he made her promise never to tell Sim about their relationship. She readily agreed to this.

Dr. G.: Do you think Sim suspects your affair?

Fran: No, I don't think so.

Dr. G.: Wouldn't he talk to you about it if he did suspect you seeing another man?

Fran: He is a very proud man and doesn't like to face things like that.

Dr. G.: You mean when he didn't discuss your sexual activities with all those men when you danced?

Fran: Exactly.

This affair kept going on for about six months. Unfortunately for Eva, people suspected this affair. Mar made many extra trips to their island and Eva just couldn't camouflage the effects and the feeling and her sporadic interest in Mar.

Dr. G.: What is happening now?

Fran: It's terrible. Mother confronted me about my affair with Mar.

Dr. G.: Does Sim know?

Fran: Everybody knows. Sim won't talk to me about it, but he is being pressured by his father, and my father is being confronted by the chief.

Dr. G.: What are you going to do?

Fran: I will have to end it now.

Eva tried to end this affair, but Mar was just too influential over her. He promised to let her get pregnant and he was good to his word.

Dr. G.: Whose baby is it?

Fran: I really don't know. It is something I want and it is taking a lot of pressure off of me and my family.

Dr. G.: Does Sim ask you who the father is?

Fran: No. I told you he supports me in all that I do. He still hasn't confronted me about the affair.

Eva stopped seeing Mar. Mar somehow lost his control over Eva. He returned to his tribe and tried to have war declared against Eva's people. One young warrior from Mar's tribe argued with him and a fight ensued. Mar was killed and the Chief was furious.

The Chief seriously considered war against Eva's tribe and the only thing that could prevent this battle was Eva. He summoned her to his island to perform her dance for him.

Eva was understandably nervous but did as she was told and danced for the Chief. The feeling returned and she engaged in several sexual acts with the Chief. War was now averted.

From the superconscious mind, I was able to identify Eva's parents as her current parents. Most notably, Sim is Allan and Mar is an ex-boyfriend from high school who treated her poorly and literally stalked her after she broke up with him.

The karmic carryover from the life of Eva was that sexual promiscuity not only felt good, but prevented a war and the loss of many lives. Two years following this regression, Fran married Allan and established a relationship based on fidelity. She no longer had to compulsively engage in sex with other men.

Chapter 7

Hysterical Blindness and a Past Life in the London Slums

Many people ask me what hypnosis can really do. If, according to recent statistics, modern medical technology is only 75 percent successful, can hypnosis make up that additional 25 percent?

There are many syndromes that modern medicine can't cure. Drugs can treat many symptoms temporarily, but such diseases as ulcers, colitis, anxiety, and depression are not caused by bacteria, viruses, or fungi. They can't be cured with medication alone. They are psychosomatic in their origin, and the subconscious mind has a great deal to do with the elimination of these disturbances.

But even more obviously in the realm of treatment through hypnosis is a category of illness referred to as "hysterical disorders." Included in this category are hysterical paralysis, hysterical deafness, and hysterical blindness. These disorders have absolutely no medical or organic cause. A complete physical examination by a specialist would reveal no medical reason for the patient's infirmity, yet the patient remains unable to function in one of these areas.

The case that I am about to describe illustrates this principle with sight loss. An attractive 25-year-old interior decorator was brought to my office early in January 1978 by her boyfriend. Her name was Judy, and Angelo was her male companion. Angelo had called me earlier that day to make this emergency appointment. It seemed that the week before, Judy had lost her sight without any warning and with no apparent cause.

Judy had never had problems with her eyes before and, in fact, didn't even wear glasses. She had been to an ophthalmologist affiliated with Johns Hopkins University and all of the tests turned out negative. In other words, there was no medical reason for Judy's blindness. I had personally spoken with her ophthalmologist and he verified these facts.

It wasn't easy to take a history from Judy because she was very upset and depressed. However, I finally found out that Judy lost her sight shortly after discovering Angelo taking amphetamine pills. She had been dating him for more than a year, but he had not informed her of his habit. Within five minutes after inadvertently seeing Angelo taking these pills, Judy screamed and lost her sight.

I asked her if she screamed because of some pain. She said that she just had an uncontrollable urge to scream but did not feel any form of pain. Judy was naturally anxious about whether or not I could help her. I explained to her and Angelo what I knew about hysterical blindness. I made no promises or guarantees, but told her I would do my best.

Introducing a hypnotic trance requires only that the patient hear the hypnotherapist, and because Judy's hearing was unimpaired, this presented no problem. Even patients experiencing hysterical deafness can be cured. The subconscious (alpha) hears what the conscious mind (beta) cannot.

Judy entered into a good medium trance rather quickly, which surprised me, considering her depression and recent traumatic experience. I conditioned her for a simple age regression to be performed on her next visit. She left my office feeling relieved and more relaxed.

The second session consisted of a simple age regression. I instructed Judy's subconscious to search through its memory banks and relive a scene or scenes that were directly responsible for her current sight problems. She reviewed a number of childhood scenes, but nothing directly related to her present loss of sight.

During the next week, I saw Judy two more times and performed a number of simple age regressions. Again, nothing of significance surfaced. Past life regression was the only avenue we hadn't explored, so we decided to try it.

Judy was very willing, but Angelo didn't share her enthusiasm. I told them to discuss it and call me when they had made their decision. The next day, Angelo called to schedule a past life regression. Judy told me she considered it her only real hope. If the ophthalmologist at Johns Hopkins couldn't find a medical cause, then the origin of her blindness must be psychological. Because she had been sightless for nearly three weeks, she was desperate. Angelo didn't think much of hypnosis, but he was willing to try anything to help Judy.

I introduced Judy into a medium-level hypnotic trance and gave her subconscious mind the suggestion to return to the true origin of her present sight problems. For about five minutes she sat motionless in my recliner with her eyes closed. I could tell she was reviewing many scenes because her eyeballs were moving back and forth rapidly.

Judy finally began to answer my questions in a high-pitched, childlike voice.

Dr. G.: Can you tell me what you see now?

Judy: Everything I like [giggling].

Dr. G.: Where are you?

Judy: I'm with my daddy.

Dr. G. And where are you both right now?

Judy: Daddy said I can have some candy. He said I can have three pieces. The shop is full of candy and stuff.

Dr. G.: What kind of stuff?

Judy: Oh, you know. Food and stuff.

Dr. G.: How long have you been in the shop?

Judy: We just got here. I can't make up my mind what to get [giggling].

Dr. G. What is your name?

Judy: Elsie. Do you want some candy too? [giggling]

Dr. G.: No, thank you, Elsie. Where do you live?

Judy: In London, of course. Aren't you silly!

D. G.: What is your father's name?

Judy: Daddy.

Dr. G.: I mean, what do other people call your daddy?

Judy: Mac.

Dr. G.: Where is your mother?

Judy: She went away. [Her voice became soft.]

Dr. G.: Where did she go?

Judy: I don't know. [Patient began crying.]

Dr. G.: All right, Elsie, calm down. On the count of five, all negative feelings about your mother not being here will disappear and you will feel happy again. One...two...three...four...five. What kind of work does your father do?

Judy: He works in a place with machines, big machines. [Patient began giggling again.]

Dr. G.: How old are you, Elsie?

Judy: I'm 6 years old. [She sounded very proud.]

Elsie responded well to my questions. She quickly changed her emotional responses from that of crying to giggling when I gave her the appropriate instructions. Further questioning revealed the following past life.

Elsie lived in a very run-down apartment on the south side of London in 1887. Her father was a factory worker in a textile mill. Her mother left her and Mac when Elsie was just 3 years old because of Mac's drinking. This was not a pleasant life for Elsie as she had no playmates and her father worked long hours. Even when he did have time for her, he was usually drunk.

It was surprising how much Elsie loved Mac, considering he beat her often and spent very little time with her. The only real pleasure he provided was an occasional trip to the candy shop at the market. It was Elsie's short memory that allowed her to forget about Mac's faults and deal only with a present pleasurable experience.

I next progressed Elsie forward in time, asking her to remember the true cause, if any, of her present sight problem.

Dr. G.: Where are you now, Elsie?

Judy: I'm outside playing. [She sounded very sad.]

Dr. G.: Is anything wrong?

Judy: No.

Dr. G.: Come on now, Elsie, you can tell me. What is bothering you?

Judy: Well, I don't have anyone to play with and everybody is in church.

Dr. G.: Why aren't you in church?

Judy: Daddy doesn't believe in going to church. He says it's a waste of time.

Dr. G.: Is this Sunday?

Judy: Yes. Can you play with mc? [Patient began giggling again.]

Dr. G.: I can't play with you, Elsie, but I would like to know some things about your daddy. Would you mind telling me more about him?

Judy: Oh, okay. [Patient sounded bored.]

Dr. G.: Where is he now?

Judy: He's in the house, probably in his room. He always spends Sundays in his room.

Dr. G.: How old are you now, Elsie?

Judy: Eleven.

Dr. G.: Does your daddy ever take you to the park or to the city on Sunday?

Judy: No, I can't remember the last time he took me anywhere.

Dr. G.: Do you love your daddy?

Judy: Well, I, of course I do. [She hesitated a few seconds before answering this question.]

I next progressed Elsie forward asking for the actual event that would explain her present sight problem. She had gone back into the apartment on this Sunday afternoon looking for her father.

Dr. G.: Where are you now, Elsie?

Judy: I'm on the couch playing with my doll.

Dr. G.: Where is your daddy?

Judy: He's in his room, I think.

Dr. G.: What are you going to do now?

Judy: I'm going to sneak up on my daddy and scare him.

Elsie went to her father's room and quietly opened the door.

Dr. G.: Can you see your daddy, Elsie?

Judy: Oh, God, what is my daddy doing? Daddy, Daddy, please don't do that! [Judy had a look of absolute horror on her face.]

Dr. G.: What is your daddy doing?

Judy: He, he's sticking himself in the arm and he has a rubber band on his arm. [Patient sounded very agitated.]

Dr. G.: What is he doing now?

Judy: Daddy, Daddy, don't hurt me! No, no, I didn't mean to scare you. [Patient now was very upset.]

Dr. G.: What is your daddy doing to you, Elsie?"

Judy: He beat me, beat me bad. I hurt all over. [Patient was wincing.]

Mac had severely beaten Elsie for walking in on him while he was in the process of injecting morphine into his arm. Elsie had never seen her father inject himself before. Apparently alcoholism wasn't Mac's only problem.

After he had beaten Elsie, Mac locked her in his closet for the rest of that day. Elsie was in a state of shock. She hadn't eaten all day and hurt from the beating. It wasn't until early the next morning that she was released from the closet.

It was necessary to give Judy (Elsie) many calming suggestions before bringing her out of the trance.

Dr. G.: Judy, on the count of five, you will be back in the present, January 1978, and you will remember everything that you experienced and reexperienced. One...two...three...four...five, awaken.

Judy: Wow, that was quite something! Dr. Goldberg, Dr. Goldberg, I can see you! You're very hazy but I can see you. [Patient was elated.]

Dr. G.: Focus on my voice, Judy. When I snap my fingers, you will be able to see me clearly.

It took Judy about three minutes until she was able to see me clearly. We went into my reception room to join Angelo and explain to him what had happened.

When Judy saw Angelo take the amphetamine pill (an additive drug) she associated this incident with watching Mac inject morphine (also an addictive drug). Judy was severely beaten by Mac for viewing something she wasn't supposed to see. Because Angelo hadn't told her about his taking amphetamines, when Judy accidentally happened in on him, her subconscious made the association of seeing something she wasn't supposed to see. Through the hypnotic regression, the cause of the blindness was removed and the symptom (blindness) disappeared.

This experience brought Judy and Angelo much closer together. They had not been getting along well, even before this hysterical blindness incident occurred. As a result of this regression, their feelings for each other grew stronger.

In addition to restoring Judy's sight, this past life regression had other unexpected benefits for her. For one thing, she reported that her claustrophobia had disappeared. It seemed that being locked in the closet caused Elsie, and later Judy, to become afraid of confined spaces. By reliving this past life, the true cause of Judy's claustrophobia was elicited and removed.

Another interesting fact was brought to my attention. Judy told me that she had quit her last job with a well-known interior decorating firm because she hadn't liked her boss. She hardly knew him and rarely saw him, but the few times she did see him he was either drinking or smoking. One day he came into the office drunk from a lunch date and she simply quit. It worried her that she couldn't explain why at the time, but he had made her feel so uncomfortable that she had had to leave. Clearly, Judy's former boss reminded her of Mac. The association that her subconscious mind made with his drinking compelled her to quit. Judy now understood what had motivated her behavior and was comfortable with her decision.

This was a most interesting and rewarding case. The fact that the cause of Judy's blindness was psychological made hypnotic regression the treatment of choice.

Chapter 8

Anorexia Nervosa: Self-Punishment for Her Last Life

Anorexia nervosa is a very dangerous syndrome. It is characterized by a patient literally starving herself to death. The patient considers herself to be very much overweight even though, in reality, she is at her proper weight or slightly underweight. When she looks in the mirror, she fantasizes that she sees an overweight figure. I have observed this neurosis in women of all ages and socioeconomic backgrounds. Most commonly, it affects young, single women of middle-class backgrounds.

There was a case that was reported to me not long ago about a 19-year-old girl who read an article in a leading magazine stating that one can never be too rich or too thin. Because this young woman was from a lower middle-class family with little chance of becoming wealthy, she decided that her only hope was to lose weight quickly by starving herself. This sudden weight loss nearly killed her. After a number of hospitalizations and psychotherapy, she realized the futility and danger of her actions and fortunately came to her senses.

I do not treat many cases of anorexia nervosa, but the number of patients calling me with this problem has definitely increased during the past five years. One warm spring afternoon, I received a telephone call from a woman by the name of Gina. Gina was a photographer and she sounded in need of help. It seemed that for the past three months she had literally been afraid to eat. Gina couldn't explain why, but she wanted to starve herself. Her appetite had all but disappeared, and it took a great deal of effort to eat any kind of food. She was 5 feet, 6 inches tall and now weighed only 92 pounds. Her weight had dropped from 120 pounds in just three months.

Gina arrived at my office the following day, immaculately dressed and, except for a rather emaciated figure, very attractive. She spoke almost in a whisper.

Gina described her problem, beginning when she started having a series of nightmares. At first, she couldn't remember anything about her dreams, but then memories began to surface. Most of the time she would see a very obese man in his 30s. The look on his face and his mere presence would frighten her. Gina didn't know what this meant, but she did know that she was afraid of this man.

My work with past life regression was well-known to Gina, because two of her girlfriends had been regression patients of mine. She thought that these scenes could be indications of a past life. I agreed with her premise and began to explain the procedure involved in regressing to a past life.

I informed Gina that it might be difficult at first to go back to this lifetime because she had many negative responses to the scenes she saw in her dream state. Because we are in the alpha state (natural hypnosis) when we dream, it is not uncommon for people to have their own past life regressions while they sleep. Unfortunately, most of the scenes that are relived during the dream state are forgotten immediately upon awakening.

Gina was highly intelligent and, although she had little prior knowledge of karma or hypnosis, followed my explanations with ease. Yet when I asked her, out of trance, about past experiences with nightmares, she had a great deal of difficulty remembering the last time bad dreams had bothered her. She very rarely remembered her dreams, and when she did, they were usually meaningless to her. Before the episode that brought her to my office, she had occasional nightmares, but none of them affected her the way these recent dreams did.

During Gina's second session, I used simple age regression to take her through various parts of her childhood. She reported scenes of little significance, but this was preparation for her past life regression. Gina was becoming more and more confident of her ability to relax with hypnosis and self-hypnosis. I always teach self-hypnosis to my patients for this very reason.

The third and fourth sessions were spent taking Gina through two past lives. The scenes and information that she reported to me were of little value as far as her anorexia nervosa was concerned. In one past life, Gina was the wife of a Massachusetts farmer in the 18th century. She lived a full life and had no significant weight problems. The second life we explored showed Gina as a seamstress in Philadelphia during the 1850s. Again no weight problems emerged. It seemed that her subconscious mind was fighting me. I gave her some specific suggestions to allow her subconscious mind to relax any inhibitions concerning exploring past life scenes directly relating to her anorexia.

We were both surprised by what Gina reported during her fifth session. I induced Gina into a medium-level trance and directed her back into a past life that would explain the origin of her anorexia.

Dr. G.: Can you tell me what you see?

Gina: I'm at the doctor's.

Dr. G.: Why are you there? Are you ill?

Gina: No. I'm just getting weighed. My mom sent me here because of my weight.

Dr. G.: What is wrong with your weight?

Gina: Well, it's high. [Gina's voice had become very deep and she spoke much slower than normal for her.]

Dr. G.: What does the doctor tell you?

Gina: He tells me I must lose 30 pounds.

Dr. G.: How do you feel about that?

Gina: I want to tell him what he can do with those 30 pounds. [Patient was very annoyed.]

Dr. G.: What is your name?

Gina: Edward. Edward Laslow.

Dr. G.: How old are you, Edward?

Gina: Call me Eddie. [Patient very demanding.] I'm 16.

Dr. G.: What year is this?

Gina: 1906.

Dr. G.: Where do you live?

Gina: Chicago.

When I asked about her weight, Gina (Edward) squirmed in the recliner. It was as if seeing herself at that weight disgusted her. Further questioning revealed that Eddie had always been overweight, and his well-to-do parents had tried everything they could think of to help him lose weight.

Eddie was rather spoiled and was used to getting what he wanted. He was also quite cruel and got into many fights at school. He seemed to enjoy bullying other children, especially younger ones. As Gina described his activities, she would continue to squirm in my chair.

I next progressed Eddie ahead five years in time. The following information was uncovered over two 45-minute sessions.

Dr. G.: Where are you now, Eddie?

Gina: I'm working in one of my father's restaurants.

Dr. G.: What kind of work do you do?

Gina: I'm assistant manager.

Dr. G.: Do you like your job?

Gina: It's okay. But I'm going to like it better when I get to be manager.

Dr. G.: Is that going to take long?

Gina: No. In fact, I'm going to see to it that I'm promoted real soon. [Gina had a very sinister look on her face.]

Dr. G.: How are you going to do that?

Gina: One of the waitresses, Mary, is a very good friend of mine. I am going to arrange for a little show for my father's benefit.

Dr. G.: What kind of show?

Gina: My father is a real prude. When he finds out that Mary is having an affair with Stan [the manager], he will most certainly fire Stan and I'll be made manager.

Dr. G.: Why are you so certain your father will fire Stan?

Gina: Because Stan is a married man and, like I told you, my father is a real prude.

Eddie was a very shrewd operator. He had a great deal of influence on Mary because she owed him some money. It was not difficult for Eddie to talk her into staging an affair with Stan. One evening Mary was entertaining Stan at her apartment when they received an unexpected visitor—Eddie's father. Eddie had one of the waiters inform his father about the affair and the restaurateur went to question Mary about this accusation.

Upon entering Mary's apartment, Eddie's father became outraged at Stan and fired him immediately. The following day, Eddie was appointed manager of the restaurant. This type of underhanded dealing was to become a trademark for Eddie.

During the next 10 years, Eddie developed quite a reputation. With his father dead, Eddie was now owner of four restaurants in Chicago. At one time, he had a partner, but this partnership broke up after it became evident that Eddie had cheated his partner out of $50,000. Each time Gina described one of these unethical or illegal dealings, she wore a look of disgust.

I next progressed Eddie to the year 1926.

Dr. G.: Eddie, where are you now?

Gina: I'm in my office counting the day's receipts. It's been a good day.

Dr. G.: I trust the restaurant business has been good to you.

Gina: It's not just the restaurants. Ha, ha! [Patient was laughing now.]

Dr. G.: What do you mean?

Gina: I run a separate business on the side.

Dr. G.: What kind of business?

Gina: A speakeasy, what else?

Dr. G.: How long have you been involved with speakeasies?

Gina: Oh, about five years now.

Dr. G.: Who do you get your alcohol from?

Gina: Frankie.

Dr. G.: Who is Frankie?

Gina: He has connections with the Capone mob. I like Frankie. He's my kind of guy.

Dr. G.: What is that?

Gina: Frankie kills people who get in his way. He is always straight with me and I like the way he handles his women.

Dr. G: How does he handle his women?

Gina: He beats them when they talk back to him. Now, that's the way to treat a dame.

Dr. G.: Do you beat your women, Eddie?

Gina: Of course I do. I only hit my wife occasionally. But I beat my other women when they deserve it.

Eddie had many affairs and most of them ended violently. He had two different apartments in the city, which were inhabited by his two mistresses. A couple of his former girlfriends were killed by one of Frankie's men. One of these girls had tried to blackmail Eddie while the other had been unfaithful to him. If there was one thing Eddie couldn't tolerate, it was a woman going out on him.

It seems, in addition, that Eddie always rewarded himself with food. He would gorge himself with food after sex, and after completing business deals or anything else he found pleasurable. He even bragged to me about a food orgy he had in 1924 after successfully arranging the killing of a federal agent who was investigating his speakeasies.

Interestingly, Eddie would not allow his picture to be taken. He may have been afraid it would be used by the police to identify him, though he had no criminal record. My interpretation is that he didn't like seeing his obese figure. All of Eddie's girlfriends were thin and beautiful. His wife was also thin and very attractive. Eddie liked surrounding himself with beautiful objects and beautiful people.

I next progressed Eddie to the last day of his life.

Dr. G.: Eddie, where are you now?

Gina: I'm in my office putting money into my safe.

Dr. G.: What year is it?

Gina: It's 1928. Where have you been? [Patient quite nervous.]

Dr. G.: Are you alone?

Gina: Of course, I'm alone. Quiet, can you hear that?

Dr. G.: No. What's happening?

Gina: It's Frankie. He came in through my private entrance.

Dr. G.: Why is he here?

Gina: He's accusing me of skimming.

Dr. G.: Have you been skimming money from Frankie and the mob?

Gina: Yes. Wait a minute, he's pulling a gun on me.

Dr. G.: Where is Frankie now?

Gina: He's standing in front of my desk. He's telling me that he'll never havc to worry about me skimming again. [Patient now very excited and begins to stutter.]

Dr. G.: What's happening now, Eddie?

Gina: Frankie, please don't shoot! No, no, ohh! [Gina was motionless for about one minute.]

I progressed Gina forward after Eddie died to find out exactly what happened. Frankie shot Eddie for cheating the mob out of hundreds of thousands of dollars. Gina seemed to be relieved when death finally came to Eddie. It was obviously an end to a most degrading life. I brought Gina back to the present.

We discussed this life in detail. She was very satisfied with her newfound knowledge. I am happy to report that during the next six weeks, she gained 25 pounds and maintained her weight at about 117 pounds. Her anorexia nervosa disappeared almost immediately and, to the best of my knowledge, has not recurred.

There were many interesting principles that Gina's life as Eddie illustrated. First, viewing scenes of her past life as Eddie in the dream state brought back the obesity and degeneracy of that incarnation. Gina couldn't deal with this so she decided to starve herself to prevent herself from becoming obese Eddie Laslow. It was not just Eddie's obesity that horrified Gina. Eddie's complete lack of ethics or morality, his infidelity to his wife, and his criminal involvements all disgusted Gina.

Secondly, Eddie never allowed his picture to be taken. In this life Gina is a photographer and loves having her own picture taken. In fact, she once worked as a model.

Thirdly, Gina had a fear of guns that she could never explain. Being shot to death by Frankie in her past life left Gina with this phobia, which disappeared shortly after this regression.

Finally, Gina's voice was naturally very soft, but when she spoke as Eddie Laslow, it became deeper and slower. In addition, she showed many facial changes, and at times, developed an almost sinister appearance when she spoke as Eddie.

Gina's life was greatly affected by her reliving her existence as Eddie Laslow. It may literally have saved her life.

Chapter 9

The 800-Year-Old Synchronicity

When I appear on radio, television, or in a newspaper interview, I am often asked to relate my most interesting case. Although I find all of them gratifying, one especially stands out in my memory, and it involves my favorite principle, *synchronicity.* Synchronicity is meaningful occurrences without apparent cause.

It is not uncommon for the same people to occur in several of a patient's past lives. Group karma works just that way—a husband and wife in one life may come back as a mother and daughter or a brother and sister in another lifetime. An acquaintance in one life will often appear again in future lifetimes. This phenomenon is well accepted. What is unusual about this particular case is the manner in which I investigated it.

Several years ago, I received a call from a man who identified himself as Arnold. Arnold worked as an appliance salesman in a Baltimore department store and was calling me for hypnotherapy at his wife's suggestion. In further conversation, it came out that Arnold was a very insecure man, and this was negatively affecting his ability as a salesman.

Arnold proved to be an excellent hypnotic patient. After six sessions, I gave Arnold many suggestions to improve his self-image and assertiveness. The tape I recorded for him contained those suggestions and helped him to believe in himself more. Regression was not used at this time because I like to stabilize the emotional level first. Once a solid emotional foundation is established, regression therapy is more efficiently carried out. Arnold expressed no interest in exploring regression at this time. His self-confidence improved and his sales record very much reflected his progress. However, he seemed troubled about something else, but was unwilling at that time to discuss it with me.

It is not my policy or purpose to pry, so I did not force the issue. I simply told Arnold that it was obvious something else was troubling him, and if he didn't feel comfortable discussing it with me, there was nothing else I could do for him. I instructed him to continue playing the cassette tape I recorded for him. This case was far from complete, but because the patient closed all avenues of communication, I had no choice. Arnold thanked me for my help and left my office for what I thought would be his last session.

Two months passed before Arnold called me again. He wanted to see me immediately. I cleared some time that evening, and a very unusual journey began. Arnold seemed embarrassed as he told me the following facts while out of trance.

People had always dominated him. Everyone from his mother, wife, boss, customers, children, and just about anyone who had any contact with Arnold dominated him. It was not clear to me what he found especially embarrassing about relating this situation, and when I questioned him, he said he couldn't explain it. It was simply that this fear of being dominated was so strong and made him feel so inferior that he had a lot of trouble expressing it to anyone. In his 18 years of marriage, he had never even discussed this with his wife. Additional sessions were not very fruitful, so I suggested the use of simple age regression. Arnold was willing to try it. I like to obtain as thorough a history as possible out of trance. This relaxes the patient and gives specific paths to explore during actual hypnotic regressions.

When I worked with Arnold initially, he easily obtained a good level of hypnosis. But now, simple age regression was difficult for him and his level of trance was light. After some further conditioning, he was finally able to achieve a good medium trance level. We discovered that his childhood was fairly unremarkable, and there were many scenes of his being dominated and manipulated by people in his family as well as by his friends. I was, however, unsuccessful in eliciting a cause for this situation.

I suggested past life regressions to Arnold. He was excited by the idea. The first few attempts resulted in very sketchy scenes, and none of them related to his problem. It was as if he was fighting me. One could deduce that, subconsciously, Arnold was afraid that I would dominate him also. A series of four past life regressions made Arnold much more comfortable with the technique and more trusting of me.

Finally, one afternoon in November, Arnold described a most unusual past life. This was a very long session and much time had been devoted to establishing the background of the scene.

Arnold's name was Thayer, and he lived in a small village in Bavaria in 1132. Bavaria was part of present-day Germany. He seemed very frightened about something as I questioned him.

Dr. G.: Where are you?

Arnold: I'm under the table.

Dr. G.: What are you doing under the table, Thayer?

Arnold: I'm eating my supper.

Dr. G.: Why are you eating under the table instead of sitting down at the table and placing your food on top of the table?

Arnold: The chains are too short and anyway I'm not allowed to eat that way.

Dr. G.: What chains?

Arnold: My hands and feet are chained to the table and the chains are very short.

Dr. G.: Who chained you to the table?

Arnold: Gustave.

Dr. G.: Who is Gustave?

Arnold: He is my master. I am his apprentice.

Thayer was an apprentice for a master guildsman by the name of Gustave. They worked with metal, mostly silver and gold. Drinking cups, plates, ornaments, and various other items for wealthy noblemen were produced by them. During the Middle Ages, it was quite common to learn a particular trade by being an apprentice for many years to a master guildsman. What was becoming rather evident was that there was more to this relationship than merely a guildsman and his apprentice.

Dr. G.: How long have you been chained to the table?

Arnold: Since we closed the shop.

Dr. G.: Why are you chained this way?

Arnold: I am always chained after the shop is closed. Master Gustave doesn't want me to leave and this is the only way he knows to make sure I don't leave.

Dr. G.: Why don't you just leave when he unchains you tomorrow?

Arnold: I can't do that. I was apprenticed to him by my father when I was 13.

Dr. G.: How does Gustave treat you in general?

Arnold: He hates me. He beats me with a whip whenever I do anything wrong. I am afraid of him.

Dr. G.: Has he always treated you this way?

Arnold: Yes. Ever since I can remember, he has always beat me and treated me like this.

Dr. G.: What happens when customers enter the shop? Does he mistreat you in front of other people?

Arnold: Oh, yes, all the time. There's nothing I can do about it. I think he gets great satisfaction out of humiliating me.

Dr. G.: Is there anyone in particular that Gustave likes humiliating you in front of?

Arnold: Well, yes. There's this girl by the name of Clotilde. He likes to let her see me being treated this way.

Dr. G.: Who is Clotilde?

Arnold: She is a very nice girl from a wealthy family and she likes me. She has bought many things from Master Gustave. He doesn't like it when she asks about me.

Dr. G.: What does Gustave do when Clotilde asks about you?

Arnold: He yells at me and tells me I'm worthless. He makes fun of everything I do and say. Then after she leaves, he chains me to the table and beats me.

Dr. G.: What else does he do to you?

Arnold: Well, he does these unnatural things to me....

Arnold was very embarrassed about this particular question. He started to stutter and after about 10 minutes, he described a number of homosexual acts that Gustave subjected him to. Gustave had never married and he used Thayer (Arnold) to satisfy his every desire. Thayer was blamed for anything that went wrong. He was degraded by Gustave whenever the master felt like abusing him. The hatred Thayer and Gustave felt for each other grew daily.

I progressed Thayer to a significant event in his life.

Dr. G.: Can you tell me what is happening now, Thayer?

Arnold: I, I am scared.

Dr. G.: Why are you afraid?

Arnold: Master Gustave, he is very angry with me.

Dr. G.: Why is that unusual?

Arnold: It's not just his usual temper. It's more than that.

Dr. G.: Why? What has happened since I last spoke with you?

Arnold: Clotilde has shown a great interest in me. She has asked Master Gustave to allow me to do some work at her family's house.

Dr. G.: How did Gustave respond to that request?

Arnold: He almost lost his temper in front of Clotilde. Her family has given Master Gustave much business over the years, and this is the first time that he has acted this way in front of her. I just know that he is going to beat me tonight.

Dr. G.: What did Gustave tell Clotilde?

Arnold: He said that I couldn't go to their home because of the tools that I would need, and he told Clotilde that I couldn't be trusted. Imagine telling Clotilde that. I hate him so.

Dr. G.: All right, Thayer. I want you to detach yourself from this scene and move forward to a resolution of this problem on the count of five. One... two... three... four... five.

Arnold: I'm being chained to the table again.

Dr. G.: Is it dinnertime now?

Arnold: Yes; somehow I feel strange. It's as if I have some extra energy. Master Gustave tells me that he is going to abuse me tonight. He often tells me that before I eat to taunt me.

Dr. G.: Tell me what happens next, Thayer.

Arnold: I don't let him chain me to the table. I'm arguing with him and he's laughing at me. Why does he laugh at me?

Dr. G.: What do you do about it?

Arnold: I attack him as he tries to chain my leg to the table. The food gets thrown to the floor and Gustave is yelling at me. I fight with him and all I can think of is killing him. [Patient is very excited.]

Dr. G.: Now calm down and slowly tell me what is happening.

Arnold: We are on the floor and I am reaching for his throat. I want to strangle him. We knocked over some tools and something is pressing against my left side.

Dr. G.: What is it?

Arnold: It's a very sharp tool. I reached down with my left hand and brushed it aside but I shouldn't have done that.

Dr. G.: Why not?

Arnold: Master Gustave, he pushed me off him and punched me in the face. I don't know what's happening now.

Dr. G.: Focus your mind on this scene, Thayer. It's important.

Arnold: He threw me against the wall and cursed me. He said I was not worth the trouble I was causing.

Dr. G.: What does Gustave do next?

Arnold: He picked up a knife-like tool. I know that it's very sharp. Oh, my God, he's stabbed me in my stomach. [Patient is very excited.] I'm bleeding and the pain is unbearable.

Dr. G.: Relax, Thayer. Detach yourself from any pain or emotion and tell me what happens next.

Arnold: He stabbed me many times. I dropped to the floor and died. He killed me. That horrible fiend killed me.

Dr. G.: How do you feel now?

Arnold: I feel as if I'm floating. I can see my body beneath me but I can't feel anything.

Because Arnold was very upset by this scene, I allowed him to view his death and to experience the complete detachment from all discomfort that typically characterizes death scenes. He stayed with this tranquil scene for about 10 minutes. I then brought him to the superconscious mind level and asked him about Gustave and Clotilde. He reported to me that Clotilde was his sister-in-law Margaret, with whom he gets along very well today. Gustave was not yet involved in his present life.

After this fateful session, Arnold felt much better about himself. He finally realized why he was so afraid of people dominating him and why he seemed to allow other people to exert their influence on him. What is interesting to note is that his sister-in-law Margaret was one of the few people Arnold has known who has not tried to dominate him. Margaret, as Clotilde, was the only bright spot in Thayer's life.

I saw Arnold a few more times to help him work out his remaining doubts. He was not interested in finding out about other lifetimes in which he might have known Gustave. Arnold felt he had learned enough about his past.

During the next six months, Arnold kept in touch with me. He had made great progress in strengthening his self-image and no longer feared people or allowed them to dominate him. He received a promotion at the store and his relationship with his wife and children had also improved noticeably. I was gratified with the results.

A year and a half after my treatment of Arnold, I received a call from an attorney named Brian, who wanted to work out some psychological problems using hypnosis. Brian specialized in corporate law for a large law firm. He was a very successful man in his late 30s, but he felt he had an undesirable tendency to manipulate people. Out of trance, he described himself as a self-made man who used people time and time again. It is ironic that the ability to manipulate people, which some consider an asset to an attorney, should be this patient's chief complaint.

Brian's conscious was working overtime. He felt guilty about his actions. Insomnia was a nightly occurrence, along with a compulsive eating problem. I also learned that his hobby was collecting antiques, mostly metal objects such as silverware, drinking cups, jewelry, and so on. He didn't care much for antique furniture. I noted this in his chart for future reference.

Brian proved to be an excellent hypnotic patient. He attained a good trance level and was easy to work with. Some progress was made with his compulsive eating habits and insomnia, but I was not satisfied with the results. I suggested age regression, and after I had thoroughly explained the process to him, Brian agreed to try this technique.

Simple age regression was helpful, but not to the extent that I had hoped. Brian relived a number of scenes concerning compulsive eating from his childhood and adolescence, though nothing of importance was discovered concerning his manipulative tendencies. He did report scenes in his adolescence and college years in which he used people for selfish purposes. Yet, I was not satisfied with this data because deeply rooted causes were not surfacing.

Brian couldn't understand my dissatisfaction. He felt he was making progress. I explained to him at this time the use of past life regression and asked him if he would consent to try it. He was skeptical about the concept of past lives, but agreed nonetheless.

In late March, I brought Brian back into a most interesting past life. He went into trance quickly and deeply. The following dialog is an excerpt from this session:

Dr. G.: What do you see now?

Brian: I'm working in my shop.

Dr. G.: What kind of shop is this?

Brian: I'm some sort of metalworker—yes, I'm a master craftsmen and I'm damn good at my work.

Dr. G.: What year is this?

Brian: 1130.

Dr. G.: What is your name?

Brian: I'm called Gustave.

Dr. G.: Can you describe your shop?

Brian: Well, it's not a very big shop. I have many fine tools that I use in my work.

Dr. G.: What especially do you make?

Brian: I mostly work with gold and silver. Noblemen commission me to make ornaments, jewelry, eating utensils, goblets, decorative containers, and other such objects.

Dr. G.: Are you married?

Brian: No. I don't have any patience for women.

Dr. G.: What country do you live in?

Brian: My land is called Bavaria.

Dr. G.: Who is the leader of your land?

Brian: King Henry.

Dr. G.: Do you enjoy your work?

Brian: Yes. I am the best at what I do and I like my craft.

Dr. G.: Do you speak with the noblemen often?

Brian: Only when they come into my shop.

Dr. G.: What do they talk about?

Brian: Oh, some damn nonsense about the election of the new Pope.

Dr. G.: Can you tell me more about your situation?

Brian: Well, not really. I don't get involved with other people's problems. I have enough of my own.

Dr. G.: What have you heard lately about the Pope?

Brian: The Pope died recently and there is some sort of fight going on as to who will be the next Pope.

Dr. G.: What kind of fight?

Brian: There were two Popes chosen and nobody knows who is going to remain as Pope. In all my years, I have never heard of such dealings. I don't like to think about those things.

An interesting historical note: In the year 1130, Lothair II was the Holy Roman Emperor, and his son-in-law, Henry the Proud, was Duke of Bavaria. Pope Honorius II died in 1130 and two elections were held. A small body of cardinals elected Innocent II while the majority of cardinals elected Analectus II. The latter controlled the Vatican and the castle of Saint Angelo. Innocent II was recognized by all of the kings north of the Alps and in Rome as the true Pope. He retired and went with Lothair to Germany until 1136 when Lothair reinstated him as the one and only Pope.

Dr. G.: Is there anything about your work that you don't like?

Brian: It's my damn, incompetent apprentice.

Dr. G.: Tell me about your apprentice.

Brian: There's not much to tell. I took this young lad into my shop and tried to make a craftsman out of him. But he doesn't seem to be able to do the work.

Dr. G.: What's his name?

Brian: Thayer.

At this point my skin began to crawl. However, my obligation was to my current patient, and it was important to continue this regression as if nothing unusual had happened. After all, Brian knew nothing of Arnold.

Dr. G.: What exactly does Thayer do that bothers you?

Brian: He exists. That bothers me. I don't know what it is about him but I don't like him. I seem to want to hurt him. He is an incompetent and will never be the master craftsman that I am.

It was significant that Brian lacked this oversize ego in his present life. Although he was unquestionably independent and successful, he was almost soft-spoken and never exhibited such self-importance. In his life as Gustave, he was coarse, crude, cruel, and sadistic. His voice was deeper than Brian's, and he spoke much more rapidly.

Dr. G.: How do you treat Thayer?

Brian: Ha, ha! You ask a very interesting question. I am too kind to the lad. I feed him, clothe him, and beat him. I am a good provider.

Dr. G.: You beat him?

Brian: You are offended? Of course I beat him. He deserves no better.

Dr. G.: Do you enjoy beating him?

Brian: Yes. He does anything I ask, and I ask a lot. He doesn't like what I ask of him, but I own him.

Dr. G.: Tell me more of your life.

Brian: I work hard. I get up with the sun and work until the sun goes down. My work is fine. I am a great craftsman. I am a master.

Gustave went on to describe the details of his life. He was a very lonely and disturbed man. People bothered him. It wasn't just Thayer whom he didn't like. He didn't like anyone. Cruelty made him feel good. Thayer provided him with companionship and someone on whom he could vent his frustrations.

Chaining Thayer to the table—which Arnold had described to me from Thayer's point of view—was an example of Gustave's cruelty. The chain was purposely made short to make it uncomfortable for Thayer. Even the simple act of eating became a humiliation. Thayer was used, manipulated, dominated, and utterly degraded by Gustave, nor was Gustave shy about describing the homosexual acts he committed with Thayer.

I next progressed Gustave to the year 1135.

Dr. G.: How is your business these days?

Brian: Business is good thanks to my skill, but not thanks to that good-for-nothing apprentice of mine. All he seems to care about is that damn girl.

Dr. G.: What girl is that?

Brian: Clotilde.

Dr. G.: Who is Clotilde?

Brian: She is the daughter of a wealthy nobleman. Her family has been doing business with me for a long time. Imagine, that incompetent actually thinks that a nobleman's daughter could actually love a commoner—and an incompetent one at that!

Dr. G.: Why is that so impossible to imagine?

Brian: Look, I am a master craftsman. If I can't have a noblewoman such as Clotilde, I'll be damned if I'm going to let Thayer have her. I will see to it that she sees him for what he is.

Dr. G.: And what is that?

Brian: A commoner. A possession of mine, and a rather worthless one at that.

Dr. G.: Wouldn't you like to be involved with someone like Clotilde?

Brian's response to that question was a string of obscenities. I seemed to have struck a nerve with that question. Apparently, Gustave's misanthropy and his homosexual tendencies grew out of his frustration at not being able to socialize with the nobility. This was a feudal society with a strict class system. Master guildsmen were not allowed to marry or consort with noblewomen. To make matters worse, Gustave was physically unattractive and crude. These frustrations, among others, led to Gustave's attitude toward Thayer and Clotilde. He used Thayer as his scapegoat.

I progressed Brian to the resolution of the situation between Gustave and Thayer.

Dr. G.: What is happening now?

Brian: I'm going to fix that Thayer once and for all.

Dr. G.: What did he do now?

Brian: It's that Clotilde. She had the nerve to ask me to let Thayer go to her house for some special work. Why didn't she ask me to go? I am the master, the best. He is just an apprentice!

Dr. G.: Is that all that's bothering you?

Brian: No! I came very close to hurting that girl. She got me very mad.

Dr. G.: Have you ever acted that way before with her?

Brian: No. Of course not. It's Thayer's fault and I'm going to fix him good.

Dr. G.: What are you going to do to him?

Brian: I'm going to feed him very well tonight. Then I'm going to give him the beating of his life.

Dr. G.: Don't you think that Thayer will sense that something is wrong?

Brian: I don't care. I just want to beat him until he begs for mercy.

Dr. G.: On the count of five, move forward to the actual confrontation with Thayer.
One...two...three...four...five. What do you see now?

Brian: I'm chaining Thayer to the table. He looks a little strange after I tell him that this will be a night that he will long remember.

Dr. G.: What happens next?

Brian: He talks back to me and keeps moving his legs so I can't chain him to the table. That crazy fool jumps at me and tries to knock me down.

Dr. G.: What do you do about it?

Brian: I laugh at the fool for his futile attempt to hurt me. Then I pick him up and throw him on the table. He knocks over the nice meal I fixed for him. He will regret this night.

Dr. G.: Where are you now?

Brian: I'm standing by the table slapping the idiot. He reaches for my throat and tries to strangle me. Now I'm really mad.

Dr. G.: What happens next?

Brian: I pick him up again and throw him against the wall. My tools are there and I tease him with a very sharp knife. He curses me and I lose my temper. I stab him again and again. It feels good to rid myself of this incompetent. He is not worth any more trouble. I killed him and I am glad.

Dr. G.: Where did you stab Thayer?

Brian: First I stabbed him in his stomach and then I stabbed him in the neck.

I brought Brian back to the present after a few minutes. He seemed drained from the session, but he was very impressed by this experience. He didn't want to pursue additional regressions. Apparently, he felt this one exposure was sufficient.

Over the next few months, Brian made considerable progress in controlling his manipulative and domineering tendencies. He has since sent numerous referrals to me. I never did tell him of the case of Arnold and his past life as Thayer. My professional ethics prevent me from revealing the details of another patient's case history.

I have already discussed the concept of synchronicity. Suffice it to say, my exposure to these two regressions was no coincidence. The odds must be millions to one against such a situation occurring. The correspondences were nothing short of startling. All the names, dates, and events matched. The main difference occurs in the two accounts of the final fight between Thayer (Arnold) and Gustave (Brian). According to Thayer, he jumps Gustave, wrestles him to the floor, and is stabbed in the stomach repeatedly after Gustave throws him against the wall. In Gustave's version, he picks up Thayer and throws him against the wall and stabs him in the stomach repeatedly and then in the neck. The only discrepancy seems to be who first accosts whom, because if the stomach wound kills Thayer, he would never know he had been stabbed in the neck!

Of course, I considered the possibility of fraud. But it seems clear to me that neither man had anything to gain from collusion. And if this was some sort of practical joke, I fail to see a motive. I had never discussed writing this book with either of them. In fact, it wasn't until October of 1980 that I even considered writing a book. And it was a year and a half between the two regressions. Finally, neither of them has ever contacted me with respect to publishing their cases. I can only think of this as an example of synchronicity.

Many people have asked me whether Arnold and Brian have ever met in this lifetime. The answer is that they have not met in this incarnation and I had no knowledge of their relationship prior to my regressing them. Furthermore, I have no intention of introducing them, for many reasons. First, if they were supposed to meet again to work out their karma, then they would have come into contact with each other long before they met me. Second, I do not attempt to play God with my patients. To introduce these two people, considering their past life history, would affect both of their karmic cycles. If this were meant to be, it would already be out of my control. Third, I would be concerned about Arnold's possible reaction to Brian, and vice versa. Considering the details of the regressions, both could be hostile and violent.

My involvement as the middleman may very well have been a test of my own karmic cycle. It was tempting to introduce these patients to each other. However, this may have done them both more harm than good, physically and psychologically. Perhaps my knowledge of both Brian and Arnold did help me understand the effects they had on each other during the Middle Ages. I did not feel that they would have benefited at all from their meeting in this lifetime. Perhaps they will meet in this life, but it won't be through me. My role in these two cases is complete. My task is to help the patient understand the root causes of his or her problems through the use of hypnotic regressions so that he or she is rid of mysterious compulsions and can lead a better existence in this lifetime.

Both Arnold and Brian's lives have, in fact, been significantly improved as a result of hypnotherapy and especially past life regression. Arnold is less afraid and more self-confident; Brian informed me that he had successfully resisted two opportunities to manipulate a new lawyer in his firm. In addition, Brian's insomnia disappeared entirely, and he lost 25 pounds. Because neither of them showed any interest in exploring additional past lives, I can only guess that they did share additional lifetimes since the 12th century and I hope they fulfilled their karmic obligations.

Chapter 10

Subpersonalities as Past Life Carryovers

There are many types of entities that assist us with our spiritual growth. These perfect beings are referred to as spirit guides or angels. In certain instances, these entities can protect us from physical harm, and can facilitate a major turnaround in our lives.

However, there are other types of entities that function to drain us, and need to be both confronted and removed. I refer to this syndrome as subpersonalities.

A subpersonality is an attached entity that negatively affects our behavior. It may be a remnant of our past-life history and personality, or it may be the energy of another soul.

As a result of this subpersonality attaching itself to our aura or soul itself, a Jekyll/Hyde-like personality change often is observed in the affected individual. One may, for example, suddenly act considerably out of character. His actions may even be self-destructive. He may suddenly know things that he would have no reason to know. Or he may begin referring to himself in the third person, saying things like, "Let Jim figure this out."

Other common characteristics associated with sub-personalities are:

1. Autism.
2. Anorexia nervosa.
3. Bulimia.
4. Emotional instability.
5. Insomnia.
6. Patterns of shifting psychosomatic complaints.
7. Memory lapses.
8. Drug abuse.
9. Migraine headaches.
10. Abusive relationships.
11. Depression.

Subpersonalities are rarely stable. Left untreated, people who have subpersonalities may exhibit bizarre and unsettling behavior. These entities can attach themselves to our very being at any time during our lives, but most commonly become part of our awareness during traumatic episodes.

Psychiatrists would label these subpersonalities as Dissociative Identity Disorder (which was previously called Multiple Personality Disorder). As is often the case, conventional therapists miss the point with these unusual cases.

There are four types. Here is a summary of these subpersonalities:

1. *Poltergeists.* Ghosts or poltergeists comprise the most common category of subpersonalities. These entities are souls who lived as humans, but crossed into spirit (died) and have refused to enter the white light (their Higher Self), which is critical for them to reincarnate. These spirits usually do not desire to take over the body of the host. They are merely dysfunctional souls that attach themselves to our auras as a comfortable place to nest.

2. *Extraterrestrials (ETs).* Occasionally ETs attach themselves to our souls' energy. This is done to study our reactions, as they appear to be fascinated by our emotional responses to stress.
3. *Past Life Personalities.* In rare instances, one of our past lives can remain as a subpersonality, and attach itself to our auras in an attempt to take over our bodies or just cancel our actions.
4. *Demons.* Demonic entities were never human. They are fallen angels, and they have been around since the universe was created. During possession, their goal is the permanent takeover of an individual's body and soul. In order for a demonic to take control of a soul, it requires permission. Playing with Ouija boards and attempting to contact spirits without the benefit of white light or other protective techniques are examples of how this permission may be granted. This is the least common type.

Examples of Subpersonality Attacks

A good example of a poltergeist attack occurred with a patient I shall call Vanessa. Through hypnosis, I learned that Vanessa had attended a funeral in 1993. The spirit of Ingrid, a psychotic woman who committed suicide at that cemetery, attached herself to Vanessa there. Superconscious mind taps and integration quickly sent Ingrid's personality to the white light. Vanessa is free of her subpersonality, and happier than she has ever been.

Fortunately, past life possession attempts are quite rare. Claudine's case is a good example of this phenomena. She was murdered in a past life by a man named Sam. Sam had killed her in a jealous rage, but he was never punished for the crime, which took place more than 150 years ago.

Claudine came to me because she had been plagued by alcoholism and depression. When I regressed her through hypnosis, we discovered that Sam's fragmented subpersonality had attached itself to her. The disturbed, murdering aspect of Sam's soul was still jealous of her, and it wanted to wreck her current marriage to Tom.

The treatment was surprisingly simple. In a single session with both Tom and Claudine, I used hypnosis to connect Claudine's subconscious mind, or soul, with her Higher Self, or superconscious mind. I asked her Higher Self what the origin of the problem was. Claudine's voice suddenly became very deep and low and Sam began speaking to me. Tom looked on, shocked, with his jaw hanging open.

I then confronted Sam. I directed Sam to enter the white light. By contacting its own Higher Self, a soul will, to a certain degree, raise the quality of its energy and better prepare itself for a future life. Once the subpersonality enters the light, it can never return to bother the host again.

Marsha's case illustrates a rather dynamic attempt at past life possession. She was a devout Christian professional woman in her early 30s. The only difficult past relationship she reported that was difficult was with a man named Hal. Dan is her fiancé, but is concerned about Marsha's recent bizarre behavior: She is blasphemous toward the church, she acts like a prostitute with strange men, and she is having nightmares about being murdered on a tropical island.

During her past life in Martinique during the 1700s, she was a young girl named Jacqueline, studying in a convent to become a nun. One night, a drunken sailor raped her. She was comforted by the priest, but decided to run away from the convent. She ended up in a brothel working as a prostitute. The owner of the brothel was obsessed with her, beat her, and murdered her during a fit of jealous rage.

For two months, the past life fragment of Marsha's soul (a subpersonality) literally attempted to take over Marsha's body. This possession attempt accounted for Marsha's behavior out of her normal character.

Dan is the reincarnation of the priest and Hal is the current life of the brothel owner. Past life regression and superconscious mind taps were the techniques used to confront Jacqueline and permanently remove her presence from Marsha's body. Marsha returned to her normal lifestyle and never heard from Jacqueline again.

Following very simple hypnotic techniques, dysfunctional behaviors stop immediately. My patients describe the effect as having a burden lifted or a blockage removed. They return to normal life, feeling stronger than ever. If you feel you have a subpersonality, I highly recommend my psychic protection from negativity and superconscious mind cassette tapes.

Chapter 11

The "Light" People

In my work as a hypnotherapist specializing in time travel, I once thought I had seen just about every type of case imaginable. Guiding thousands of patients into past and future lives, accessing spirit guides and time travelers from our future (see chapters 16 and 17), detailing abductees' encounters with extraterrestrials and training them to slow down and reverse the aging process and so on seemed to complete the spectrum.

What I didn't discover was the true origin of our karmic cycle and cases of patients' first lifetime on Earth until I did a "light" people regression. I have always been a proponent of extraterrestrial (ET) origins of our species, along with reincarnation paradigms.

Although this is one of the most controversial theories in parapsychology, the case history of one of my patients might lend it some credence. The true origin of life on this planet will surprise you. My research shows that certain ""light" people," originating from other solar systems, appear to be responsible for not only our evolutionary advancement, but for the karmic cycle itself. The "light" people posses no physical body, but are pure energy in the form of light.

Interestingly, most of the cases I have done with "light" people regressions involve people who show no interest in ETs or reincarnation. These cases simply surface by themselves and are most commonly preceded by the patient having strange dreams about these light beings.

A "light" people regression is the most difficult type to conduct. There seems to be a bubble-like energy field surrounding the patients that compromises their ability to communicate. The patient is censored by a group of "light" people known as the "Planners," which makes getting information rather difficult.

The only reason I can elicit any information whatsoever is because I have conducted numerous "light" people regressions, and I can relate to them on their level of awareness.

I have regressed more than 1,000 patients to past lives as "light" people, and the reports I received showed consistent characteristics, which will be detailed at the end of this chapter.

From my research, I learned that the "light" people are sent to Earth from another galaxy to experience life in human bodies. Their goal is to assist us in our evolutionary development. When light" people leave their human bodies, they return to an examination room (although this is not a physical room as we know it). Their progress is evaluated by a group of monitors or Planners. If they do well, their vibrational rate is raised, but if they fail, it's reduced. These Planners are directed by Master Planners who communicate with them from the home planet many galaxies away.

When I sense a "light" people regression is about to transpire, I never prepare the patient for the experience. My reasoning is to eliminate imposing my belief system on them and preventing any possibility of preconceptions on their part.

When Ed called my office, it was simply to utilize age regression to retrieve a lost watch given to him by his grandfather, who had since passed away. That goal was accomplished easily in a single session. He requested another hypnotherapy session to explore his childhood and this is what surfaced:

Dr. G.: Where are you at this time?

Ed: I am in an examination chamber.

Dr. G.: How old are you?

Ed: I have no age. Why are you asking me these questions?

Dr. G.: What is your name?

Ed: I am a Planner. Why can't I see your essence?

By now I correctly deduced that this was a "light" people regression, so my subsequent questioning took a far different path, as compared to a regular regression to one's childhood.

Dr. G.: I am a Master Planner, far above you in vibrational rate.

Ed: Why have I not been told of your presence?

Dr. G.: You function on a need-to-know basis. Now, no further questions. I will ask the questions and you will answer.

At this time there was about a five-minute delay in Ed's next response. "Light" people are always restricted in what they can say and a Planner is no different. Because he was not prepared for a Master Planner, he became concerned that he may be under investigation.

Dr. G.: What is going on in the examination chamber at this time?

Ed: It's XL-47. He has done well on this planet, and I am in the process of raising his vibrational rate.

"Light" people came to our planet to facilitate our evolution, and they inhabited the bodies of primitive humans while altering genetic coding and other biological processes to promote our development.

After a period of time within our bodies, these beings of pure light were somehow extracted and taken to an evaluation chamber in the form of a fifth dimensional "room" of sorts.

The room is more like an *energy point*. It consists of swirling lights, most of which are white, but other colors are present. There are *black voids* in this room, which function as entry and exit points for Planners and other more advanced "light" people.

Dr. G.: What is XL-47's status at this time?

Ed: His essence is yellow and will be raised to green shortly.

The "light" people have a hierarchy of colors to their essence. White represents the top of this pyramid and is reserved for Master Planners and other highly evolved beings. The lowest level is red and is followed in increasing quality by orange, yellow, green, blue, indigo, and violet. You may recognize these as colors of the rainbow.

XL-47's current frequency vibrational rate appears as a yellow (third level) essence and will undergo some sort of fifth-dimensional manipulation to be raised to a green (fourth-level) color. I cannot detail the precise mechanism, as that type of data is restricted and anything about this group of ETs is hard to obtain.

Dr. G.: Will XL-47 have to return to a physical body?

Ed: Oh yes. He still has a long way to go, but he is progressing at a rapid rate.

Dr. G.: Have you had any problems lately with any of your group?

Ed: Yes. MR-62 was examined not long ago and he failed many tests.

At this time, I should explain that "light" people can enter and leave the physical body just about any time they desire. They must perform certain functions and assist the human they are occupying in its intelligence and social functions.

Sometimes these "light" people get carried away with the physicality of the body and violate moral and ethereal codes (such as obsessions with sex, drugs, or murder), or merely refuse to perform the functions for which they were trained. When this happens, the Planners punish these "light" people.

Dr. G.: What tests did MR-62 fail?

Ed: He spent too much time eating and enjoying other physical pleasures (sex), and delayed his required reporting to me.

Dr. G.: What did you do?

Ed: Because MR-62 failed basic assignments, he was punished by being forced to remain in the physical body. His actions resulted in certain physical ailments (upset stomach), so he was not permitted to leave his body.

Dr. G.: What else did you do?

Ed: I brought him to the examination chamber and lectured him about his responsibilities.

Dr. G.: How did he respond?

Ed: He tried to leave, so I immobilized him with my thoughts and placed him in a state of suspended animation for hours at a time.

Apparently, MR-62 was in deep trouble. He failed to perform adequately and his vibrational rate was now in danger of being lowered. This technique of a Planner immobilizing a light being has been reported to me almost every time I have conducted this type of past life regression. I continued my questioning of Ed.

Dr. G.: Have you had any more extreme examples of failure with your group?

Ed: Why all these concerns? Am I being threatened with some form of discipline?

As a Planner, Ed was now becoming a bit paranoid. It seems that "those who live by the sword die by the sword" was applicable to the "light" people hierarchy.

Dr. G.: Remember, I am a Master Planner. I will ask the questions. Your role is to answer them and report to me. Understood?

Ed: Yes. I apologize for my insubordination. In response to your question regarding more extreme examples of failure, I do have a report to make.

Dr. G.: Go on.

Ed: One of my agents, QZ-468, failed every test he was assigned.

Dr. G.: How did you handle him?

Ed: His essence was reduced to red (the lowest level) and he was given a final notice that if he failed again, he would be abandoned.

Dr. G.: What happened then?

Ed: He failed again, and I had no choice but to banish him by imprisoning him permanently in the physical form and deleting all memories of his true origin.

The mechanism of the origin of our karmic cycle now became clear. Advanced ETs from a distant galaxy in the form of light energy experimented with humans to aid us in our evolution. Many of these "light" people took advantage (or were overwhelmed) by our physicality and ran afoul with what the Master Planners had in store.

The Planners, as supervisors to the progress of these "light" people, had the power to trap these light beings into our physical bodies and remove their memories so they would not be psychologically compromised as they began life as a human.

If they learned karmic lessons as a human, their vibrational rate could still be raised. This sounds very similar to the karmic cycle with reincarnation being the modality.

Although the transcript between Ed and me seems easy to follow, this was not an easy past life regression. "Light" people regressions are always difficult and time consuming. It's as if everything even a Planner says is being censored.

"Light" people regressions represent fewer than 5 percent of the 35,000 regressions I have conducted. They often appear at significant moments in a person's life. Usually, patients who have had a previous life as a light person want to explore their first human incarnation on Earth. They show little interest in extraterrestrial life.

Here are some other observations I have made concerning the "light" people:

- They communicate entirely by telepathy.
- They are unquestionably from another galaxy.
- They are not time travelers and do not originate from the future.
- They function on a different dimension (fifth dimension). The only things that can confine them are *magnetic fields* and *thought patterns* controlled by the Planners. Planners can immobilize "light" people merely by directing certain thoughts at them.
- There is a definite hierarchy, with Master Planners being above Planners.
- The highest ranking "light" people are referred to as the "source" or "All That Is."
- "Light" people describe themselves as pulsating lights with varying degrees of intensity. Their essence may be white or any rainbow color. *Rank is determined by their frequency vibrational rate.*

I have concluded that "light" people—trapped in human bodies—represent the beginning of our karmic cycle. We are fortunate that these aliens tampered with our evolution. Our present level of technology might have been unattainable without their aid.

Chapter 12

Seeing Into the Future

Age Progression

In the field of parapsychology, the term *precognition* is used to describe the accurate descriptions by a test subject of events in the future. I personally feel the term "age progression" is preferable to "precognition" in describing moving forward in time with hypnosis. Many people consider precognition to be a unique mystical experience, and find the expression age progression easier for the average person to relate to.

How Progression Works

My experience with guiding patients into their future has given me a certain vantage point of the universe that is enlightening and worth sharing. Basically there are six ways to learn about the future. These are:

1. Clairaudience—Hearing sounds or voices that are undetectable by our ears concerning the future.
2. Clairvoyance—Discerning objects or events that are not present to the normal five senses.
3. Forecasting—Making predictions of the future by use of mathematical projections or other objectively obtained data, as in predicting the

winner of an election with only a small percent of the precincts reporting in.

4. Prophesying—Reading the future from subjective impressions or feeling in an altered state of consciousness.
5. Age/Future Life Progression—Using hypnosis to actually see into the future before it occurs.
6. Fifth Dimension Travel—This out-of-body experience is associated with increased sensory awareness and a loss of a sense of time so that it is impossible to differentiate the future from the present. When the scene from the future actually becomes reality, you feel as if you have seen this before.

Several theories of precognition have been advanced. Most are abstruse, some ingenious, none adequate. Basically, these theories fall into two categories. The first looks on the future as an already existent reality, one that exists as fully and objectively as the present does. The future is not a potentiality, but an actuality. Fate corresponds approximately with our concept of what has been decreed, or our past action (karma). We feel we are victims of fate, caught in its web, or net.

The second theory postulates a "plastic" or provisional future that exists now in somewhat the same way that a human being exists the instant the sperm meets the ovum. A lot can happen to a fetus between conception and birth, and possibly the same sort of incident—abortion, miscarriage, premature delivery—can occur to an event gestating in the "womb of time." The term *destiny*, which corresponds loosely with the Indian notion of *dharma*, is flexible and our free will has a great effect on its eventual manifestation.

A plastic future rejects the notion that the future already exists. It says that tomorrow is real only in potentiality. The future is capable of taking many possible final forms. Only when it congeals into the present does it really exist as an actuality. In other words, we live in a framework of potentiality and it is our actions that determine its final form. We can change our future.

We can test the validity of age progression by simply comparing the recorded data to events that actually transpire days, weeks, or months in the future. There simply have been far too many documented examples of specified prognostications that came true to ignore this discipline.

A good example of a documented age progression is that of the 18th century scientist and philosopher Emanuel Swedenborg's prediction of his own death. In early 1772, John Wesley, founder of the Methodist church, requested a meeting with Swedenborg for sometime in the summer. Swedenborg informed him that he would die on March 29, 1772 so he would not be able to keep this date. Swedenborg did, in fact, die on March 29, 1772 of natural causes. We have this case documented because it appeared in Wesley's own personal journal.

Here are some other examples of age progressions:

Jules Verne

This 19th-century French stockbroker turned novelist authored several novels about the future. In one of his lesser-known books called *An Ideal City*, Verne depicts music recitals being heard around the world as a result of being transmitted down a wire from the artist to certain pianos. Does this not sound like a primitive reference to MP3 music on the Internet?

In 1865, he wrote his classic *From the Earth to the Moon*, in which he described intimate details that paralleled those of America's first flight to the moon by Apollo 11 in July of 1969. For example:

- The initial breakaway velocity of Jules Verne's craft was 36,000 feet per second while Apollo 11's third stage velocity was 35,533 feet per second.
- The huge cannon that fired Verne's capsule into space was called the Columbiad, while the

Apollo 11 mission was carried out by the Columbia. Both capsules orbited the moon several times, occasionally at the same altitude. Both teams took photographs, and the Verne capsule crew even charted the Sea of Tranquility, where the Apollo 11 crew landed.

- The launch sites were almost identical. Verne chose a spot in Florida about 140 miles due west of Cape Kennedy. In Verne's story, Texas fought for the honor. Today Mission Control is in Houston, Texas.
- Both capsules splashed down in the Pacific and both crews were picked up by American Navy ships.

The Sinking of the *Titanic*

Morgan Robertson wrote a novel in 1898 titled *Futility*, in which a supposedly unsinkable ocean liner struck an iceberg on its maiden voyage and sank, carrying the elite society of two continents to their deaths.

Fourteen years later, in 1912, a similar "unsinkable" liner sailed from England with 3,000 passengers aboard. Like Robertson's craft, it was 800 feet long and weighed 70,000 tons, but with far too few lifeboats. The real boat, like Robertson's, struck an iceberg and sank with the loss of more than 1,000 lives. Robertson had named his boat, the *Titan*. The real ship was the *Titanic*.

Edward Bellamy

Looking Backward, written in 1888 by Edward Bellamy, was one of the most influential American books on social reform prior to the 20th century. He wrote this masterpiece from the perspective of the year 2000, and it was an attempt to detail an ideal path of social development from 1888 to the beginning of the 21st century.

Bellamy described a music room in the home that contained three or four skillfully placed audio amplifiers concealed in the walls. Adjacent to one are several knobs, which, when turned, will bring in any one of four different musical programs at the volume desired. A listing of the programs available at each hour is delivered daily to every home that subscribes to this service. All programs are supplied throughout the 24-hour day and are sent also into the bedrooms where a smaller speaker or even headphones are provided. This may seem commonplace today, but we must remember it was written in 1888!

The houses in Bellamy's description had electricity and a central heating system. Public laundries, equivalent to modern day Laundromats, were delineated, as were the common usage of restaurants. Restaurants were a relative rarity in his day. Electric alarm clocks and credit cards that are accepted throughout the world were also components of Bellamy's depiction of the year 2000.

My own age progression while driving

My own trip into the future occurred while driving to Ft. Lauderdale, Florida from the University of Maryland School of Dentistry, where I was a student in the early 1970s. Because Christmas vacation represented the only significant break until the summer, I looked forward to these trips.

My method of maximizing this vacation time consisted of driving straight to Florida from Baltimore, stopping only four times for gas on the 1,000 mile trip. This particular trip was significant because, while driving in the very early hours of the morning, I nearly dozed off on the highway. Occasionally, a jolting sensation sharpened my conscious awareness.

The next thing I was aware of was arriving in Florida, renting a room in a private residence, and being frustrated at not being able to fall asleep due to my now-alert mind. I noticed an unusual design to the wallpaper in the room as I lay on the bed trying to provide my fatigued body with its needed rest. I did eventually fall asleep.

Back on the highway, I was jolted back into a hyper-alert consciousness and completed my trip to Florida. My first thought was, "Did I dream that scene or did I really go into the future?"

Upon arrival in Ft. Lauderdale, every detail of my "dream" manifested into reality. When I purchased a paper, I haphazardly called the telephone number from an ad showing a room to rent in a private home. After arriving at this house, I dragged my fatigued body to the bed and found it difficult to sleep, because my mind was still in a hyper-alert state. Lastly, I noticed the wallpaper of the bedroom bearing the exact unusual design I had "seen" on the highway in Georgia several hours before! I had never been to this house before. These events convinced me that I definitely viewed my future.

An age progression saves a life

Consider the case of a patient who worked with me several years ago. Tami had just graduated from college in June of 1996. She lived in New York and came to my Los Angeles office to learn how to see into the future. I completed her training by the second week in June, and she returned to New York.

One issue Tami had was what to do during the summer, as she was entering graduate school that September. After a few days of contemplation, Tami decided to travel to Europe and spend the last half of the summer there.

She practiced the technique we worked on during her stay in Los Angeles, and became a fairly experienced hypnotic subject by the end of June. At that time, she decided to fly to Paris first, as some of her friends were there and wanted her to join them on their European trip.

One thing that shocked Tami was that she saw her plane take off from JFK airport in New York, and quickly crash, killing everyone aboard. At first, this bothered Tami. She became excited about going to Europe, but her previous use of my age progression methods had already demonstrated their accuracy, during which she was able to see into the future and affect minor changes in her life.

Her solution was to not leave for Europe until the end of July. Tami's original plans called for her leaving New York on July 17th on TWA Flight 800. I'm sure this flight will be familiar to you. It crashed, killing all 230 passengers and crew. Had Tami ignored the information she obtained from her hypnotic age progression, she would be dead now.

Tami was very thankful to me when she called my office to inform me of these events. I didn't hear from her until late September, and tried to reiterate the fact that it was her abilities and spiritual growth that saved her life, not me. I merely trained her.

The Space-Time Continuum

Many dreams seem to contain fragments of futuristic material, just as they contain fragments from the past. In sleep, the mind appears to wander freely back and forth over the "equator," an imaginary line between the present and the future. At the deepest level of consciousness, there is no sense of the flow of time, only an "eternal now" in which all events coexist.

Modern day physicists use the term *space-time continuum* (coined by Albert Einstein) to illustrate the fact that there is no such thing as the past, present, or future as we know it. All of our lives are being lived at the same moment but at different frequencies. Thus, your past lives are occurring right now on a different frequency along with your present and future lives. They are all affecting each other. You are thus able to change the past and future by changing the present (see Figure 2).

Suppose, for example, that you are in a helicopter above a major highway. You look down and see that traffic is stopped because of an accident. At this time, you could radio someone in a car five miles behind the scene of the accident and inform the driver of the upcoming traffic problem. Because you are in a helicopter above the traffic flow, you are actually detached from the scene itself. The driver that you are warning is immersed within the flow of traffic. In a sense, you are reading the future of this car. If the driver of that car keeps driving on that highway, he will encounter the congested traffic that you are now observing. The helicopter represents another dimensional plane, and on a different plane, there is no time as we here on Earth (or on the highway, in this analogy) know it.

To extend the analogy further, note that from the vantage point of the helicopter, you could also see what the traffic flow is like behind the car to whose driver you are talking. This would represent the past. The traffic ahead of the driver represents the future, and the traffic that the driver is experiencing now represents the present. You are, in effect, reading the past, present, and future from the helicopter. By leaving the Earth plane, or entering into hypnotic trance, you can read the past or future without the restrictions that occur in the waking state.

The confusing aspect of progression (perceiving one's future) is that the effect appears to precede the cause, violating causality laws of conventional physics. Because space and time do not exist independently, but as a continuum known as space-time, this fourth dimensional paradigm allows an effect to come before a cause. Our brain is constructed to deal with only three dimensions (length, width, and depth). This fourth dimension known as time (in reality, the fourth dimension of the space-time continuum) often confuses our three-dimensionally oriented brain.

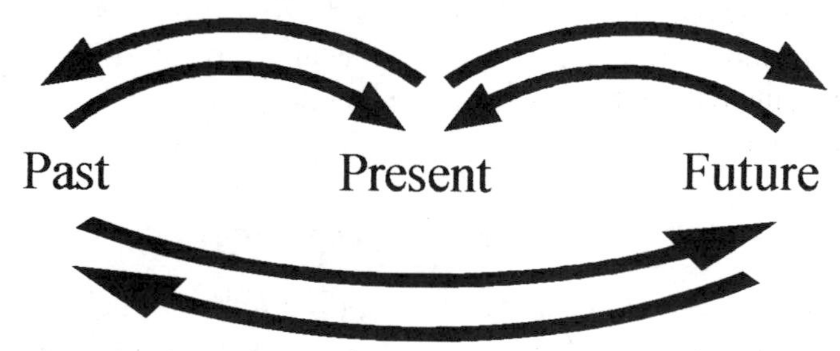

Figure 2. The Space-Time Continuum.

We can show how the brain can do this futuristic viewing by applying a theory developed by Professor John Taylor of King's College, London. He hypothesizes that our brain emits *tachyons*, impulses traveling faster than light, thereby reaching into the future and then being reflected back to the brain, giving foreknowledge.

If some form of energy is transmitted from the human body capable of traveling faster than light, it might not emanate from the brain itself. It could originate from the Akashic records (see page 258) stored on the fifth dimension. Not having traveled faster than light, and so into the future, would the impressions and messages necessarily be received directly by the brain, but by the subconscious mind. The brain might pick up the impulses after the outgoing energy waves had been reflected back, radar fashion, to the bodily source of transmission. Quantum physics clearly demonstrates that any tachyon would move in reverse time sequences.

Forbidden Knowledge

The concept of "forbidden knowledge" is often mentioned by my patients. People ask me, "Isn't knowledge of future events prohibited by the universe?" The answer is simple. If you are supposed to know something, such as your future, your Higher Self will see to it that you receive that data. If, however, you are not supposed to be aware of certain future events, then no person, place, or thing will give you that information (unless and until you are ready to receive it). Even with my highly sophisticated techniques and extraordinary success rates, I cannot arrange for you to receive information that you are not supposed to have. When the student is ready, the teacher will be there.

A Future Life Progression

Age regression is simply viewing the future of one's current life. When you perceive a life in some distant century in a new physical body, the term *future life progression* is applied. I discovered this discipline back in 1977 when I asked a patient to go to the origin of a difficulty and she went forward to the 23rd century! The future life illustrates a karmic lesson or pattern, which is usually manifested in their current life. This often includes the same people, and provides a way to learn from the future to correct the present, thereby affecting the future.

The interesting aspect of future life progression hypnotherapy is not merely the technological advances one observes, but the growth in the soul's way of dealing with and hopefully resolving issues from its many prior lifetimes.

Traditionally, most of my patients are fascinated by their past lives. They usually are not interested in exploring future lifetimes. Much of this has to do with fear. When they resolve this fear, they are more open to the experience.

Mark's case is interesting in many ways because he illustrates growth from his present incarnation. His background is a rather conservative one. He is a CPA from Florida and was divorced, having two very unsuccessful marriages. His three children couldn't relate to him and he rarely spent time with them.

You could accurately describe Mark as a loner and very depressed. He expressed no interest in exploring previous lives and just desired to see if a future life would be happier than his present one.

Mark described his present life as rather boring. He was quite competent as an accountant, but lacked passion for his work. Everyone he knew considered his profession as lacking in excitement and this added to his feelings of isolation. He informed me that in college, he was rejected from two fraternities and all he could recall was how much he studied while most of the people he knew were partying.

Mark's trip to my Los Angeles office in 2000 seemed to be a very special highlight in his otherwise routine and dull life. After preparing him for a future life progression, I began my questioning.

Dr. G.: Where do you find yourself?

Mark: I'm in an underwater city.

Dr. G.: How old are you?

Mark: 15.

Dr. G.: Where are your parents?

Mark: I have none.

Dr. G.: What is your name?

Mark: Elam.

Dr. G.: What year is it Elam?

Mark: 2837.

Elam lives in what we call Greenland today in an underwater city. Greenland is a member of the Atlantic Federation and this democratic government replaced the League of One during the 28th century about 100 years earlier.

The reason why Elam says he has no parents is because he is a test tube baby who was developed in an artificial host and never knew who the donors were. A type of foster-home approach exists here to raise these children.

Dr. G.: Do you know why you were selected to be a test tube baby?

Mark: It had something to do with assuring I would have special skills and potential for a productive career.

As I progressed Mark forward I found out that he was just average, and that the test tube baby experiment apparently failed in his case. By the age of 18, he was sent above ground to be trained as a pilot.

Dr. G.: Elam, tell me about your new home.

Mark: I like living above ground. The monorails are fun, as well as efficient in getting around town.

Dr. G.: How else do you travel?

Mark: Well for short local trips, I use the teleportation station in my den. We have large ships (planes) for longer trips and I hope to fly them someday.

Dr. G.: Do you have any cars?

Mark: Yes, we have vehicles that don't contain wheels. They are antigravity cars that travel a few feet to several hundred feet above ground.

I next progressed Mark to the completion of his training as a pilot and his future job.

Dr. G.: Tell me about your work, Elam.

Mark: I am very upset. I couldn't qualify for the pilot position for the large ships I discussed.

Dr. G.: So what kind of work do you do now?

Mark: I am a copilot on a charter transport service.

Dr. G.: Where do you travel to?

Mark: We take people from the Earth to recreational areas and resorts on the moon.

Dr. G.: That sounds interesting.

Mark: It really isn't. The crafts mostly fly themselves by way of the computers and it's really a boring trip.

Dr. G.: Is there anything about your job you like?

Mark: Well yes. After we arrive on the moon, there is a layover of several days and I mostly party with the other guys and some of the guests.

Mark was describing the equivalent of a fraternity party on the moon while waiting to return to Earth with tourists whose vacations had ended. Perhaps this made up for Mark's lack of a fraternity party life in college. Even with this fringe benefit, Elam was still unfulfilled.

Dr. G.: Do you have a girlfriend, Elam?

Mark: Yes. Her name is Zia and she is beautiful.

As I continued questioning Mark about Zia, I discovered that they got along quite well. The only problem was that Zia wanted to get married and disliked Elam's job. He was away so much and she also knew about the partying.

Dr. G.: How are you getting along with Zia now?

Mark: It's terrible. She keeps trying to get me to quit my job and use my talents on Earth.

Dr. G.: What talent is that?

Mark: Oh, didn't I tell you? I am an inventor.

Dr. G.: Is that why you were a test tube baby? Was the purpose to have you become an inventor?

Mark: Yes, but it never quite worked out.

I could see a past life carryover developing in Mark's future life as Elam. In both lives, he feels as if he is a failure, and appears to be trying to make up for lack of social experience in his current life as Mark and in his future life as Elam.

I then progressed Elam forward to a significant event in his relationship with Zia.

Dr. G.: What has happened since I last spoke with you?

Mark: It's terrible! I had a big fight with Zia over marriage and told her that I simply am not cut out for it.

Dr. G.: What did she do?

Mark: She broke up with me.

Mark's two unsuccessful marriages may have carried over into his future life as Elam as fear of commitment and of the institution itself.

Following his breakup with Zia, Elam had a nervous breakdown. I progressed him to the resolution of this issue.

Dr. G.: What did you do to treat this mental collapse?

Mark: I went to TASK.

Dr. G.: What is TASK?

Mark: It stands for Terrestrial Alliance for Scientific Knowledge and functions as both a research and treatment clinic.

Dr. G.: What did your therapy consist of?

Mark: They used a combination of color programming and music to realign my brain and balance my energy centers to reestablish normal functioning.

TASK sounded interesting. This research center was apparently quite large and well known. It stored massive amounts of data dealing with all forms of medicine and alternative disciplines of healing, as well as other scientific disciplines.

Dr. G.: Are you back to normal now?

Mark: Oh yes.

Dr. G.: What will you do now?

Mark: I decided to devote myself to my inventing.

Dr. G.: How will you earn a living until you actually market one of your inventions?

Mark: TASK solved that problem.

Dr. G.: How so?

Mark: I told you they do a lot of research. During my therapy, they analyzed my brain waves and determined that I had natural talents for inventing. Then they offered me a job.

TASK's offer was well-timed and attractive. In addition to a good salary and fringe benefits, Elam would receive a royalty on each product he invented that was sold worldwide.

Dr. G.: How is it going with TASK?

Mark: Great! I have completed several small inventions and now I regularly receive royalty checks as a bonus.

Dr. G.: Are you dating anyone at this time?

Mark: Yes. After giving our relationship a great deal of thought I contacted Zia and told her I wanted to marry her.

Dr. G.: Is that true?

Mark: Yes. Maybe it was my therapy at TASK, but I now have no fear of marriage and want to be with Zia.

Dr. G.: How did Zia respond to the proposal?

Mark: She was excited. We began dating again and are now planning our wedding.

As I moved Elam forward in time, he was now in his early 30s. He and Zia did get married and appeared to be quite happy. In addition, Elam received several promotions and honors at TASK for his work. During the next five years, Zia gave birth to a son and daughter and this further added to their marital bliss.

Dr. G.: Elam, can you tell me about an invention of yours that you are most proud of?

Mark: That's easy. It's my tele-immersion unit. I received national recognition and became quite wealthy as a result of this device.

Dr. G.: What does a tele-immersion unit do?

Mark: This device enables the user to share precisely the visual experience another is having, regardless of how far the other person is in distance.

Dr. G.: In other words, are you saying you are seeing the world through their eyes?

Mark: Exactly.

Dr. G.: Does this work on the moon and other planets?

Mark: So far TASK's initial testing shows that it does without any significant distortion in the signal.

One could see both the military and industrial applications of the tele-immersion unit. So it looks as if Elam, the test tube baby, finally lived up to his potential both personally and professionally.

One last invention Elam shared with me is something he calls the Cyborg connector. This device consists of a computer connection implanted in a person's head so that data can be downloaded from a small hand-held computer directly into their brain. This gives new meaning to the term "artificial intelligence."

So the circle is complete, and Mark left my office with the knowledge that he will resolve his issues as Elam. About a year later, he reported to me feeling as if he had a new lease on life. This case represents one of the many advantages of doing future life progressions.

Chapter 13

The Future Lives of a TV Personality

Early in January 1981, Harry Martin called me expressing interest in progressing into the future through the use of hypnosis. He had done so well with past life regression that he wanted to see if it could work "in reverse." After seeing himself as a self-made warehouse owner in the 18th century, a 19th-century blind piano player, and an RAF radio operator during World War II, Harry was ready for an entirely different experience. I explained the theory concerning the space-time continuum and he seemed very enthusiastic about attempting a journey into the future.

Harry was the cohost of a local talk show called "Hello Baltimore" on WBAL-TV. At our first session, I wanted to establish the validity of this technique. I decided to progress Harry just one week into the future to the WBAL newsroom assignment board to see if he could read news items about events that hadn't occurred yet. This seemed to be a fair test of hypnotic progression and Harry agreed to it wholeheartedly. My next step would be to progress Harry into a future life. All of these sessions were tape recorded and I gave Harry a copy of these tapes.

On February 2, 1981, Harry began his first trip into the future. I progressed him one week forward, to February 9, 1981, which was a Monday. The technique simply consisted of Harry's reading either from the newsroom assignment board one hour before air-time of his broadcast or his reading from the actual script of that day's newscast. (The first 15 minutes of "Hello Baltimore" consisted of a news update.)

Dr. G.: Tell me exactly what you see on the assignment board.

Harry: Plane, and the number 406.

When I asked Harry to read the news script about this item, this is what he reported.

Harry: State aviation officials are investigating the crash of a small plane this morning near Route 406.

This item never made it on the air, but on February 9, a small plane did crash in Bowie, Maryland. This crash was investigated by state aviation officials.

Dr. G.: What is the next item on the assignment board?

Harry: It's the name of a place, I think, but I can't make it out.

Dr. G. Can you spell it?

Harry: It's a long name. It's a very weird combination of consonants. It's the name of a man.

Dr. G.: What letters can you make out?

Harry: ST W KI...it's a long Russian-type name.

On February 9, Stanislaw Kania, Poland's labor leader, was told that he might soon be fired unless he instructed his workers to return to work.

Dr. G.: Move down to the next item that you will be reading on the air. Tell me what the script says.

Harry: This is an accident. It's on 695 [the Baltimore Beltway] between the Pikesville and Security Boulevard exits, but I don't know where.

Dr. G.: What vehicles are involved in the accident?

Harry: One large vehicle and one small one. There were no deaths.

On February 9 a school bus on its way to Randallstown (between Pikesville and Security Boulevard) hit a car at 200 Embleton Road in Owings Mills (just north of Pikesville). No deaths were reported.

Dr. G.: What is the next news item, Harry?

Harry: It has to do with Governor Hughes and the budget.

Dr. G.: What about the budget?

Harry: Governor Hughes says he's holding the line this year on the budget. The legislature is going against him for some reason, saying that they don't have to hold the budget on some raise proposal.

On February 12, Governor Hughes vetoed a $40- to $60-million raise for state employers. The Maryland Classified Employees Association (MCEA) had obtained the support of the State Legislature in voting for a salary raise.

Dr. G.: What is the next news item?

Harry: It's something about Jerry Falwell.

Dr. G.: What about Jerry Falwell?

Harry: It has something to do with Falwell's interview that appeared in *Penthouse*.

On February 4, Jerry Falwell withdrew his lawsuit against *Penthouse* magazine. (Remember, this session was taking place on February 2.)

Harry's next progression session was the following Monday, February 9. There was much excitement and enthusiasm in his voice when he discussed last week's "hits." I was also stimulated and elated with the results of the last session.

Anyone can do what Harry accomplished. The hypnotic state allows the psychic component of the brain to be tapped. We all have this progression ability. Naturally, I do not use this technique to predict stock values or lottery numbers. First, I consider this an unethical use of our natural psychic abilities. Second, the dates are not always accurate.

A progression of one week in the future may, in actuality, be three days or 10 days hence. What the patient perceives as one week in advance can actually take place a few days on either side of that precise date.

I then progressed Harry to February 16 and again had him read the news items on the script that would be used on the air.

Dr. G.: What news item appears next on the script?

Harry: A fire in the city.

Dr. G.: What kind of building was involved?

Harry: A house fire; a row house.

Dr. G.: Do you see the name of the person who owned the house?

Harry: I want to say Johnson. They don't own it; I think they just live there.

Dr. G.: Anything else?

Harry: There are two little girls involved.

Dr. G.: Are they hurt?

Harry: No, they escaped safely, but somebody was hurt. I don't know who, though.

Dr. G.: Can you see anything clsc?

Harry: I see two little girls being dangled from the second-story window of this row house. They're being rescued by someone. They had ribbons in their hair.

On February 13, a child named Kenneth Blanda died in a second-story fire on 540 Pulaski Street in the western part of Baltimore City. A space heater had caused the fire. Patricia Johnson, a neighbor, was interviewed about the fire. This fire did occur in a row house.

What is especially interesting is that in four of the six hits, the dates matched perfectly. With one of the misses, the date was five days before, and with the other, it was three days before the predicted date. I consulted with a professor of mathematics at a local university and he stated that the odds were hundreds of thousands to one against this type of thing happening by mere chance. These hits don't *prove* progression but, in my opinion, they lend significant credence to the theory.

On March 9, Harry came to my office for a progression into a future lifetime. He was excited about this adventure. I induced him into a medium trance and began questioning him. During this entire session, Harry spoke in a slow, almost monotonous voice, expressing no emotion whatsoever.

Dr. G.: What do you see before you?

Harry: A pyramid.

Dr. G.: Is this pyramid isolated or are there other structures around it?

Harry: It's isolated.

Dr. G.: Where is this pyramid?

Harry: It's in the desert.

Dr. G.: What is the purpose of this pyramid?

Harry: It has something to do with energy. It's getting energy from the sun.

Dr. G.: Are there any other structures by the pyramid that are related to its energy functions.

Harry: There are pipes on the bottom of it.

Dr. G.: Why are you there?

Harry: I'm just observing. It's like a tour.

Dr. G.: How long have you been there?

Harry: I've just arrived.

Dr. G.: How long are you going to be there?

Harry: Another hour and then we're going to leave.

I next progressed Harry to the tour itself.

Dr. G.: What do you see now?

Harry: The pyramid is made of glass.

Dr. G.: Are you inside the pyramid now?

Harry: Yes. There are living quarters in the far corners with plants and all sorts of supplies.

Dr. G.: How tall is the pyramid?

Harry: 70 feet high.

Dr: G.: What is the source of energy for this pyramid other than the sun?

Harry: Nothing.

Dr. G.: How many people live inside the pyramid?

Harry: 300.

Dr. G.: What is the purpose of this pyramid?

Harry: It's a self-sufficient structure. These 300 inhabitants are specially selected scientists.

Dr. G.: What is the name of the pyramid?

Harry: Phobos.

Dr. G.: Can you describe the leader of the tour?

Harry: A man wearing yellow coveralls leads us.

Dr. G.: How many of you are on this tour?

Harry: There are 10 of us.

Dr. G.: Can you see any personal effects in this pyramid that would indicate that people are currently living here?

Harry: Yes. There are plants in various quarters.

Dr. G.: What form of communication exists in the pyramid?

Harry: We don't speak. We think and our thoughts are transmitted as images. That is the purpose of this scientific team—to explore silent communication.

Dr. G.: Can you see what the people on the tour are wearing?

Harry: We all wear a one-piece coverall suit of a certain color.

Dr. G.: What kind of footwear do you have on?

Harry: Rubber ankle-high boots that are the same color as the suit.

Dr. G.: Does the color of the suit have any meaning?

Harry: Yes. Each color signifies your function and rank on this project.

Dr. G.: What is your color?

Harry: Beige.

Dr. G.: What colors are the other people on the tour wearing?

Harry: We are all wearing beige. Red is the lowest color. Next is beige, orange, yellow, green, and violet. As we progress in our duties, we move on to the higher colors.

Dr. G.: What do the scientists in the pyramids do as you observe them?

Harry: They just seem to be walking back and forth.

Dr. G.: Do they make any sounds?

Harry: No.

Dr. G.: What year is this?

Harry: 2153.

Dr. G.: How do you communicate any problems with your supervisors?

Harry: You think about it and they will know it.

Dr. G.: Are you the only inspector?

Harry: Yes.

This was Harry's first job in this future lifetime. He had very little formal training for this inspector position. I next progressed Harry forward in time by 10 years.

Dr. G.: Where do you find yourself now?

Harry: I'm inspecting the irrigation system.

Dr. G.: Has anything changed since I last spoke with you?

Harry: Yes. The pyramid is now being used for farming purposes.

Dr. G.: Could you elaborate?

Harry: All of the plants are grown in water, not soil. The water has all the necessary nutrients in it.

Dr. G.: What exactly do you do now?

Harry: I help monitor the ratio of various nutrients in the water so that the correct proportions are present.

Dr. G.: Do you do this yourself?

Harry: No, the computer does this. I just double-check the computer.

Dr. G.: What do you do if the computer is malfunctioning?

Harry: I repair it.

Dr. G.: What color is your suit?

Harry: Yellow.

Apparently, Harry had been promoted to a much more sophisticated position in the pyramid. I now progressed Harry to the last day of his future life.

Dr. G.: Where are you?

Harry: I'm reporting to the termination room.

Dr. G.: Are you still in the pyramid?

Harry: Yes.

Dr. G.: Why are you in the termination room?

Harry: It's my turn to change units.

Dr. G.: Can you describe this procedure?

Harry: I lie down on a table and they put something on my fingers and I just go to sleep.

Dr. G.: What does this do to you?

Harry: It takes all of your energy out of you.

Dr. G.: Why is this done?

Harry: You can now be placed in a more appropriate unit. You don't grow old or grow up. You are just transferred.

Dr. G.: Is this then a mechanical body?

Harry: No. It's a totally biological unit.

Dr. G.: What happens in between going from one unit to another?

Harry: You are stored on tape.

Dr. G.: Do you have a choice as to whether or not you will enter a certain unit?

Harry: No.

Harry's voice and delivery in answering my questions were particularly interesting to me. They were vastly different as compared to his normal speech patterns. I was also fascinated with Harry's report of the experiments in mental telepathy and the use of solar energy as the only energy source. The isolation of this future life was similar to Harry's past life as Hap, the blind piano player. Even though he was born blind, Hap exhibited no remorse. As a 22nd-century irrigation inspector, Harry easily accepted this "termination." The 18th-century life as a warehouse owner and director of an import-export business required that he be an inspector . It was also lonely at work. This karmic lesson still needed to be learned 400 years later.

When Harry received his promotion to irrigation supervisor, this reminded me of his start in newscasting as a radio personality. He was then promoted to television reporting. Today, Harry is a well-organized television newscaster. He acquired this discipline from at least three previous lifetimes. As an RAF radio operator, he was well trained in scientific discipline.

Assertiveness is a trait Harry Martin possesses today. It is a necessary quality for a television personality. Yet during the 19th, 20th (as the RAF radio operator), and 22nd centuries, this characteristic was lacking. The karmic lesson was learned and didn't have to be repeated.

Harry's second future lifetime was revealed two weeks later. He came to my office on this spring afternoon feeling quite relaxed. I induced him into a medium trance and proceeded with the questioning.

Dr. G.: What do you see?

Harry: I see white curtains that look like lace in front of a window.

Dr. G.: What else do you see?

Harry: I'm inside this room and I'm looking at my work.

Dr. G.: What kind of work is that?

Harry: Silver plates. There are these silver plates on the wall.

Harry's answers were again almost mechanical without any expression of emotion. His speech pattern was very slow and his voice very deep. This was to continue throughout the session.

Dr. G.: What is characteristic about these plates?

Harry: They have emblems on them, but no writing.

Dr. G.: Can you describe the furniture?

Harry: The design on the couch and chairs is cubical.

Dr. G.: What is this place?

Harry: It's my home.

Dr. G.: What is special about this particular day?

Harry: This is a rest day.

Dr. G.: What kind of work do you do?

Harry: I'm a sort of craftsperson.

Dr. G.: What do you construct?

Harry: Those plates. Those silver plates on the wall.

Dr. G.: Who do you do these for?

Harry: People. People request my services.

Dr. G.: Are there many craftsmen like you?

Harry: No. There are only a few of us who do this kind of work.

Dr. G.: What do people call you?

Harry: Amygdala.

Dr. G.: Is that your complete name?

Harry: Yes.

Dr. G.: What year is this?

Harry: 2271.

I next progressed Amygdala forward in time by two years.

Dr. G.: Can you tell me more about your work?

Harry: These plates are made of silver. They are a means of currency.

Dr. G.: Are there other forms of currency?

Harry: Yes. You see, these silver plates are a way of holding massive amounts of wealth.

Dr. G.: The fact that you have some of these silver plates on your wall, does that mean that you are wealthy?

Harry: Yes.

Dr. G.: Why do people come to you for your work? Why don't thcy just store their own silver?

Harry: What happens is my making these plates increases the value of the metal.

Dr. G.: What kind of work do some of your clients do?

Harry: Law and some of my people are in manufacturing and transportation.

Dr. G.: What kind of transportation are you referring to?

Harry: Molecular reassembly. This type of transportation is new, but is being used more and more.

Dr. G.: Are there any other uses for molecular reassembly?

Harry: Sustenance. We have small units that help nourish us while we sleep.

Dr. G.: Could you describe your own molecular reassembly unit?

Harry: It's a platform, a round platform. There is a coordinate tracking system to set it.

Dr. G.: Do you need someone else to activate it?

Harry: No.

Dr. G.: When you do use it, how do you get reassembled?

Harry: It's programmed into the unit by the tracking system.

Dr. G.: Can you describe the last time you used the molecular reassembly unit for transporting yourself?

Harry: I recently went into the city for a meeting.

Dr. G.: Was anyone else present?

Harry: There were two other people. One is a man dressed in a gray suit made of very shiny material. [Patient paused.]

Dr. G.: And the woman, how was she dressed?

Harry: Oh, I'm really confused. [Patient exhibited emotions for the first time since the session began.]

Dr. G.: Why are you confused?

Harry: How did you know it was a woman?

Dr. G.: You said one of these two people was a male, so I assumed that the other was female. How was she dressed?

Harry: This other person in the room is not really a woman.

Dr. G.: Is she human?

Harry: Partially. She is part human and part machine.

Dr. G.: Can you describe her?

Harry: The top half of her body is of human form but the way she gets around is by machine. Her head is shaved. Her eyes are slanted and her skin is very pale.

It seemed the lower part of this being consisted of a mechanized apparatus similar to a wheelchair.

Dr. G.: Is there anyone else in the room?

Harry: No, just the computer.

Dr. G.: What is the purpose of this meeting?

Harry: It has something to do with insurance.

Dr. G.: Personal insurance or work-related insurance?

Harry: Work-related.

Dr. G.: Can you read the policy right now?

Harry: There's no writing. You plug it in. [Patient sounded bored.]

I next progressed Amygdala to the time when he would return home and review his policy.

Dr. G.: What are you doing now?

Harry: I'm plugging the policy into the wall. The screen asks for my ID number so that only I can review it.

Dr. G.: What specifically does it state?

Harry: Amygdala...insured against defects in workmanship. Mars 1522.

Amygdala didn't know what Mars 1522 referred to. I returned Harry to the present.

In this life, Harry (Amygdala) showed more of his creative potential as the silver craftsmen. This society seemed to value silver more than any other metal, and crime was almost unknown. In his present life, Harry is also quite creative. He is currently writing a novel, plays the drums, and is much involved with the production aspect of a news miniseries. As the 19th-century piano player Hap, Harry was also showing his creativity. The RAF radio operator died before he could leave his mark on society. Harry's career as a television personality is his way of contributing to the world. This 23rd-century life was the culmination of at least 400 years of creative talent. The great wealth that Amygdala accumulated, in addition to the recognition he was shown, were karmic paybacks for centuries of hard work and dedication.

In the current 20th century, Harry is well on his way to "doing his thing." From his past and future lives, he has learned the value of creativity and recognition. Now, as a media personality, he can put these lessons to use. Of the many benefits he received from hypnotherapy, Harry states that focusing his concentration, acquiring more discipline and energy, and the realization that maybe he should start loving life (taking time to smell the roses, and so on) were most significant. Developing a more open attitude toward hypnotherapy and a better understanding of himself must be added to these advantages. Perhaps the knowledge that there will still be a world in 300 years is enough to give us all an optimistic view of the future.

My reaction to Harry's progressions and regressions was one of satisfaction. Harry has previously stated positive changes in his behavior and attitude toward life. These positive results make me feel proud to be a hypnotherapist.

Most patients don't want to know about the future. That is unfortunate because of the tremendous therapeutic potential progression represents. Whether you believe in progression, regression, or hypnosis doesn't really matter. Anyone can obtain the benefits Harry Martin received through hypnotherapy.

Chapter 14

A Contaminated Future

A compulsion is defined as a repetitive and seemingly purposeful behavior that is performed according to certain rules or in a stereotyped fashion. The behavior is not an end in itself, but is designed to produce or prevent some future event or situation. The activity is quite excessive and is not connected in a realistic way with what it is designed to produce or prevent. The individual generally recognizes the senselessness of the behavior and does not derive pleasure from carrying out the activity, although it provides a release of tension.

With this background, you can now appreciate Pete's predicament. Pete called me in August of 1984. He was a clinical psychologist and had a hand-washing compulsion. He knew the definition of a compulsion very well, but could not help himself. Pete had spent years in therapy with no results. He would constantly wash his hands, day and night. He changed his clothes two to three times a day to "remove the dirt."

Pete was a truly pleasant man. I could see him relating rather well to his patients. He was always neatly dressed, well-groomed, and soft-spoken. Under no circumstances could he treat a patient with a compulsion. It was just too close to home and he would refer them out. There were many interruptions in his practice because he would wash his hands at least once during a session, usually after shaking hands with the patient.

Pete's biggest fear was the possibility of being contaminated. There was absolutely no logic to his concern. He felt that if he didn't go through his daily rituals, he would somehow be contaminated and wouldn't be able to function. Another unusual aspect of his psychological profile was the number eight. This number haunted him. He was born in August (the eighth month). Every time he obtained a telephone number or a new address, the number eight was always well represented. His grandmother died in August, and there were many other deaths in his family during the eighth month of the year.

As a result, Pete always exhibited a form of anxiety and depression every August. His first call to my office to set up his initial session occurred at the end of August. Another strange occurrence was the name Teresa. This is not a particularly common name, but one that Pete associated with negativity. A girl he dated in graduate school rather cruelly ended their relationship just prior to his oral exam for his doctorate. Her name was Teresa. Throughout his growing up years, the name Teresa would send chills down Pete's spine. He could not explain why.

Pete recovered from the Teresa who had ended their relationship, but the name still haunted him. He had one car accident in his life and the woman involved was hospitalized with numerous injuries. Her first name was Teresa, and there were two eights on her license plate. In addition, this automobile accident took place late one August evening.

By the time Pete actually entered my office in September of 1984, he was desperate. He just had to rid himself of this compulsion once and for all. It was causing him to lose sleep, and additionally, it was certainly not helping his therapy practice. Many people are given a poor impression by a psychologist who washes his hand immediately after greeting you.

Pete proved to be an average hypnotic patient. By that I mean, his trance depth fit into the light to medium range. The majority of the population can easily attain this level. As I have mentioned before, one does not need to reach a deep level of hypnosis to regress into past lives or progress into a future lifetime. In Pete's case, this was more than sufficient for his explorations.

Pete's first past life helped explain a lot about his current symptoms. The year was 1888 (note the presence of the number eight) and the city was Paris. Pete was a female singer named Marie Duvall. Marie was very successful on the stage, but her morals left something to be desired. She was a prostitute for years before she became known for her musical and acting talents.

Even after achieving a name on the stage, Marie still used her body to get what she wanted. She was very ambitious and aggressive (a complete opposite of Pete today). Pete cringed at the thought of what Marie did and represented. She was vain, selfish, cruel, and ruthless. She slept with men indiscriminately just to get what she wanted from them. She was never satisfied; she always had to have more.

Pete would comment to me during these sessions about how "dirty" Marie was. She would have sex with one man and without washing herself, sleep with another during her prostitute days. One of the events that truly saddened Marie was the death of a lover. She became infatuated with a man who worked for the government. He was powerful and Marie couldn't get enough of him. She loved power. One day he was killed by a German agent.

The French government knew about their affair and convinced Marie to work for them. She readily agreed because revenge was a part of her personality. She acted occasionally as a spy for the French government and only wanted assignments against Germany. One night she was sleeping with a German agent and her assignment was complete. She obtained the needed information, but decided to kill him herself. In a series of violent thrusts Marie stabbed the German agent to death. Her naked body was covered with his blood. She stood and laughed about this. It was at least an hour before she washed herself off. During this scene, Pete was cringing in his chair. He couldn't stand the sight of Marie standing there drenched in blood laughing about a murder she had just committed.

Shortly thereafter, Marie informed the French government she could no longer work for them. She continued with her life, satisfied that her lover's death was avenged. As the years went by, she began to have nightmares about that murder. Feelings of guilt flooded her mind. She didn't know what to do.

Although she was not a religious woman, Marie felt a trip to a convent outside the city would be the solution. She wanted to confess her sins, especially the murder. When she arrived at the convent, the sister in charge spent a great deal of time listening to her story. At the end of this she told Marie that they could not absolve her of her sins. The date was August 8 and the nun was named Sister Teresa.

When Pete came out of that trance, he was made aware of a number of facts. First, the number eight had played a rather prominent role in Marie's life. Second, a person with the name of Teresa had finally emerged as a possible source of his anxiety. Last but not least, a source of his hand-washing compulsion reared its head. (You will note that I say *a* source and not *the* source. Pete's case was far too complicated to be explained by one past life regression.) One interesting aside on this life was Marie's failure to find peace with Sister Teresa. Perhaps that was the main reason Pete chose psychology as a profession: Now he could help people when he himself couldn't obtain that needed aid 100 years ago.

The rest of Marie's life was inconsequential to Pete's condition, so we left her alone and explored another life. In an African life, Pete was a female and a mother. Her husband was killed in a war and she was left to raise her baby daughter. Loneliness was a definite problem, but even more significant, a plague annihilated her baby daughter and most of her village. She survived a good many years, but lived in constant fear for her life and always blamed herself for the death of her daughter, even though there was nothing she could have done to prevent it. Eventually, this woman died. The key point in this life was the plague and the blame she projected onto herself. Here we have another cause-effect relationship with the current compulsion.

For Pete's third trip back in time he described a life in England during the 15th century. This time Pete was a male named James. James was a nobleman and spent most of his time in the king's court. He had an older brother, Robert, who was also at the king's side. Later, the king became sexually involved with James and his brother. Pete again began to cringe when he described this homosexual relationship. He called it "sick" and "dirty."

As time passed, a power struggle developed between James and his brother. Because both were lovers of the king, they received special treatment and favors. Robert was older and was thus given more power and authority. This angered James and a battle of wits ensued between the brothers for power and position.

James (Pete) lost this battle and was banished from England. He grew depressed and, in France, planed his next move. He returned with some men and murdered Robert. The king was furious and had James beheaded.

Pete cringed in my recliner as he perceived his death. He described the blade as being "filthy with the blood of its previous victims." Here again we can see cause-effect relationships to explain Pete's current compulsion. Do not ignore the guilt he felt from violence (killing his brother) and his homosexual relationship with the king. Sex, violence, guilt, and a dirty blade were the karmic carryovers from this English life.

The stage was set for the most significant life relating to Pete's present-day compulsion. As I stated elsewhere in this book, because all time is simultaneous, the cause of a present-day problem could very well rest in a future lifetime. Although all of the lives we explored were causative, they were not the only or most significant factors. In Pete's case, the most significant life turned out to be a future life.

By this stage in our hypnotherapy, Pete was beginning to show marked progress in sleeping better and in the lessening of the frequency and intensity of his compulsive symptoms. He was eager to continue his therapy and most probably expected to regress to another past life during the next session. Such was not the case. Pete traveled forward instead to the latter part of the 21st century.

Dr. G.: What is your name?

Pete: Ben. Ben Kingsley.

Dr. G.: Where do you find yourself?

Pete: I am in school and I like what I'm studying.

Dr. G.: What is it that you are studying?

Pete: It's a science course and I like the work.

Ben was in a high school physics course. He had a natural talent for science and loved putting things together, taking them apart, and calculating the probability of various experiments.

Dr. G.: Where do you live, Ben?

Pete: Tulsa. Tulsa, Oklahoma.

Dr. G.: What year is this?

Pete: 2074.

Dr. G.: Tell me about your family.

Pete: What do you want to know?

Dr. G.: What does your father do?

Pete: He is a psychiatrist.

Dr. G.: And your mother?

Pete: She works as an architect.

Dr. G.: Any brothers or sisters?

Pete: I have one brother, Roger, and one sister, Tenina.

Dr. G.: Are they older than you?

Pete: No, they are both younger.

Dr. G.: What do you want to do with your life?

Pete: I want to go to college and do something in the scientific field. I don't know exactly which field yet.

As I continued questioning Ben, I found out that he was a very conscientious young adult. He didn't seem to have any bad habits. He was a good student and got along well with his family. Ben exhibited a great deal of respect for his father and mother. He admired their dedication to their respective careers but, at the same time, did not feel neglected. Ben was kind and helpful to his younger brother and sister.

Ben was progressed beyond his high school years to any relevant advanced education or occupation. He described going to college and majoring in physics.

Dr. G.: How do you like school?

Pete: I love it.

Dr..G.: What is your major?

Pete: Now I'm concentrating in nuclear physics.

Dr. G.: With what goal?

Pete: When I graduate, I want to work as a technician in a nuclear power plant.

Dr. G.: With your skills, why not become a nuclear physicist?

Pete: I couldn't do that.

Dr. G.: Why not?

Pete: Because I'm not cut out for that kind of responsibility.

Dr. G.: Don't you think you could handle the training?

Pete: I'm sure I could but, you see, I get a little nervous sometimes when things don't go well.

Dr. G.: What do you mean by a little nervous?

Pete: Well, every once in a while, when I get nervous and frustrated, I develop a panicky feeling.

Dr. G.: What do you do?

Pete: I lose my temper sometimes and don't think too clearly for a few minutes.

Dr. G.: This sounds like a real problem. Have you told your father about this?

Pete: Yes, he knows about it.

Dr. G.: Has he done anything about it?

Pete: I am seeing one of his colleagues, a Dr. Margolis.

Dr. G.: What does Dr. Margolis tell you about your condition?

Pete: He tells me it's not very serious, but that I should keep my stress levels down and avoid repeated confrontations.

Dr. G.: Doesn't that preclude a career as a nuclear plant technician?

Pete: It would if it was found out, but that won't be a problem.

Dr. G.: How so?

Pete: Dr. Margolis is a very good friend of my father. He owes Dad a big favor. Also, he is well aware of my academic record.

Dr. G.: By that you mean he will keep your therapy off the record.

Pete: That's correct.

Dr. G.: Is there anything else about yourself that might surface as a problem in your chosen profession?

Pete: Nothing that I can think of.

I was looking for some carryover of Pete's compulsion, but found none. Ben was only occasionally out of control with these temper episodes and nobody seemed to be concerned. No one except me, that is.

None of Pete's characteristics seemed to have expressed themselves in Ben. If anything, he was quite the opposite of Pete's present-day personality. I next progressed Ben to a significant event in his college career.

Dr. G.: Where are you now Ben?

Pete: I'm meeting Gail.

Dr. G.: Who is Gail?

Pete: She is my fiancée.

Dr. G.: Does she know about your temper episodes?

Pete: No. I don't know why you keep stressing those rare behaviors. When Gail is around, I am calm and in complete control.

Ben was quite right. When he was with Gail, he was a different person. He was calm, confident, and sensitive to her needs. Even if things weren't going well for Ben, Gail's presence made it easier to take. She was obviously the best thing that had ever happened to him.

Dr. G.: How are things going with Dr. Margolis's treatment?

Pete: Okay, I guess.

Dr. G.: What does he do when you see him?

Pete: He uses a form of biofeedback with me.

Dr. G. Does he put you on any medication?

Pete: Only occasionally. He only prescribes drugs when I report a series of episodes.

Dr. G.: Have you done that recently?

Pete: No. I have been doing fine lately.

Ben was correct: He had been feeling better. Gail had moved in with him and Ben felt on top of the world. Dr. Margolis was pleased, and monitored Ben once a month. Gail had no idea that Ben was seeing Dr. Margolis. She had her own career as a computer programmer and kept quite busy.

Gail never saw Ben at his worst. He studied in the library, and when he got frustrated in the lab, it was usually when he was alone. Ben's father was proud of his son and felt everything was progressing nicely.

Ben was a very happy man. He graduated from college and married Gail. His family was proud of him and he was well on his way to achieving his lifelong goals. I next progressed Ben to his working environment.

Dr. G.: Tell me about your work.

Pete: I absolutely love it. I work as a technician in the nuclear plant outside of Tulsa.

Dr. G.: So you have remained in Tulsa.

Pete: Yes. I am a junior technician and I am supervised by Ralph.

Dr. G.: How do you get along with Ralph?

Pete: We have a good working relationship. He is an excellent teacher and we have become good friends.

Dr. G.: Do you ever get upset at work?

Pete: Sometimes I feel a little frustrated at the vast complexities of the plant, but I don't really get upset.

Dr. G.: How about at home?

Pete: No, Gail and I love each other.

Dr. G.: Do you still see Dr. Margolis?

Pete: Just three or four times a year. He says I am doing fine.

Dr. G.: Then, why does he keep seeing you at all?

Pete: My father wants to make sure that I am really all right. Because Dr. Margolis's therapy is strictly off the record, Dad feels responsible for my psychological well-being.

As I progressed Ben forward in time, he reported a true love for his life. Although his family life was important, he was truly dedicated to his job. I perceived a little too much dedication. Ben had an obsessive-compulsive personality, but that is not uncommon among scientifically trained people. What I was concerned with was the excessive workaholic traits he was exhibiting, coupled with a high-strung nature that was potentially explosive and dangerous.

None of my concerns manifested themselves during my questioning of Ben. I then progressed him forward five years.

Dr. G.: What has happened since we last spoke?

Pete: I really do enjoy my work. I have received three promotions and am the second in command in my unit.

Dr. G.: Who do you work under?

Pete: Ralph is still my supervisor.

Dr. G.: Do you still get along with him?

Pete: Yes. We are very good friends and our families spend a fair amount of time together.

Dr. G.: You said families. Does that mean you have any children?

Pete: Gail and I are the proud parents of two sons, Aaron and Ronald.

Dr. G.: Does it bother you that you are not in charge of your unit?

Pete: No. You see, I have been assigned to a new research unit and am being trained to head my particular section.

Things had very much worked out for Ben. He was only with Ralph about one half of the week. The rest of his time was spent in a brand-new nuclear research facility located about 20 miles from the plant. This facility was studying various techniques to harness and control nuclear power safely. This was a very special unit and it was quite an honor to be chosen to work in it. Ben's ambition and skills had allowed him to rise up the promotion ladder quickly, which quite pleased him.

Dr. G.: How does Gail feel about your two jobs?

Pete: Oh, she is all for it. She is always supportive of my career and I love her for it.

Dr. G.: What about the long hours?

Pete: I don't mind them at all.

Dr. G.: Doesn't Gail object to your absence from your home?

Pete: Gail has her own career and taking care of the boys keeps her busy. We really don't have any problems.

Dr. G.: What about your temper episodes? Is that still a problem?

Pete: Not at all. I haven't had any episode in more than three years.

Dr. G.: Are you still seeing Dr. Margolis?

Pete: No.

Dr. G.: Does your father approve of your termination of therapy with Dr. Margolis?

Pete: He hasn't said anything about it for a long time. Dr. Margolis consulted with Dad before ending the therapy, so I guess I'm okay.

Dr. G.: Has anyone in either of the two facilities you work in found out about your past psychological problems?

Pete: Not a chance. If any knowledge of my treatment were known, I would be removed from my positions.

Dr. G.: Even though Dr. Margolis feels you are "cured"?

Pete: It doesn't matter what Dr. Margolis thinks. The history of psychological problems would be totally destructive to me professionally.

Dr. G.: How does Ralph respond to your research position? Is he jealous of you?

Pete: He really is proud of me. After all, he trained me. In answer to your question, I don't feel Ralph is the least bit jealous of me. Ralph is much more of a family man and he would never work the kind of hours I do.

As we discussed this part of Ben's life, I could tell he was really happy. His workaholic tendencies didn't seem to bother Gail, his friends, or his other family members. Ben's father was very proud of him, as were Ben's peers. I, however, was still not convinced that Ben was as psychologically stable as Dr. Margolis had assumed.

Ben had a complete life. He loved his work and enjoyed his family life and his friends when he wasn't working. His ambitions were being fulfilled, and Ben was unquestionably in control of his life.

As I progressed Ben forward to a significant challenge or difficulty in his life, some interesting patterns were beginning to emerge.

Dr. G.: What has happened since we last spoke?

Pete: I don't know what I'm going to do about Aaron.

Dr. G.: Aaron, your oldest son?

Pete: Yes.

Dr. G.: What about him?

Pete: He is not doing well at all. He is so bright. There's just no excuse for it.

Dr. G.: What do his teachers say?

Pete: They say he is just not trying. He is preoccupied with other things.

Dr. G.: How do you handle this situation?

Pete: I tried talking to the boy. He seems to understand me, but he just doesn't do anything about it.

Dr. G.: Have you thought of taking him to a psychologist?

Pete: I don't want even to discuss that option.

As I inquired further into this situation, I seemed to have struck a nerve. Aaron was named after Ben's father. Ben wanted Aaron to excel at everything he did and subconsciously exerted performance pressure on him, which resulted in Aaron's rebelling. By not performing well, Aaron could only go up in his performance. This did not sit well with Ben.

Gail allowed Ben to handle the educational guidance of the boys. The thought of Aaron needing counseling brought back the memories of Ben's treatment with Dr. Margolis. Ben became somewhat frustrated and angry. He came close to losing his temper.

Dr. G.: How did this situation resolve itself?

Pete: Aaron and I had some long talks. I began to treat him differently, letting up on some of the standards I set for him.

Dr. G.: Did it work?

Pete: Yes. He began to improve in school and things went back to normal.

Dr. G.: Did this cause a strain in your relationship with Gail?

Pete: At first it did, but later we worked things out.

Dr. G.: Did this affect your working relationships?

Pete: Well, I guess it did. It is hard working the hours I do. Maybe I was a little too sensitive.

Dr. G.: Could you give me an example?

Pete: Ralph had to correct some of my calculations and reports at the plant. I argued with him about it, thinking that he was picking on me.

Dr. G.: Why would he do that?

Pete: I thought he was jealous of my position at the research facility. That was dumb. Ralph is my best friend and only wants the best for me.

Dr. G.: Did you ever have a temper episode with him?

Pete: No, but I felt close to one at certain times.

Dr. G.: Have you thought about going back to Dr. Margolis?

Pete: Not a chance. I can handle myself now. I do not need therapy.

Ben was still quite sensitive about any mention of therapy. Even the thought of therapy for Aaron made Ben quite upset. The problem with Aaron did resolve itself nicely without the involvement of a therapist. It is interesting to note that in this life Pete is a psychologist, but was very averse toward therapy in his next lifetime.

Ralph didn't seem to be concerned with Ben. The incident was a minor one and Ralph was used to the egos of some of his crew. Nobody suspected Ben was having any significant problems.

I progressed Ben forward again to a significant event in dealing with his emotions and his temper.

Dr. G.: Where are you now, Ben?

Pete: I am at home and arguing with Gail.

Dr. G.: What is this all about?

Pete: She got into a car accident. It was so stupid. She just ran out of the house after we had words and didn't think clearly about the other vehicles.

Dr. G.: Was she hurt?

Pete: No, thank goodness.

Dr. G.: Did you have a temper episode?

Pete: Yes, and Gail was shocked. She didn't really think it was a serious matter. She just wrote it off to the accident itself.

Dr. G.: Have you now thought of seeing Dr. Margolis?

Pete: No, and I don't want to talk about me going back into therapy. Is that understood?

Ben was getting very emotional about his psychological state. He even threatened me. I was concerned about his explosive nature and after years of calm, the storm began to rise on the horizon.

I can understand Ben's concern about his career. However, he was acting irresponsibly in not going back to Dr. Margolis. His therapy could still be kept confidential, but Ben wouldn't hear of it.

For the next year or so, things quieted down. Ben felt better and he naturally assumed that there would be no further problems. I didn't assume that at all.

I next progressed Ben to another significant event in his life.

Dr. G.: What is going on with you, Ben?

Pete: [Crying] I don't want to talk about it.

Dr. G.: What happened?

Pete: It was such a waste. How could these things happen?

Dr. G.: What has happened?

Pete: My father was killed in a plane crash. He was returning from a medical convention.

Dr. G.: When did you find out about his death?

Pete: Just a week ago. His funeral was very difficult for me to attend.

Dr. G.: And your mother?

Pete: She is taking it a lot better than me. I don't know how she does it.

The death of his father was very difficult for Ben. He took some time off work and spent some time with his family. This was a very emotional time for him. Interestingly enough, Ben did not exhibit temper problems during his grief. He felt emotionally numb, but functional.

After several weeks, he returned to work. It was business as usual. He worked his long hours, did his job well, and dealt with life. On the surface, all seemed to be in order. However, it was clear to me that Ben was repressing his feelings. He was ignoring his inner needs and playing a role. This was not natural and, considering his past psychological history, potentially very dangerous.

To the outside world, Ben was fine. His relationship with Gail improved. He was the old Ben, so it seemed. A year later, Ben received a very significant promotion.

Dr. G.: What is your career like now?

Pete: I have been promoted to chief technician at the research facility.

Dr. G.: How does that affect your other job?

Pete: I now spend all of my time at the research facility. Although I am on call at the power plant, very little of my time is spent there.

Dr. G.: Are you now working fewer hours?

Pete: Somewhat fewer, but I do spend a lot of time at the research lab.

Dr. G.: Do you see much of Ralph?

Pete: Yes, we still socialize. He is quite interested in my work, and our families do see each other now and then.

Dr. G.: Ben, tell me about the research facility.

Pete: What do you want to know?

Dr. G.: Is this work classified?

Pete: No. We just research safe and more effective uses of nuclear power.

Dr. G.: Is this funded by the government?

Pete: Yes. We have a tremendous budget and we are the most highly regarded research facility in the country.

Dr. G.: Do you worry about being laid off?

Pete: Absolutely not. It is a very secure position. My only concerns are related to doing my work to the best of my ability. After all, I am the chief technician in my unit and a lot depends on my capabilities.

Dr. G.: What does the facility look like?

Pete: We have a rather large building subdivided into various corridors. Each corridor represents a different division and all divisions are color-coded.

Dr. G.: Do these divisions have names?

Pete: Yes, of course. There is Norad-Alpha and Norad-Beta, Gani-Alpha and Gani-Beta, and my unit is Teres-Alpha.

Dr. G.: Is there a Teres-Beta?

Pete: Yes. Didn't I mention that? I apologize for the oversight.

Dr. G.: Do you occasionally make small oversights at work?

Pete: Now don't you start that again [getting angry]! I am competent to do my work and I don't need to see Dr. Margolis.

Dr. G.: I didn't say anything about Dr. Margolis.

Pete: I know, but you were going to, weren't you?

Dr. G.: Ben, have you had any difficulties at all at work?

Pete: Sometimes I miss a calculation and my men correct me.

Dr. G.: Does that get you angry?

Pete: Not enough that it shows, but, yes, I do get down on myself.

Dr. G.: Are you a perfectionist?

Pete: I don't think so. I just want everything to be done correctly.

Dr. G.: What is the difference?

Pee: I guess none. I will admit to being a perfectionist. Does that make me mentally unfit?

Dr. G.: It could if it makes you angry enough to let your emotions rule your behavior unchecked.

Pete: Well, that doesn't happen, so I guess I'm okay.

Ben went on to tell me more about his position. He was in charge of the Teres-Alpha division, which dealt with researching how to contain nuclear power and more effectively eliminating nuclear waste products. Ben was indeed a good supervisor. He was young, aggressive, knowledgeable, and totally dedicated. If you could ignore his emotional problems, he was absolutely perfect for the job. I couldn't ignore his psychological profile and my concern was growing by the minute.

As I progressed Ben forward, he described being in many different types of activities at the facility. He sat in on board meetings, participated in planning major projects, correlated the data from his division, and handled public relations, among other things. In other words, Ben had a lot of responsibilities. In my opinion he was "biting off more than he could chew," considering his emotional state.

I progressed him forward to the most significant event in this life.

Dr. G.: What year is this, Ben?

Pete: 2088.

Dr. G.: What is going on in your life at this time?

Pete: I'm really excited about my project.

Dr. G.: What is it exactly?

Pete: I am working on a way to compartmentalize and quantify the flow of nuclear material from one reactor site to another.

Dr. G.: That sounds complicated and dangerous.

Pete: It is. But it is also exciting.

Dr. G.: Are all of your men working on this project?

Pete: No, just me and Chet. I do most of the calculations.

Dr. G.: Are you putting in a lot of overtime on this?

Pete: Yes.

Dr. G.: Have there been any problems?

Pete: Just the usual frustrations—nothing major.

Dr. G.: Does Chet work overtime with you?

Pete: No, he goes home on time. I stay late by myself.

Dr. G.: So you work better when you are alone?

Pete: You know, I never thought about it, but I do. I really do like it better at night when only a skeleton crew is around.

Dr. G.: You mean there aren't people working there at night?

Pete: No, not really. We have the usual security people on board in the evening, but very few researchers or technicians are around at night.

I then progressed Ben forward to an actual event that would be meaningful to him. He reported being at the facility late one evening in 2088. He was alone and there were some problems.

Dr. G.: What is it, Ben?

Pete: Something is very wrong here.

Dr. G.: Exactly what is it that is wrong?

Pete: The level of nuclear wastes has risen and the diffraction chamber I developed isn't working.

Dr. G.: What do you mean, isn't working?

Pete: Apparently, my calculations were off and there is an overflow of the backup of these waste products.

Dr. G.: Can you handle this emergency?

Pete: I am sure I can. Wait—it isn't working. What am I going to do?

Dr. G.: Move forward, calmly, to your actions.

Pete: The dials are going crazy. The danger signal is about to be reached.

Dr. G.: Can you call for help?

Pete: I can handle this. I can do this myself. After all, I am the chief technician.

Dr. G.: Go on.

Pete: It's no use; the system is backing up.

Dr. G.: What does that mean?

Pete: A meltdown could occur. Everything will be contaminated. I can't let that happen.

Dr. G.: What do you do?

Pete: The signal is sounded. The security men will be here shortly. I can't let them see what I have done.

Dr. G.: What will you do?

Pete: I will isolate myself from them.

Dr. G.: Is there anybody with you now?

There was silence for a very long two minutes. When Ben finally responded he described a bizarre set of circumstances. There was a security guard making his rounds in the Teres-Alpha unit. Ben knocked him unconscious with a hard metal object. He then went completely out of control.

The frustration of his personal failure got to him. Ben couldn't handle the situation. It was his fault that this meltdown and contamination was occurring. He alone had handled the calculations that resulted in misprogramming the computer. When he calmed down, I continued the questioning.

Dr. G.: What is happening now, Ben?

Pete: I am totally isolated. I have sealed off this unit and it will take hours for them to get in here.

Dr. G.: What will that solve?

Pete: Nothing, but I must be alone.

Dr. G.: What have you done to correct this situation?

Pete: I turned all of the power and diffraction switches on high.

Dr. G.: Won't that add to the overload?

Pete: It sure will. This baby will blow and I'm going with it.

Dr. G.: Don't you want this to end a different way?

Pete: No. Nobody is going to fire me. Nobody is going to tell me I was wrong.

Dr. G.: What about the guard and the others?

Pete: I don't care. I don't care.

Ben had a nervous breakdown. He would not listen to reason. Pete, sitting in my recliner, was in no danger. It was Ben who couldn't be reasoned with by logic. As a result of Ben's actions, there was a complete meltdown of the research facility. The skeleton crew and Ben were killed. The nuclear contamination from Ben's miscalculations affected the entire Tulsa area. The water supply was contaminated. Concomitantly, the food supplies were then contaminated. Everything was contaminated. From the superconscious mind level, I spoke to Ben.

Dr. G.: Ben, what did you learn from this?

Pete: I learned how to contaminate a major city by my stupidity. I learned nothing but how to hurt innocent people.

Ben didn't quite understand another connection from this future life. He died in August of the year 2088. The eighth month and the year 2088 were very significant associations of the number eight. In addition, he worked in the Teres-Alpha unit. This spells out as Teresa, the name that haunted Pete most of his life.

Pete was brought out of trance feeling drained and unsure of what this all meant. I explained to him that this future life was the real cause of his present contamination compulsion and the origin of his difficulties with the number eight and the name Teresa. He understood the connection and complimented me on my ability to perceive his true underlying psychological problems when everyone else had been fooled.

However, I wasn't looking for compliments. I pointed out that Ben should have continued to see Dr. Margolis, but even that may not have prevented the blowup. Ben was a powder keg just waiting to explode. Finally, he did.

Pete was confused. How could this future life help him now? It was a terrible thing to look forward to. He sure didn't want to experience this in 100 years. I agreed with him. Although I did effect some cleansing from the superconscious mind level, that wouldn't solve his problem. The answer lay in the application of the principles of quantum physics.

You will recall that in all of the other future life progressions documented in this book, the results were positive. In other words, the resulting life represented a culmination of the patient's achievements. The patient was programmed for this frequency and that became their reality.

But that was just one probability of at least five major probabilities. In Pete's case, he perceived a negative frequency or probability though he had at least four others from which to choose. The solution to Pete's problem was really quite simple. All I had to do was to have him perceive the other four choices and then, after he selected the ideal frequency, program this frequency to be his reality. By doing this I would, in a way, help Pete to switch frequencies so his future would be quite different than if we did nothing.

I realize that this sounds confusing. You may say, how can I do this? How can I change the future? What you must consider is that every time you make a choice you are, in effect, changing the future. In Pete's case, progressing him forward to the other parallel existences, he would have at the end of the 21st century would accomplish that very goal.

Pete progressed nicely to four other lifetimes in that same time frame. After each life was reviewed, he carefully considered the one he felt was ideal and then I progressed him to that frequency. Remember, Pete was the one who chose the ideal frequency. I will never make that choice. The various environmental factors can be quite similar in these parallel frequencies, as was the case here. However, there will always be major differences, and each action by Pete in a certain frequency will have a certain effect on the total outcome of his life.

Thus, there is no predestination. The soul always has free will. What will be somewhat predestined is the basic framework of the frequency. The specifics can be changed by varying the choices along the way, but the basic framework can't be altered. You cannot just choose the best aspects of all five frequencies. You can only choose one frequency and accept the good with the bad. That is one reason why I always have the patient make this choice.

The typical pattern of the five frequencies is as follows: one is very bad, one is below average, one is rather neutral, one is above average, and one is excellent (not perfect). It is not difficult for patients to classify their frequencies into the above categories. It is pretty cut-and-dry.

I won't bore you with the details of Pete's other frequencies—just the one he chose. Remember, the basic environmental details were similar. His name, family members, and parents' occupations were identical. It's Ben himself in this ideal frequency who exhibited some noticeable differences.

Dr. G.: Where are you now, Ben?

Pete: I'm a senior in college.

Dr. G.: What is your major?

Pete: Nuclear physics.

Dr. G.: With what goal?

Pete: I want to go to graduate school and become a nuclear physicist.

Dr. G.: Do you ever get upset and lose control of your temper?

Pete: No. What a silly thing that is to ask.

In this frequency, Ben didn't settle for just being a technician. He went for the brass ring and became a nuclear physicist. In addition, he didn't exhibit any of the signs of emotional instability that he did in the previous frequency. Thus, there were no visits to Dr. Margolis and no temper episodes.

Gail still entered Ben's life and they got married when Ben finished graduate school. They were very much in love and Ben's parents approved of this relationship. I next progressed Ben to the year 2084.

Dr. G.: Tell me about your work?

Pete: Well, I am a nuclear physicist at our new research facility outside of Tulsa.

Dr. G.: How are things going?

Pete: Quite well. I have an excellent staff and couldn't be happier.

Dr. G.: Tell me about your staff.

Pete: My chief technician is someone I have known for a few years. He is also my best friend.

Dr. G.: Who is that?

Pete: Ralph. Ralph Straeger.

So you see, the pattern changed somewhat. Now Ralph had the position that Ben had occupied in the previous frequency. Ben was a highly competent and emotionally stable nuclear physicist who was also Ralph's boss. Ben and Ralph were still the best of friends. Their families socialized often and Ben was a very happy man.

Dr. G.: Tell me about your father.

Pete: Dad is a psychiatrist. We get along real well.

Dr. G.: Did he ever want you to follow his footsteps and go to medical school?

Pete: He let me decide what I wanted to do with my life. He was totally supportive.

I next progressed Ben to the year 2088.

Dr. G.: Tell me about your family.

Pete: You mean my wife and children?

Dr. G.: Yes.

Pete: Well, my wife, Gail, is a dream come true. We have two sons. I don't know what else you want to know.

Dr. G.: Do you ever get into big arguments with Gail?

Pete: Not really. We have minor disagreements like all couples do, but we never get mad at each other. We are very much in love.

Dr. G.: How are your children doing in school?

Pete: Just fine. Especially the oldest, Aaron. He is so bright, even I have a difficult time keeping up with him.

Dr. G.: Does your father spend much time with them?

Pete: What an odd question to ask. My mother and father visit us occasionally. You must realize that my dad is a very busy man. He attends many medical meetings.

This frequency was indeed ideal and different. By August of 2088, things were very different. Ben had no emotional problems. His son Aaron was an excellent student. His father was alive and well. Ben's relationship with Ralph was excellent, and all of the previous frequency's problems seem to have been avoided.

I next progressed Ben to the end of 2088.

Dr. G. Tell me about your work.

Pete: I have been working on a technique to help divert nuclear waste safely and to more effectively contain nuclear waste.

Dr. G.: How is it going?

Pete: Quite well. Thanks to an excellent staff and my good friend Ralph, we have successfully tested the techniques.

Dr. G.: So, it is a success?

Ralph: A great success.

Dr. G.: What is the name of your unit?

Ralph: Why, it is called Teres-Alpha.

So the pattern was complete. Pete passed the magical year of 2088 without causing the disaster he had in the previous frequency. He, as Ben, still worked in Teres-Alpha, but that name didn't act as a jinx. In fact, you might say it was a good-luck charm.

This frequency had many other positive aspects to it, but they are not relevant to Pete's problem. I ended the trance and programmed him to this ideal frequency.

Pete made rapid progress after this session. He no longer feared the number eight or the name Teresa. He understood what it really meant and why the contamination compulsion was so deeply ingrained within his psyche.

Pete's past lives were causative factors. I cannot ignore them. However, I must put a greater weight on his future lifetime as Ben Kingsley as the cause of his former problems. Being the sole cause of the irreversible contamination of an entire city is far more significant than murdering one man or living an immoral life.

Also, Pete made much more progress after experiencing his future life than in perceiving his past lives. There is no doubt in my mind that the future lifetime of Ben was the main cause of Pete's problem.

Pete today is totally recovered. He did this himself with a little assistance from regression and progression therapy. I like this case because it illustrates the principle that the future is now. We can change the future, but we must perceive it first.

The new age of Aquarius that we are in gives us the potential for tremendous opportunities. It is a 2160-year astrological era of spiritual harmony that began on February 4, 1962. If you ignore these opportunities, then your life won't change much. You will stay on your average or below-average frequencies. However, if you follow the laws of karma, you will switch to a much more desirable frequency, which will not only assure you of a better life in this incarnation, but it will result in more positive future lifetimes. The choice, as always, is yours.

Chapter 15

Past Life Therapy in the 22nd Century

Kim's case is one of my favorites because it illustrates so many of the principles of karma and the space-time continuum. It is not that unusual for a patient to express interest in exploring a future life. What is fascinating, more often than not, are the results.

In 1982, a somewhat overweight saleswoman named Kim called my office with a request to explore her future life. She hadn't read the first edition of *Past Lives—Future Lives*, but she had heard of it. If there was such a thing as future lives, she wanted to experience it.

My explanations of the theory behind future life progression, the space-time continuum, and hypnotherapy were met with enthusiastic interest. Kim didn't have any background in this field whatsoever. She had just heard about me and my work. Kim had never read books on reincarnation or parapsychology, so she began therapy without a lot of preconceptions.

In late July of 1982, Kim began her trip to a future lifetime. She proved to be an excellent hypnotic patient, exhibiting REM throughout her trance.

Dr. G.: What do you perceive?

Kim: I see a young female with dark, shoulder-length hair, dark eyes, small frame, and approximately 18 years old.

Dr. G.: What is your name?

Kim: Barbara. Barbara Parkhurst.

Dr. G.: What are you wearing?

Kim: I'm wearing a white jumpsuit with a white shoe-boot. The clothes are very lightweight. The boot has a special water bubble-like sole for maximum arch support and protection.

Dr. G.: Are these your daily clothes?

Kim: These are my work clothes.

Dr. G.: What kind of work do you do?

Kim: I work in an underground research facility.

Dr. G.: What year is it?

Kim: 2119.

Dr. G.: You stated that you are underground. Is there some specific reason for this?

Kim: Yes. We require isolation. We have no contact with the outside world.

Dr. G.: What do you do exactly?

Kim: We are a think tank. Our purpose is to research and develop new concepts, which are highly technical, for the ultimate betterment of all humankind.

Dr. G.: Do you work for the government?

Kim: No. We have no political or government affiliation. We are an independently funded research organization.

Dr. G.: Tell me more about your underground location.

Kim: Our complexes are all underground and completely indestructible. Should the entire world see holocaust, we would be completely unharmed. Hopefully, our work will preclude human destruction.

Dr. G.: What about your family?

Kim: We have no families. We are the result of genetic engineering. Only genius-level banks are used and properly matched. We are all dedicated to science.

Dr. G.: What do you feel your purpose is?

Kim: Humans, in their natural state, are destroying their own species gradually. We're working to help humankind alleviate primal emotion. It is humankind's only hope of survival. The thrust of our work involves positive emotional responses. We are aware of human behavioral patterns and select the positive response enhancement for our research.

Dr. G.: How many of you are there?

Kim: There are many researchers in many areas. We are all specialists. It is quite rare for someone outside of our group to appear on the screen.

The screen referred to a monitor for communication from one area to another. On very rare occasions a scientist from the surface might communicate with this group.

Dr. G.: What is your specialty, Barbara?

Kim: My work is with light refraction. I specifically work with ionization of molecular structure.

Dr. G.: For what purpose?

Kim: By altering the molecular structure of certain components of the brain, we hope to permanently remove destructive human qualities.

I next progressed Barbara to the age of 22. She further described the underground complex as a series of tunnels (like a maze) ending in laboratories. There were living quarters for the researchers and viewing screens were set up at strategic locations in the complex. Transportation within the complex was provided by small vehicles powered by air cushions. These vehicles did not touch the ground and were nearly noiseless. One could detect a faint "whooshing" sound when one of these cars came by. This apparatus had also been developed by one of the research groups in the complex.

Dr. G.: How do you learn from the others in your group?

Kin: Learning and analysis are done by programming discs. There is no "personal" teaching. All of our work is placed on discs and we have free access to any disc we choose.

Dr. G.: What about your personal life?

Kim: There are no male-female relationships as exist aboveground. We do have feelings of deep-rooted respect and admiration for one another.

Dr. G.: Is there someone you respect and admire more than the others?

Kim: Howard Pennington. There is a special, almost indescribable, feeling on my part for Howard Pennington. It is not physical attraction, but one of intense professional worship. I wish to sit at his feet and learn—a master-disciple relationship in its pure form—this is a pure love uncluttered by physical attraction. I wish to spend every free second in his presence.

Dr. G.: What does Howard work on?

Kim: Howard Pennington is so advanced that it is very difficult for us to comprehend his work. He formerly developed a vibrational response technique to simulate aboveground "family emotional responses." He was able to place these on discs for our experiments. He feels my ionization concept may be able to produce similar effects. I am honored that he would be so familiar with my work.

Dr. G.: What else did he work on?

Kim: Howard has been working on a time biotelemetry concept.

Dr. G.: What is that?

Kim: He is attempting to condense a thousand years of time into a few hours. This way a subject can benefit from one entire spectrum of human emotions in a very brief period of time.

Dr. G.: Do you want to be his assistant?

Kim: More than anything in the world.

Dr. G.: Why doesn't Howard have an assistant now?

Kim: Because of our response modes.

Dr. G.: What do you mean?

Kim: We are all in awe of Howard Pennington and his work. This affects our response modes. Most of our response modes fall into a negative range, usually in the inferiority complex division.

Dr. G.: Are you qualified to work with Howard?

Kim: It's not that simple. My response modes are quite consistent. My only problem is in the frustration mode. However, my consistency rates are superior to all others in the complex. If any of us will be chosen to work with Howard, it will be me.

During further conversations with Barbara I found out that she was able to use her own ionization of molecular structure technique on herself to qualify as Howard's assistant. She began working with Howard and with her assistance, his work advanced rapidly.

Dr. G.: How are things going?

Kim: Quite well. We have modified some of our initial approaches to make the outcome more feasible.

Dr. G.: What do you mean?

Kim: Howard preferred discs to allowing a subject to actually experience different lifetimes for every emotion known. The time it takes to do this is just a few hours.

Dr. G.: But isn't the subject confused?

Kim: Not really. It is not necessary for the subject to remember or even understand the lives. We are only interested in the emotional cleansing and reprogramming.

Well, it looked as if past life regression therapy was alive and well in the 22nd century. The principles I practice today are utilized by Howard, with some condensing of time commitments. Barbara and Howard worked very well together. They perfected this technique and had many successful responses from their subjects.

Dr. G.: What will happen now?

Kim: The results are being sent to the surface and will be used at special treatment centers.

These treatment centers functioned like psychological clinics. Patients with emotional problems were treated using Howard's past life therapy discs. It proved quite effective.

Dr. G.: Are you still working with Howard?

Kim: Yes, I'm so excited about his success. Now I'm even more thrilled.

Dr. G.: Why? Did something else occur?

Kim: Yes. Howard has consented to utilize his technique on me. I can't believe it. Imagine, shortly I will be made to reexperience my past lives and benefit by the resulting emotional cleansing.

Dr. G.: But won't it be difficult for you to remember them being that this is a condensation approach?

Kim: Normally, yes. Because I have been such a help to Howard, he has made several arrangements to slow the procedure down so I can remember these lives.

Thus began the past life explanation of a future life researcher named Barbara Parkhurst. I will attempt to describe the regressions as facilitated by Howard's discs. This most unusual approach proved very informative and therapeutic to Kim.

Barbara regressed back to the early 18th century in France. She was a teenage servant girl to a French nobleman named Charles. Her name was Antoinette and the chief servants were Sofie and Josef.

Dr. G.: Tell me about your life, Antoinette. What do you enjoy about it?

Kim: I like being a servant. Charles is kind to all of us. I also like eating the leftover pastries.

Kim had a sweet tooth and the origin of it was not difficult to elicit. Antoinette was very fond of Charles because he treated her and the other servants so well.

Dr. G.: Does Charles ask you to do anything of a special nature?

Kim: If you mean does he take me to bed, the answer is yes. It's part of my duties. I do not mind. Charles is a kind man and I am honored that he allows me to please him.

Apparently, Charles treated Antoinette especially well. She was his favorite and Antoinette fell in love with him. I progressed Antoinette forward to a significant event.

Dr. G.: Antoinette, has anything important occurred since I last spoke to you?

Kim: Yes [crying].

Dr. G.: What is it?

Kim: I'm going to have Charles's baby. I'm so happy.

Dr. G.: What about Charles's wife?

Kim: No one must know that I'm pregnant. Charles's wife is quite frail and all of their attempts at children resulted in stillborn babies. She must not know of the child.

Dr. G.: How will you hide this pregnancy?

Kim: Charles is taking me to his summer house. His wife never goes there. Tom, the head of the stable, will look after me. Charles will tell his wife that I was dismissed.

So Antoinette moved into the summer house. Tom took care of her and Charles visited Antoinette about every 10 days.

Dr. G.: Wasn't this a bit unusual?

Kim: Charles took care of everything. It was very lonely, but Charles arranged for Tom to marry me so the child wouldn't be a bastard. Only Sofie, Josef, and Tom knew about the baby.

Dr. G.: What else did Charles do?

Kim: He gave Tom a beautiful horse as well as the servants' quarters for him to live in. I stayed in the big house. Charles told Tom never to touch me and he never did even though I was his wife. Charles could never marry me. He married for land.

Dr. G.: How did Charles treat you at the summer house?

Kim: He treated me as though I were a lady instead of a servant. He brought me fine clothes, sweets, and exotic foods. He never gave me a wig. He didn't like them on ladies. Charles liked real hair.

I progressed Antoinette forward to the birth of the baby.

Dr. G.: Tell me what has happened.

Kim: The baby was a boy and we named him David. Charles brought me a ring with a ruby in it. I felt like I was his wife. The women who helped me deliver David were sent away by Tom so that no one would see Charles. He stayed with me for two days. He never did that before and I never wanted him to leave us. He always came to see us when he went hunting, but he always returned the same day.

Dr. G.: What about other visitors coming to the summer house?

Kim: Charles didn't bring anyone to the summer house anymore. He told these friends that his wife was too sick and all of his socializing was done at the estate.

When David was two years old, Charles's wife died in childbirth and their baby died also. Charles decided to remarry to acquire more land.

Dr. G.: Whom did Charles marry?

Kim: Charles married a foreigner. She was beautiful and wealthy. She was also quite ruthless and Charles seemed a little afraid of her.

Dr. G.: Didn't that worry Charles?

Kim: No. Because she was a woman, she had no real power as long as Charles was lord.

Dr. G.: What about you?

Kim: Charles didn't really like her. This was strictly a business deal. I was unhappy because I felt jealous, afraid she might have a son and Charles would leave us and forget all above David and me.

Dr. G.: What else did you feel?

Kim: I felt sorry for his other wife. She was so sickly. I felt better than her because I'd given Charles a son. I never feared his first wife. The new woman made me fear losing Charles. She suspected Charles was seeing another woman, but she expected it to be a lady—not me.

Dr. G.: What did Charles do about her suspicions?

Kim: He rejected her because she confronted him and fought with him. She hurt his pride. A French lord should never be questioned by a woman.

Dr. G.: What happened as a result of this?

Kim: He came to us more often and he loved David more and more. He brought us more gifts. We never asked him for anything. Charles kept telling me how much his wife was frustrating him. I started to feel safe again. He told us that he would always take care of us and that his wife would never be able to hurt us.

Dr. G.: Were you always faithful to Charles?

Kim: Yes. I never had any man but Charles and I never asked for any gift except my little goat, Julia. When Charles first brought me to the summer house, he said I could have a gift and because I knew I'd be lonely, I asked for Julia. I used to play with her at the estate. She was company for me.

Dr. G.: Did he bring Julia to you?

Kim: Yes, he did. I told him Sofie knew which goat was Julia. He had Tom bring her to me over his horse. Besides the goat, I never asked for anything. I did love and appreciate everything Charles brought us. He couldn't stay with us much, but he thought he'd done everything to make us happy and he did all he could.

Dr. G.: Didn't Charles have other lovers?

Kim: He had a lot of women for bedding. He wasn't faithful to anyone, but I think he truly loved us. The rich ones all had a lot of women. Charles wasn't bad, but I still wished he could be faithful to me as I was to him.

As time went on, Antoinette became more and more attracted to Charles. She was very much in love with him, even though she was quite aware of his faults and his lifestyle. I next progressed Antoinette to the most significant event that was to occur in her life.

Dr. G.: Where are you now?

Kim: Oh, my God! I don't know what to do. Please help me.

Dr. G.: What happened?

Kim: Charles is dead. He had a heart attack and died in my arms.

After calming her down I tried to follow the next chain of events carefully. Tom helped Antoinette dispose of Charles's body. It could not be found in the house. Tom buried Charles in the woods.

Dr. G.: What is going on?

Kim: We had to get all of our personal effects out of the house quickly. I packed everything and ran to the servants' house with Tom. I changed into my old clothes and put all of my fancy clothes and gifts from Charles in bags. Tom buried these bags in the woods.

Dr. G.: Please tell me what is happening.

Kim: Charles's wife was sending four men to look for Charles's kept woman and Tom was afraid they would kill us.

Dr. G.: But didn't you tell me that all wealthy French lords had many women? Why should she care about you?

Kim: They had many women, but a kept woman is something else. I represented more of a threat to her. In addition, she heard rumors about a son by this kept woman and this made me especially dangerous to her.

Dr. G.: Does she know about Charles's death?

Kim: No, that would be impossible. He just died a few hours ago.

Dr. G.: What did Tom do next?

Kim: He told me that these men were searching all of Charles's houses with orders to kill the girl and the child. Tom made us stay in the servants' house. He covered my hands with dirt and messed up my hair. He dressed little David in old clothes and made him look dirty, too. He told me I wasn't to cry for Charles or show any emotions when the soldiers came.

I next progressed Antoinette to the arrival of the soldiers.

Dr. G.: What did the soldiers do?

Kim: The soldiers burst into the big house and searched it. Then they came to the servants' house and questioned Tom. David and I were working in the garden and we could hear Tom telling the soldiers that we were his wife and son. He told them a lady came to the big house to see Charles a long time ago, but hadn't come for a long time. He said Charles had never allowed him to see her and he didn't know who she was.

Dr. G.: What happened next?

Kim: The soldiers believed Tom and left. They never came back. We were still afraid and never returned to the big house. We stayed in Tom's house and wore ugly clothes and ate awful food.

Dr. G.: Did Tom get close to you?

Kim: Oh, no. He stayed in the stable. He was honorable to Charles's wishes. Tom acted like our servant.

Later Charles's wife took over the estate. She was quite cruel and ruthless. The soldiers reported their conversation with Tom to her. She thought Tom was purposely hiding the true identity of Charles's kept woman from her. She sent Tom away on a long journey for special materials for her clothes. Antoinette never saw Tom again.

Dr. G.: What did you do?

Kim: I sold the ruby ring Charles gave me to buy food. We were cold and had no place to go. David later died.

Dr. G.: Then what?

Kim: I buried him next to Charles. I then sat in a corner of the servants' house and cried. I never ate again.

Antoinette died of starvation pining away for Charles and David. In the superconscious level, I was able to find out that Charles was Kim's ex-husband. She divorced him because he cheated on her once too often. He was a very materialistic and manipulative man. David came back as Kim's son, Jeremy. They are very close.

The important point in this life was Antoinette's early attraction to sweets. For a servant girl, sweets were a welcome change to the dull food normally eaten. As Charles's kept woman, they represented a special reward and reminded her of him. The starvation end to that life carried over in Kim's constant and losing battle with dieting.

Barbara Parkhurst was very much affected by this life. Howard Pennington was most pleased with this experience and the following day he "disced" Barbara back into another one of her past lives.

This lifetime took place in Rome in the early part of the 16th century. Barbara was Paolo, a 19-year-old guard to the pope. His life seemed without purpose. He did his job well, but didn't seem to have any friends; he just seemed to be existing.

Dr. G.: Paolo, tell me about your family.

Kim: I didn't really know my family. I was raised by the Church. My mother was a prostitute in Florence and my father was a nobleman.

Dr. G.: Does that make you a bastard?

Kim: Yes. I'm the bastard son of a nobleman and a prostitute. Some combination, huh?

Dr. G.: Did you ever go back to visit your mother?

Kim: No. The Church forbade me to ever go back to Florence.

Dr. G.: Does that bother you?

Kim: No. I don't miss not having real parents; I just do my job.

I then progressed Paolo forward to a significant time in his life. He reported being sent on some assignment with a number of other soldiers. They were sent by the army to kill the inhabitants of a small village.

Dr. G.: Why are you sent here?

Kim: I do not question my orders.

Dr. G.: Do you really want to kill these defenseless people?

Kim: No, I don't, but if I disobey my orders, I will be killed.

Paolo was the youngest soldier sent to exterminate this village. He had never killed anyone before and didn't want to begin now.

Dr. G.: Tell me what you did.

Kim: Well, there weren't that many people in the village to begin with. The other soldiers rounded them up and killed them. I was supposed to kill this woman and her child.

Dr. G.: Did you?

Kim: No.

Dr. G.: How did you manage that?

Kim: I put my sword into the body of a man lying dead on the street. Then I told the woman and the boy to hide and wait for us to go. I also told her to move to another village the following day and never to return to this place again.

Dr. G.: And your sword?

Kim: The blood on my sword from the dead man's body was used to convince my fellow soldiers that I had carried out my orders.

This plan apparently worked quite well. Paolo returned to Rome and remained a guard in the Vatican.

Dr. G.: What has happened since I last spoke to you?

Kim: I met a beautiful girl named Julianna. We were married and I am very happy.

Dr. G.: Do you have any children?

Kim: Yes, we have one son, Antonio.

As the years went by, Paolo finally had a purpose. He loved Julianna and Antonio. The problem was his attitude toward his employers. When Antonio expressed interest in becoming a guard like his father, Paolo told him to find another occupation.

Dr. G.: Why do you discourage Antonio from following in your footsteps?

Kim: These men I guard, they are not holy.

Dr. G.: Are you referring to the pope?

Kim: No. The Church noblemen I guard now seem to be more like politicians. I do not trust them. I do not think they are real God-fearing men. I do not respect them and I don't care if they live or die.

Dr. G.: Isn't that a big problem, being that you guard them?

Kim: I do my job, but I don't like it. The only thing I care about is Julianna and Antonio. Antonio and I sometimes go to the market. He carries bread and fruit in a bag. I love him and feel very proud of him. Nothing else in my life has any meaning.

Later on, Antonio became an apprentice craftsman. Paolo was proud of his son. He was still a guard and quite frustrated in his job. I next progressed Paolo to a significant time in his life.

Dr. G.: What has happened since we last spoke?

Kim: I am very sad.

Dr. G.: Why?

Kim: My wife and son are gone. They both died of a fever. Here I am, 35 years old, and now life is completely meaningless.

I asked Paolo about whether he contemplated suicide and he said no. He did report that he didn't like working with the foreign guards in the Vatican. I then progressed Paolo forward to the end of his life.

Dr. G.: Where are you now, Paolo?

Kim: I'm on guard duty.

Dr. G.: Tell me what happens next.

Kim: I was making my rounds one night and all of a sudden someone jumped me by the edge of the building. He put his sword through me above the stomach and between my ribs. I started to fall when he pulled it out, but then I started drifting up and there was no pain. I felt free and glad to be free. I knew instantly that I was dead and was pleased to be rid of that life.

It is interesting to observe the complete lack of emotion exhibited by Paolo. He was, indeed, most happy to be rid of the life of a burned-out guard in 16th-century Rome.

From the superconscious mind level, Kim (Barbara) reported that Antonio was her current son, Jeremy. She did not identify Julianna or the village woman and her son whom she had saved. An interesting sidenote to this is that Kim attended a Christian seminary and earned a degree in theology. Although she never used this background professionally, she had a strange attraction to formal study of the Bible. To this day, she keeps away from all forms of formal religion.

I did some checking myself on the events in Rome during the early parts of the 16th century and ascertained some interesting facts. In 1527, Charles V of France ordered the sack of Rome. He took Pope Clement prisoner. Swiss guards along with local guards protected the pope. The *Encyclopedia Americana* stated that the Swiss guards suffered heavy losses in 1527. Paolo mentioned being separated from the foreign guards, but on that fateful day, he was with them.

Another fact of interest in validating the accuracy of this life was the description of the Vatican by Paolo. Paolo did not remember a statue of Saint Paul atop the column of Marcus Aurelius. As it turns out, one of the Popes had the statue of Marcus Aurelius removed and replaced it with Saint Paul's statue in 1589, about 62 years after Paolo's death. Thus, Paolo correctly would not have seen Saint Paul's statue during his lifetime.

Barbara Parkhurst returned to the 22nd century a little confused and a little drained. She and Howard discussed these two lives in great detail. She was quite anxious to continue with her past life exploration, so the following day was set aside for her third trip back in time.

Barbara's next past life took her back more than 1,000 years. She was a Chinese girl named Soon Lin. Soon Lin was about 14 years old and worked in rice paddies doing some sort of farming. She was dressed in rough-looking dark clothes that resembled pajamas. She wore no shoes and she spent most of the day standing in water.

Soon Lin described her family as large and close. They were very poor, but proud people. I progressed her to an important day in her life.

Dr. G.: Where are you now?

Kim: I'm working in the fields. What's that?

Dr. G.: What's what?

Kim: Those warriors are coming this way.

Dr. G.: What warriors?

Kim: I noticed them before. It is not uncommon to see warriors ride by the fields. They rarely stop, but today is different.

Dr. G.: Where are they now?

Kim: They stopped by the edge of the fields. They are staring at me and the other girls. I am afraid.

Dr. G.: What happens next?

Kim: One of the warriors charges into the water and nearly tramples one of my sisters. He's heading toward me. I am afraid.

The warrior grabbed Soon Lin and pulled her onto his horse. He brought her out of the fields and stopped his horse in front of her parents.

Dr. G.: What did he do next?

Kim: He tossed a small pouch at my father and nodded his head toward me. I guess that meant that he was paying for me with those coins.

Dr. G.: What did your father do?

Kim: He just nodded in agreement and the warrior rode off with me.

So without a word being said this Chinese warrior bought Soon Lin. He took her with him and joined his fellow warriors and rode away. Some hours later they stopped to set up camp. The warrior took Soon Lin's clothes off and stared at her body. Apparently, this was to see if she was a virgin. She passed the test.

Soon Lin was taken to some kind of village. There she was resold by the warrior to an elderly, obese, and quite ugly Chinese man. Soon Lin fainted when she realized that she had been sold to this grotesque man. The next thing she remembered was waking up in a tent, lying on a bunch of satin pillows.

Dr. G.: Where are you now, Soon Lin?

Kim: I...I don't know. I guess it must be this man's home. His name is Chu.

Dr. G.: Where is Chu now?

Kim: He is in this tent with two other women. They are older than me and very pretty. Oh—his nails are disgusting.

Dr. G.: What do you mean?

Kim: He has fingernails that go all the way to the ground. It looks disgusting.

Dr. G.: What happens next?

Kim: Chu comes toward me and hits me across the face. Then he rips my clothes off and rapes me right in front of the other two women. They laugh as he physically abuses me and totally ignore my screams.

Dr. G.: How long does this continue?

Kim: I don't know. I fainted again, and when I awoke, I had bruises and scratches all over my body.

This went on for more than a week. One night Soon Lin couldn't take it any longer and ran away.

Dr. G.: Where did you go?

Kim: I ran away to a neighboring village and found a kindly old man who lived with his son. He agreed to let me stay there and hide away for a while.

Dr. G.: Did the old man keep his word?

Kim: Yes, for a few days anyway.

Dr. G.: Then what?

Kim: Some soldiers came later and the boy told me to run away fast. His father had accepted some money from the soldiers and told them where I was hiding.

Dr. G.: Did you escape?

Kim: No, I didn't have a chance. The soldiers caught me, hit me, and took me back to Chu.

Dr. G.: What happened to the old man?

Kim: They killed his son for trying to help me. Then they took the money they gave him back. He was broken-hearted, but still alive.

Apparently, Soon Lin was considered Chu's property. She was bought and now his. He could do whatever he pleased to her. When she returned to Chu's tent, her right leg was broken. She healed very slowly and walked with a decisive limp. This was done so she couldn't run away again.

Dr. G.: What did you do then?

Kim: I stayed and took care of Chu's women. I was some sort of a servant, but still his toy. He physically abused me whenever he felt like it. He made fun of my leg and beat me for sport. I hate him.

This went on for about a year. Soon Lin tried to run away again. This time she didn't get very far. She was caught and her right leg was cut off in front of the other women. She slowly bled to death.

From the superconscious level, she identified Chu as her ex-husband and the boy who had tried to save her when the old man had sold her out to the warrior, as her son, Jeremy. The lesson she was supposed to learn was humility and submission. She did learn the former, but not the latter.

An interesting aside on this life is that Kim later reported to me that she hated long fingernails. She had a favorite aunt who would wear them and she would feel very uncomfortable until her aunt took them off.

Barbara Parkhurst was getting quite a lot out of these past lives. She and Howard discussed them in detail after every session. Howard was beginning to see the benefit of these slower regressions as compared to the instant regressions he had initially programmed into the discs.

The stage was set for another regression. Howard prepared Barbara for her fourth trip back in time.

This time Barbara had also chosen ancient China. She was a male named Yun Chang. He was in training to be an advisor to the emperor. Yun Chang was at some sort of a monastery, surrounded by beautiful statues, Oriental rugs, and other fine things.

Dr. G.: What is it that you study?

Kim: I study everything. The fine arts, history, philosophy, meditation. All knowledge is at my disposal.

Dr. G.: You sound like a man of peace.

Kim: I am.

Dr. G.: But is the emperor also a man of peace?

Kim: I do not know much about him. It does not matter. I will advise him according to my training.

Dr. G.: Do you train with others?

Kim: Yes, there are three others. We will all advise the emperor.

Dr. G.: Is your training identical to that of the other three students?

Kim: No, not quite. We all have our specialties, but we also have a common goal.

Dr. G.: And what is that?

Kim: We will advise our leader so that he may best serve the common good.

As the years passed, Yun Chang and his three colleagues graduated and advised the emperor. However, Wu Dee was not an emperor of peace. He liked war and made it clear to his advisers that he would not take kindly to being advised to keep peace when war was a viable option.

Dr. G.: If Wu Dee wants to declare war all the time, then why does he need advisors?

Kim: He doesn't look for war all the time. There are many matters of state that require our expertise and we are consulted.

Dr. G.: But haven't you sold out to the system?

Kim: We have compromised to serve the common good.

So all of Yun Chang's idealism went down the drain. He sold out to the system. His advice was governed by fear—fear for his own life.

I next moved Yun Chang forward to the most crucial time in his life.

Dr. G.: What is occurring now?

Kim: Wu Dee has called us together to sanction a rather large war.

Dr. G.: Does Wu Dee need your sanction?

Kim: No, but if we do not agree, he will execute us.

Dr. G.: How did you decide?

Kim: We took a vote. Two said no and two said yes, including me. I allowed intellect to cloud my judgment and convinced them that we must all say yes to war.

Dr. G.: Did they all agree?

Kim: Yes, and I was honored for my judgment.

Wu Dee accepted their sanctions and declared war. He was very successful and honored his advisors. Yun Chang was made chief advisor.

Dr. G.: What else happened?

Kim: I was given a special house to live in with servants. I falsely convinced myself that we were wise to sanction war.

This went on for years. Every time they agreed with Wu Dee, they were honored and given additional privileges. From the superconscious level, Yun Chang realized he failed to accomplish or display any wisdom. Wisdom is not mere intellect, but a combination of intellect, understanding, and compassion.

Yun Chang's intellectual judgment was neither wise nor deserving of honor. He misused his influence over others to allow a unanimous sanctioning of war. Arrogant pride and fear perpetuated this rubber stamping of Wu Dee's ruthless endeavors.

It is most interesting to note that the Yun Chang life preceded the life of Soon Lin. Perhaps the life of Soon Lin was both karmic retribution as well as a true lesson in the unlearned humility corridor of Kim's karmic cycle.

Meanwhile, back in the 22nd century, Barbara Parkhurst and Howard Pennington began comparing notes of the former's past lives. They worked together but nothing romantic developed. This was a different type of society. Barbara had reached her pinnacle of success by working with Howard Pennington.

Howard also benefited by this arrangement. He was able to see his research as it applied to a distinguished colleague, not just a subject sent down from the surface. After a period of further testing, Howard modified his discs to slow down the process of regressing. It wasn't as slow as it is today, but it also wasn't as condensed as the "90-mile-an-hour" method he originally conceived.

Barbara learned a lot from Howard. They worked together for many years in their isolated facility underground. The past life regressions taught her many lessons. She learned about her past, her deficiencies, and her challenges. As Barbara, Kim learned what it would be like to work with a man she held in high esteem, with a higher love.

In spite of Howard's superior mind, Barbara did not shy away from the challenge or allow herself to fall into the negative response mode characterized by an inferiority complex. She rose above this. As a result of the trust and reverence in which she viewed Howard, Howard only reinforced her commitment to dedicate her life to bettering humankind.

But who was Howard in Barbara's past? He did not show up in any of her four past life regressions. Did he suddenly just materialize in the 22nd century? The answer was no. Kim informed me from the superconscious mind level of Howard's real identity. Many years ago, Kim dated a man named George. George was a truly kind and beautiful man. They had been engaged.

But fate would not allow this union. George contracted a rare form of leukemia and was hospitalized. Kim visited him every day with tears in her eyes. She prayed every night for his speedy recovery. Perhaps it was a flashback to Antoinette's desire for Charles or Paolo's yearning for Julianna, but George just wasted away and slowly died.

Kim could not hold back the tears as she described this to me. "So close and yet so far," was all she could say. She never really got over George. Her ex-husband never knew about her previous lover and fiancé. It was for the best that she kept George a secret.

The relationship between Kim and her son, Jeremy, was quite close. Kim could see him as David and the son of the old Chinese man. This was the only saving grace from her marriage.

The result of this future life progression was amazing. Kim lost weight. She dressed better and developed a positive self-image. She made much progress in her career as a saleswoman, giving up her tendencies to procrastinate.

She described her views as follows: "Love is the key to everything. This really makes me feel like I'm on the right track. One aspect of love that I felt for Howard during the progression was complemented by the love I have for God."

Kim improved because now she has a true purpose. It will take 130 years, but she will be with George again. George will be Howard Pennington. They will complete their mission together.

Chapter 16

Time Travelers from Our Future

Is it possible that some day we will eventually master time travel? My research has uncovered the fact that time travelers do exist and originate from 1,000 to 3,000 years in our future.

I refer to these futuristic time travelers as *chrononauts*. Many have abducted us throughout history and even traced us back to our past lives. These very same chrononauts have actually abducted us in several of our previous lifetimes. The main purpose of these chrononauts is to assist us in our own spiritual growth. They are us in the future.

Here is a summary of the four different types of time travelers my patients have related to me in hypnosis:

1. *The grays*. This is the classic "insect" alien with large black eyes. They stand around 3 to 5 feet tall with grayish skin, no ear lobes, four fingers and toes on each hand and foot, and are the most commonly observed time travelers. Some of these chrononauts appear as "little whites" or "little blues." Neither type has body hair. Some of these aliens are female.

Other grays have been observed of various heights, some rather tall and slender. These are usually in charge of the smaller aliens and often perform examinations on human abductees. They all wear one-piece uniforms with insignias that often are triangular in shape.

2. *Hybrid time travelers*. These are a genetic mixture between humans and beings from other planets. Their skin ranges from whitish hues to bronze, and they range from 5 to 6 feet tall. Some hybrid chrononauts look quite human from a distance, but resemble aliens upon closer inspection. Many have large faceted eyes and odd-looking foreheads. My patients report seeing female hybrids.
3. *Pure humans*. About one quarter of the time, travelers from our future are entirely human by genetic makeup. They look like us in every respect. These chrononauts have interbred with our species throughout time, and this may explain some of our genius protégés in various fields.

A common trait to these pure human time travelers is their height. They appear to be between 6 and 7 feet tall, compared to the 3 to 5 feet of the insect aliens types and 5 to 6 feet hybrids. They are blond, blue-eyed, tanned, clean shaven and always appear to be dressed in white robes. The many references in almost all ancient books concerning the presence of "Giants" lend support to these reports.

There are reports from my patients of these pure humans working along with aliens and/or hybrids. Whenever this occurred, the pure human time travelers always appear in charge of their activities.

4. *Reptilian time travelers*. These beings have vertical pupils and lizard-like skin. The little data I have about them suggests they are *not* out for our best interests. These beings are 100 percent extraterrestrial, and have nothing to lose by our lack of spiritual growth. They are never part of a

time traveler team and are commonly fugitives escaping from certain imprisonment.

They are infrequently reported by abductees as originating from other less-friendly planets in our present century. I do not argue this point, but they also exist in our future and travel back in time. These time travelers are most definitely to be avoided, as they eat humans.

I have no data on time travelers before the 31st century or beyond the 51st century on our planet. The explanation for that is an educated guess that we won't master time travel for another 1,000 years, and after 3,000 years we will all probably ascend, so there will be no one left on Earth to travel back in time. Another possibility is that we simply lose interest in time travel after the year 5000 A.D.

The time travelers from about 1,000 years in our future conduct many experiments on us, and have been engaged in this activity for many thousands of years. Most of their experiments have failed. All of our ancient and advanced civilizations were time traveler experiments. We are their most recent project.

The chrononauts from 2,000 to 3,000 years in our future make fewer mistakes. They are poorly represented, and still in need of spiritual fine tuning. Although much more evolved than we, they are helping us grow spiritually so their eventual ascension will be faster.

You might assume that these chrononauts travel back in time in flying saucers, but only the ones from about 1,000 to 1,500 years in our future do. The others have mastered teleportation and can "beam" themselves anywhere they want to instantly.

Those of you who like conspiracy theories will be happy to know that each group of time travelers is in communication with our government and exchange scientific data. These chrononauts are responsible for the quantum leaps in our technology throughout this century.

Here is a summary of my patients' regressions depicting the actions and motives of time travelers:

- These time travelers (chrononauts) function as our "guardian angels" by placing attackers in suspended animation states to allow our escape. They can manipulate our physical laws to assist us in times of need.
- These chrononauts follow us from lifetime to lifetime. They trace our soul back to our previous lives and monitor our spiritual enfoldment.
- The origin of these chrononauts is Earth from 1,000 to 3,000 years in the future.
- The past 500 years has seen a significant increase in the quantity of their monitoring and abductions.
- Fertility problems are quite common in these futuristic grays.
- A state of suspended animation can be induced instantly on anyone they choose.
- They have mastered hyperspace travel between dimensions, and can move through walls and solid objects.
- By existing in the fifth dimension, they can observe us and remain invisible.
- They can levitate themselves or us at will. Genetic manipulation of our chromosomes is a routine procedure for them. They have greatly sped up our rate of evolution.
- The less advanced groups make many errors with experiments, but the more advanced ones manipulate time and space with proficiency.
- The ultimate purpose of these time travelers is to facilitate the perfection of the human soul to

> allow for ascension and the end of the karmic cycle. As we grow spiritually, so do they. They are us in the future.

The three-dimensional world we normally observe consists of length, width, and depth. Time is added as the fourth dimension to this paradigm. In reality, time is the fourth dimension of the space-time continuum. To our concept of existence, we must now add a fifth dimension of anything beyond time, such as parallel universes, as well as hyperspace in general.

The very idea that our species in the future can travel back in time physically to interact with us seems preposterous to many. This paradigm is based on solid mathematical models.

The idea that time travel does not violate causality has been demonstrated by Kip Thorne, the well known Caltech Astrophysicist.[1] The Cambridge University professor and author Stephen Hawking[2] also agrees with this hypothesis and he is considered one of the greatest minds of the last half of the 20th century.

Kip Thorne's research theorizes a form of hyperspace travel through hyperuniverses by these futuristic humans, thus avoiding the need of time machines per se.

We already defined hyperspace as everything that is beyond our four-dimensional space-time universe. We can equate hyperspace with the term *fifth dimension*. Time travelers use some form of hyperspace engineering and enter an enlarged wormhole to transport themselves back in time through some type of hyperuniverse to our century. Mathematical models for this paradigm are well established, so let us discuss this in detail using the subatomic model.

Consider a black hole with a singularity at its center. Singularities are those areas of space-time where large distortions and possible tears in the fabric of space-time appear. The very same mechanism that creates black holes produces white holes. One difference between the two is that the time sequence is reversed—black holes send you into the past; white holes send you into the future.

A wormhole is a connection between white holes and black holes that is constantly materializing and dematerializing. It connects every black hole with its white hole counterpart. These wormholes are time machines that do not violate causality. We travel in time to the past and the future, when there is a jump through a singularity in the interior of a rotating black hole—where all universe layers meet.

When we journey from the present to the future and back to the present, we are experiencing a time-loop. This could also be exhibited by traveling from the present to the past and back to the present, as in the case of chrononauts.

This very same mechanism is used by chrononauts on a macro universe scale to physically travel back in time to study us. They use this principle to go forward in time too, as some of these time travelers from 1,000 years in our future have indeed communicated with chrononauts from 2,000 and 3,000 years in the future!

Taatos, the First Time Traveler

Time travel will be discovered in approximately the year 3050 by a man named Taatos. He is the Hermes of ancient Egypt, and the very first chrononaut (time traveler).

Taatos was a brilliant scientist, artist, writer, and archeologist and had many other talents. Prior to his actually traveling back in time, holographic images were sent into the past. This is why the ancient Egyptians, Greeks, Romans, and so on, described "visions" by their oracles, soothsayers, and psychics.

Objects were transported back in time after the technology was perfected. Finally, humans made trips to centuries past by way of saucer-shaped crafts through the black hole-wormhole-white hole paradigm I discussed earlier.

Taatos was the first human time traveler. Following his success, four other chrononauts were selected to function as a team on this craft. Their names were Geb, Isis, Osiris, and Horus. You may recognize these names from Egyptian theology.

Although scholars are aware of the names Taatos and Hermes (the Greek name for Taatos or Thoth), they consider him a legend only. Taatos did function as pharaoh in Egypt several times from about 9000 B.C. to 5500 B.C.

During one of Taatos' many trips back to ancient Egypt, he appeared as Imhotep, the Grand Vizier and High Priest to pharaoh Zoser. Imhotep (Taatos) was a renowned architect who designed and built the funeral complex and Step Pyramid at Saqqara. He was also a talented physician and later the Greeks called him Aesclepius, the god of Medicine.

After advising George Washington to visit West Point in 1780, Taatos was directly responsible for the future first President of the United States discovering that General Benedict Arnold was about to turn over West Point to the British. This could have cost the colonists the American Revolution. Taatos guided Washington through his eight years as President and then ascended.

Whenever time travelers reach their level of perfection, they most often choose to ascend. Such was the case with Osiris and Geb at about 6000 B.C. Horus ascended before the First Dynasty. Isis stayed around until about 400 A.D., then also ascended.

What is interesting to note about time travelers is that they are not only influential in our technological development, but they are responsible for naming all of our cities, countries, and continents. I quite realize that what I am reporting is extreme, but consider what it means.

Our traditional paradigm of the past preceding the present, which comes before the future, is incorrect. The future, especially with the advent of time travel, can influence the past and present so that we never really know when something originated. This does suggest a violation of causality, but Kip Thorne's research and mathematical models demonstrate clearly that it does not.

Traksa, a Teleporting Time Traveler

By utilizing my own self-hypnosis tapes, I was able to communicate with several time travelers. The first time traveler I met in hyperspace (the fifth dimension) was a pure human calling himself Traksa. He lives in the 36th century on Earth when time travel is manifested by way of teleportation. This means that Traksa can beam his physical body back to our century without requiring a spacecraft. He is pictured on my Website.

Most of the initial contacts we make with a futuristic time traveler take place during our dream (REM) cycle. At that time, we actually leave our physical bodies and enter hyperspace gaining the ability to communicate with fifth-dimensional people, including chrononauts.

Traksa works with several people in our present time, myself included. For more than 20 years, he has guided me during my dream levels to get the message out regarding time travel and spiritual growth.

Many chrononauts used cryptograms of their names representing their current mission. This name will often change as the mission changes. For example, one of Traksa's assignments consisted of introducing me to Art Bell. Art was the original host of Premier Radio Networks Shows *Coast to Coast AM* and a Sunday evening talk show known as *Dreamland*. The listeners exceeded 20 million and the topics covered dealt with metaphysics, especially UFOs, and conspiracy topics. If you spell Traksa's name backwards it reads "ASK ART!"

The mechanism of time travel by teleportation is apparently rather complex. What I have discovered from Traksa and other teleporters is that they use a type of fifth dimensional computer chip to determine precisely where to travel back or forward to in time. They carry a small camera-like device that connects them to a rather advanced master computer. This is roughly similar to our computer-controlled jet airliners today.

Time Traveling Case Histories

I would like to comment on time travelers' interactions with us that result in abductions. This is not like the brutal anal probing you hear about involving present-day grays. Time traveler abductions aboard a craft or military installation (yes, our government works with chrononauts) mostly involves sperm and egg samples for infertile futuristic grays to create hybrids, and spiritual growth enhancement of the abductee. Always remember that time travelers have a self interest in our growth. They are us in the future and their world is greatly affected by what we do today.

One last point to bring out is that Traksa and other time travelers have informed both my patients and me that they are around today, but spend most of their time in the fifth dimension so we cannot see them. They do not make their true identity known to us, but do work with many of the governments around the world.

Here are two incidences of time traveler contacts that my readers were kind enough to share with me:

I too have been visited by a "Time Traveler." It occurred about 13 years ago. At precisely 3 a.m., I was alone in the house and awakened by an electrical feeling, a zap on the nape of my neck. There in the bedroom doorway was a figure dressed in a white robe standing more than 6 1/2 feet tall. His hands and face were covered with his apparel. I tried to communicate telepathically, but I was too scared to be receptive. I then said, "What do you want?" To that, he shook his head as if to say nothing and sparkled into nothingness—as if he were beamed up. I stayed awake the remainder of the night to know I was dreaming. Yes, this experience inspired me to evolve spiritually.

and

Your story of time travelers struck a cord with me and I would like to share my experience with my fellow time travelers. I am not a very successful out-of-body traveler, but I recalled a very profound event that started as a dream.

I came upon a mountain that was conical in shape and varying shades of grey. There were trails that switched back on this mountain and people traveling them on their way to the top. The trails were very muddy and these people slogged through them with great difficulty. Their clothes were dripping with mud and they were very weary and troubled.

At the side of the mountain, I saw a trail and as I approached, I saw that it went straight up to the top of the mountain. As I got closer, the trail turned golden and began to glow as I stepped upon it. I turned and looked up the mountain and saw two beautifully robed people with golden hair. One was a man who sat on an ornate chair and peered over the landscape holding a staff. I knew that he was a very tall man and if he were to stand he would have been 7 or 8 feet tall. Next to him stood a beautiful woman dressed in white robes motioning me to come up the path to them.

As I took a few steps, I began to float and literally flew up the trail. As I approached them, she pointed toward the sky, indicating I was to continue past them upwards. When I did, I popped into another dimension. It was as real as the one I am in now. I floated over a landscape and a beautiful colored horizon of salmon and turquoise colors. I could feel the wind on my skin and hear it in my ears.

I was so delighted that I began to think how I wanted to share this with my husband. As soon as the thought started to form in my mind, I heard and felt a great sucking sensation and was pulled out of this reality, back to that dream state, down the mountain and into what appeared a waiting room with large windows and hard wooden pew like benches against the walls. I could see out to what looked like a loading dock at a train station and the mountain beyond. I just thought I'd share this with you and do hope someday I will encounter those two tall, beautiful beings again. The first time is an experience I'll never forget.

A Teleporting Time Traveler Saves Two Lives

Two nine-year-old classmates were walking home from school in Texas when suddenly an older teenager around 18 ran up to them and pushed both of them aside. This teenager was wearing a light blue tennis outfit and just as she pushed both of these girls (Brenda and Amy) aside, a car driven by a drunken teenager jumped the curb and would have killed these girls by hitting them head on. As Brenda and Amy turned to thank this teenage girl, the older girl disappeared.

Ten years later, I worked with Amy who related this story. What brought this to her attention was that she remained friends with Brenda and they recently decided to play tennis. Amy picked up Brenda at her parent's home and saw Brenda in the exact same blue tennis outfit worn by the teenager who saved both of their lives 10 years earlier. Brenda told Amy that she blacked out for a short time earlier that day and had a dream that she saved the lives of two younger girls.

Amy now realized that it was the 19-year-old Brenda that saved them. Brenda had entered into a tear in the fabric of space-time and traveled back in time 10 years to save herself and Amy from the drunken teenager in the car.

A Conversation with a Time Traveler

Nineteen-year-old Sherry reported several missing time episodes in her life. The most significant one I explored through hypnotic age regression took place just three weeks prior to her session with me.

Sherry described being abducted from her bedroom by two grey extraterrestrials who simply appeared from nowhere. These dimensional travelers took her to a spaceship and placed her in a type of conference room.

A 7-foot-tall, blond-haired, blue-eyed man dressed in a white robe began showing Sherry holograms depicting several of her past lives in which she was again abducted by this same team of time travelers.

All communication was by telepathy and the tall blond man informed Sherry that he and his team originated from the 32nd century. The purpose of this abduction, as well as the ones in her prior lives, was to stimulate her spiritual growth. Following that abduction, Sherry stopped smoking, achieved better grades in school, and made improvements in most aspects of her life.

A Time Traveler Meets Her Younger Self

In 1996, a 72-year-old woman came to my Los Angeles office for past life regression hypnotherapy and reported a most unusual incident that took place a few months earlier. This patient, whom I shall refer to as Eva, always wears a yellow scarf and has since her teenage years.

Eva is a slender woman now, but had a weight problem until she was about 50. A few months ago, she went to a local mall in her home town to do some clothes shopping and wore her customary yellow scarf. Eva has always lived in the same city. She went to her favorite department store and saw a woman who looked exactly as she would have 30 years ago!

This young woman in her 40s was overweight and wore a dark brown miniskirt, along with a yellow scarf and light green blouse. There was a blue ink stain on the back of this skirt. Eva recalled that she had such a skirt and it was her favorite. The only problem with it was that it had a blue ink stain on the back of it!

Eva approached this woman and stood right in front of her. She got a good look at her and clearly identified this person as herself as she looked 30 years ago. As she was about to speak to this individual, the younger Eva appeared to fade away and disappear. This was witnessed by another woman who immediately ran out of the store.

Eva hadn't thought of that brown miniskirt in many years. She doesn't have any pictures of herself at that age, but her family does. After researching family photo albums, Eva finally found a picture of herself in her early 40s wearing a yellow scarf, the brown miniskirt, and the exact same light green blouse she saw on her younger self in the mall.

My explanation of this event is that Eva somehow teleported herself at age 42 from 1966 to 1996. I suspect they could have talked to each other, but the universe had other plans. The young Eva teleported back to 1966 in the same way she arrived.

I asked Eva if she ever recalled such an incident 30 years ago. She stated that one afternoon she did "black out" for an hour or so, but all medical tests were negative. There never was another similar occurrence.

For an hour in 1966, Eva became a time traveler who traveled ahead 30 years and returned to her point of origin. Perhaps she entered a tear in the fabric of space-time.

The Time Traveler Exchange Program

Has a family member, neighbor, friend, or colleague been acting strange lately? They may very well be a time traveler from the future who has changed places with the person you have known for years.

Many time travelers from the years 3050 to 5000 A.D. have come back in time to interact with us. Through a discipline known as Quantum Medicine, these time travelers can regenerate lost limbs and resuscitate the dead (if they are treated within 24 hours of physical death) by tapping into what we call intergalactic lines—energy fields in our universe that originate from the God-energy complex.

These intergalactic lines represent creative energy and allow a chrononaut to shape shift or morph their physical appearance to duplicate that of a 21st-century individual. This also includes the current century individual's fingerprints, DNA, and complete memory.

You would not be able to prove that this time traveler is anyone but the person he or she says they are. The only thing these futuristic people cannot perfectly duplicate is behavior and mannerisms unique to that person. This is why someone you know may be acting "odd."

All chrononauts adhere to what are known as Timeliner International Security Codes (TISC), which forbid chrononauts from revealing either their true identity or advanced technology to the residents of the century in which they currently are visiting.

Chapter 17

A Future Life as a Time Traveler

Before I begin to describe a future life of one of my patients as a time traveler, a comment on the government's attitude toward UFOs and ETs is in order. We are all too familiar with various governments' dismissive comments and denials regarding UFOs and the existence of ETs.

One surprising law that was passed in the United States and adopted on July 16, 1969 concerned contact with ETs. Title 14, Section 1211 of the Code of Federal Regulations states that any U.S. citizens making contact with ETs or their vehicles is guilty of a crime. Such a person automatically becomes a wanted criminal to be jailed for one year and fined $5,000. A NASA administrator is empowered to determine with or without a hearing that a person or object has been "extraterrestrially exposed" and impose an indeterminate quarantine under armed guard, which could not be broken even by court order.

Whatever happened to the U.S. Constitution? This ridiculous and Fascist law was repealed on April 26, 1991, after being on the books for 22 years! By itself, this piece of federal legislation does not demonstrate the existence of UFOs or ETs, but it is a rather interesting expression for an entity that maintains ETs do not exist. They don't exist, but if you touch one, you are a criminal!

Jon came to my office in 1996 to explore his past lives. He had no interest in future lives and was surprised when my instructions to explore a life that would provide insight to his karmic purpose led him to the 35th century!

He had seen my CBS television movie *The Search for Grace* a few years earlier, which depicted a documented case of reincarnation (see Chapter 4) and wanted to learn more about his past lives. The first hypnotic time travel session with Jon resulted in a totally unexpected future life as a chrononaut.

Dr. G.: Where do you find yourself at this time?

Jon: In Muvia at the training center.

Dr. G.: What year is it?

Jon: 3478.

Dr. G.: What type of training center is this?

Jon: It's where I am being educated for my career.

Dr. G.: And what career is that?

Jon: I am training to be a time traveler.

From both my and my patients' communication with chrononauts, I learned that Muvia is actually the ancient continent of Lemuria or Mu located in the Pacific Ocean that sunk approximately 11000 B.C., but surfaced some time during the 28th century. By the year 3050 it was the seat of time travel research and Taatos's work on discovering how to send first images, then objects, and finally humans back through time.

Initially, time travel consisted of enlarging wormholes lined with *exotic matter* (possessing negative mass and moves forward in time—the complete opposite of *anti-matter*) and sending chrononauts and their flying saucer crafts back in time through hyperspace.

By the early 35th century, time travel shifts from enlarging black holes, which result in tears in the fabric of space-time, to teleportation. Teleportation has no effect on the space-time continuum.

By the 25th century, teleportation is actually utilized for transportation, but not time travel. By then, most homes are equipped with teleportation units that permit people to travel locally instantaneously. It required an additional 1,000 years before this method could be applied to time travel itself.

The Muvian training center can be compared to NASA's Lyndon B. Johnson Space Center in Houston, Texas. The chrononaut candidates were selected through a highly competitive process that evaluated their education, training, experience, and unique qualifications.

All chrononaut applicants must have earned a doctorate in hyperspace physics to be eligible for admission. The training they receive during their four years at the academy consists of three main components. The first deals with advanced physics, quantum medicine, and history/archeology. They must know a great deal about the historical period they work in for obvious reasons.

Physical conditioning is the second phase, and is much less rigorous than that required prior to the discovery of teleportation for time travel. The body is not subjected to any unusual forces when teleportation is utilized, whereas much stress was experienced when enlarging black holes was the mechanism for time travel. This could be the equivalent of the G (gravity) force of modern day astronauts. Chrononauts will be trained to be resourceful and still must be in good physical shape.

The most important phase of chrononaut training is their spiritual growth component. Because the main purpose of a chrononaut is to assist us in our spiritual growth, they must practice what they preach. Chakra balancing, self-hypnosis, and other methods are used to achieve this.

Training is also given in human and ET psychology, and in adherence to timeline laws. For example, a chrononaut is trained to avoid major interference in a society's angst whenever possible. These time travelers attempt to guide and stimulate humans to grow intellectually and spiritually. They will not simply manipulate our actions.

Dr. G.: What is your name?

Jon: Kamar.

Dr. G.: How old are you?

Jon: 26.

Dr. G.: How did you get interested in time travel?

Jon: Other members of my family expressed interest in this field, but none of them could qualify. I used to fly with my father.

Even though teleportation units were utilized in the future for travel, it was confined to local trips. Large air ships piloted by thought are used to transport large groups of people for long distances. Kamar's father was a pilot for one of these ships.

Dr. G.: Kamar, it's a far cry from piloting a ship to time travel. What sparked your interest?

Jon: As I mentioned, for as long as I can remember, my family tried to get into the Muvian program. But a strange incident seemed to focus my attention on time travel.

Dr. G.: What was that?

Jon: I went shopping one afternoon when I was in high school and a show on GCN peaked my interest.

Dr. G.: What is GCN?

Jon: GCN stands for Global Communications Network and its host, Tzaxa, did a program on time travel. He interviewed three time travelers and their stories simply fascinated me.

A detailed discussion followed during which I discovered that Kamar went to the equivalent of a shopping mall. The GCN show was a type of radio show produced live in the mall with a hologram of Tzaxa projected through the shopping center.

Tzaxa's show is heard worldwide and is very popular. He wears a one-piece gold jumpsuit and is very animated—a true futuristic showman. The interview Kamar described presented a life of danger, adventure, education, and spirituality. This interested Kamar and he now dedicated himself to becoming a chrononaut (the equivalent of today's astronaut).

Dr. G.: How many people are on the planet at this time?

Jon: About a billion.

I should explain at this time that the reason for this small population, as contrasted with six billion people today, is not due to wars, disease, or comets crashing into our planet. It is due to the tendency of people to have small families. Futuristic humans no longer suffer from poverty or lack of education. They do not have large families for religious or other reasons. They emphasize quality of live versus quantity.

Dr. G.: Have you gone back in time yet?

Jon: Just a month or so as part of my training.

Dr. G.: Tell me how it felt?

Jon: The first time I teleported, it was the strangest experience.

Dr. G.: How so?

Jon: The entire trip was characterized by a strange feeling throughout my body. It was as though something twisted my body.

Dr. G.: What else did you experience?

Jon: It felt almost like I was caught in a giant web. Suddenly, the world exploded into countless pieces of glowing threads. They stretched away in all directions, and they intersected everything, including me.

Dr. G.: Go on.

Jon: I could now perceive that the strange, twisting sensation that I was experiencing was correlated with the motion of these threads. And they were in constant motion. I could feel the world. I could see the room around me, superimposed within the pattern of these threads. I was also aware of things beyond the room. In fact, it seemed like I was aware of everything, although not in any detail. It's somewhat difficult to explain. The overall effect was very similar to looking at a hologram, except it was visceral as well as visual—you could see/feel the image, but you could also see/feel the interference pattern. The difference was that the "interference pattern" was not flat, but extended in all directions.

Dr. G.: Anything else?

Jon: Part of me was totally confused, and another part of me was completely familiar with whatever this was. There was a very odd sense of my consciousness being split. What I mean by that is that two contradictory thoughts were present in my mind simultaneously.

Dr. G.: How long did these effects last?

Jon: They disappeared almost immediately upon my arrival at both locations (one month ago and Kamar's return to his starting point).

Dr. G.: Did these symptoms repeat upon further teleportation trials?

Jon: They became less and less. Eventually, I became so accustomed to the experience that they nearly disappeared.

Dr. G.: Was your response unusual?

Jon: Not really. I related my experiences to the base doctors and was informed that they were well within normal range.

I then directed my questioning to the Muvia base and asked Jon to describe where he lived.

Dr. G.: Tell me about Muvia and its buildings.

Jon: Most of the base consists of mushroom-like structures several hundred feet high. There are no other artificial structures except for the pyramid shaped Psiocoms.

Dr. G.: What are Psiocoms?

Jon: Highly advanced computerized navigation and information structures.

Dr. G.: How is security maintained on the base?

Jon: There are antigravity orbs patrolling the base and monitoring activity. Trackers are always present.

Further discussion revealed that these orbs were spherical devices that functioned like a satellite. Trackers were security personnel who patrolled the base in antigravity hover bikes.

Dr. G.: Kamar, tell me about your personal residence.

Jon: My home is small, but comfortable. The land is dominated by beautiful gardens. The house is positioned in such a way as to accent the garden.

Further questioning revealed that the walls of all homes in the 35th century consisted of a uniformed surface with the windows blended into the walls so that the smooth surface was maintained. A single color characterized the interior of Kamar's home. The interior was plain and rather conservative.

Dr. G.: Kamar, how do you prepare your meals?

Jon: I use the food simulator.

Dr. G.: What is that?

Jon: This device creates most any meal you desire from your thoughts alone.

Dr. G.: What do you do for relaxation?

Jon: I use the holographic relaxation center.

The holographic relaxation center is equivalent to the holodeck portrayed in the *Star Trek* television series. Because each home was small in size, virtual reality techniques made them appear larger. Devices also existed to shrink items for storage and later enlarge them to their original size.

I next progressed Kamar to his first mission back in time as a full-fledge time traveler.

Dr. G.: Can you tell me about your first mission?

Jon: It took place in Sumeria[1] at about 3000 B.C.

Dr. G.: How many were in your team?

Jon: There were four of us and I was the youngest.

Dr. G.: What were your instructions?

Jon: I was being trained in the art of communicating with these primitive men during their dream state.

Dr. G.: How does that work?

Jon: I travel through hyperuniverses in the fifth dimension by way of teleportation. While in this hyperuniverse, I was being trained to implant dreams into selected Sumerians to facilitate their development of writing.

Dr. G.: How did your work progress?

Jon: Very well. We traveled to several time eras from approximately 3400 B.C. to about 3000 B.C. to supervise the evolution of pictographs to cuneiform.

Prior to the development of writing, a picture-writing system existed. This picture-writing was essentially a drawing of objects and actions accompanied by strokes and dots to represent days and distances (quantitative concepts).

We can see examples today on a menu in which a picture of a man standing might indicate a buffet, or a hotel rating in a travel guide would be followed by four or five stars to indicate its quality.

Between approximately 3500 B.C. and 3000 B.C., Sumerian picture-writing on clay with small styles made it difficult to make curved marks. Picture-writing was replaced by wedge-shaped marks known as cuneiform. The Sumerian language was well adapted to this type of writing. It was a language of vast polysyllables and many of the syllables taken separately were the names of concrete things.

Another advantage of this cuneiform development was that once the clay tablets hardened they were nearly indestructible, and many have survived today. The cuneiform depictions are far more standardized and recognizable as compared to the pictographs. Cuneiform writing spread throughout the Middle East, and by 100 B.C., it was replaced by the North Semitic script used in the Aramaic language.

Kamar's first mission involved the development of writing. This was an honor, and he must have earned this privilege through his training at the Muvian academy. By far the most important thing taking place during this time of man's social development was the invention of writing and its gradual progress to importance in human affairs.

I next questioned Kamar about his progress as a time traveler. He described many missions, all increasing in complexity during the next 100 years of his life. It must be mentioned that 35th century humans live for hundreds of years. This is mostly due to a device known as an alpha syncolarium. Think of an isolation tank that emits energy signals accompanied by sounds through our body. The result is a stimulation of our gonads and adrenal glands to produce more DHEA (the intermediate phase of the sex hormones estrogen in women and testosterone in men). DHEA fosters the production and action of T-lymphocytes in our immune system and wards off any type of viral disease, thereby lengthening our life span.

I next progressed Kamar to his most significant mission as a chrononaut.

Dr. G.: Where are you now, Kamar?

Jon: On Mu.[2]

Dr. G.: You mean back on the base?

Jon: No. I mean the ancient continent of Mu before it submerged.

Dr. G.: Approximately what year is this?

Jon: It's about 101000 B.C.

Dr. G.: What is your mission?

Jon: I was sent back here with three of my colleagues to assist our species in fending off the *Electric Wars*.

The Electric Wars is a generic name applied to battles between various ET groups and us for control of our planet. These wars occurred at various times in prehistory and up to about 1500 B.C. Two main ET groups dominated our planet 100,000 years ago.

One group called Lyrans were selfish, power hungry, dogmatic, and authoritarian. Their goal was to enslave us. Sirians comprised the other group and functioned as our protectors. Unfortunately, the Lyrans came to Earth before the Sirians, so the Sirians had to play catch up and were often outnumbered by the Lyrans.

Mu was a civilization that the Sirians influenced and therefore became very spiritual. Mu's main colony in the Atlantic was Atlantis and it was influenced by the Lyrans. By 100000 B.C., Atlantis declared war (Electric Wars) on Mu, and advanced ET technology appeared in both cultures.

This turf war in Mu and Atlantis, known as the Electric Wars, lasted nearly 50 years. Whenever light flashes and pulsations were observed, it indicated an interdimensional interface had taken place. Many of these ETs, and the eventual peacemakers we will soon meet, traveled interdimensionally, as did our time travelers. Interestingly, other time travelers have informed me that when we observe lightning, thunder, and magnetic variations today, we are witnessing the residual effect of action taking place within other dimensions.

An interdimensional time portal existed, allowing other beings (human and ET) from different dimensions, or our past and present, to enter our world and interact with us. They may even originate from a parallel universe!

Dr. G.: Kamar, move to an event that will be significant on this mission.

Jon; I am speaking to my supervisor about the wars.

Dr. G.: Who is your supervisor?

Jon: His name is Muat.

Many chrononauts assume a name when they travel back in time that represents their mission. Muat stands for Mu and Atlantis.

Dr. G.: What does he tell you?

Jon: Muat is very concerned for my life. These Electric Wars are dangerous and he has lost men before.

Dr. G.: Can you give me an example?

Jon: Yes, he once mentioned Etwar, who was killed prior to my arrival.

Etwar was Traksa's first life as a time traveler. He originated from the 32nd century in that life and adopted the name Etwar (ET War) while he worked with Muat in Muvia. Traksa's second incarnation as a time traveler was during the 34th century where he assumed the name Lyrat (which stands for Lyran and Atlantis) and functioned during the Atlantis war with ETs in approximately 35000 B.C. He was killed in both lives. Traksa's third life as a chrononaut in the 36th century is his most successful.

Muat obviously does not like losing any of his agents. He assumed a protective role over Kamar, but still allowed the latter to do his job.

Dr. G.: Tell me more about the ET problem at this time.

Jon: The problem is far more complex than mere technology and weapons. We chrononauts have many devices that can counteract anything the Lyrans present.

Dr. G.: So Kamar, what is the most significant issue?

Jon: The Lyrans have propagated genetic manipulation of humankind and this makes it difficult to deal with local population.

Dr. G.: Can you tell me more about this ET form of genetic manipulation?

Jon: It is referred to as *impulse codes* and manifests as a three-dimensional distortion of reality to unsuspecting humans. Even without their conscious awareness or permission, this technique is coded into the memory so that past experiences can be wiped out and brainwashing scenarios substituted.

Dr. G.: So this is beyond mere suggestion or hallucinations.

Jon: Yes. It's an actual alteration of the DNA and neurological system of the individual.

Dr. G.: Is there anything your group can do to neutralize this effect?

Jon: Yes. We have techniques to do just that, but they take time and we simply cannot work with every one of the millions of inhabitants of Earth to do so.

Dr. G.: So what is the solution?

Jon: Fortunately, our group works with dimensional traveling ETs who possess more efficient methods to deal with this issue.

Dr. G.: Can you tell me more about these ETs?

Jon: Certainly. One group is known as Aethien and they resemble praying mantis insects. They are white to gold in color and are about two feet tall.

Dr. G.: Are they related to the Zetas (the classic grey ET)?

Jon: No. They are emissaries of peace and work along with the Ranthia.

Dr. G.: Tell me about the Ranthia.

Jon: The Ranthia are dimensional travelers and peace ambassadors that are not fully matter based. They often appear as a ghost, but possess the ability to manifest as a human, animal, or solid object. These *shapeshifters* also have the ability to appear as a hologram.

Dr. G.: They sound interesting.

Jon: Oh, they are more than interesting. Because of their ethereal makeup, they can undo what the Lyrans perpetuated on these humans and reverse the impulse code procedure on a massive basis.

Dr. G.: Are these Ranthia also peace emissaries?

Jon: Yes. They are strange to look at, but they are most helpful when negotiations of peace become the issue.

Dr. G.: What is the status of the Electric Wars now?

Jon: The wars are at a high point and my group must assist the Sirians in their defense. We cannot utilize the counsel of the Aethien and Ranthia until the fighting ceases.

Kamar next described many battles during which chrononaut technology and that of the Aethiens was utilized to defend both continents (Mu and Atlantis). Even though it appeared on the surface that Atlantis was attacking Mu, in reality, both civilizations were being invaded by the Lyrans.

This was a critical time in man's development because a successful Lyran takeover of our planet 100,000 years ago would cause numerous rifts in the space-time continuum and result in many deleterious effects on us today and in the future.

Dr. G.: What is going on at this time?

Jon: It's the most amazing yet depressing thing I have ever seen.

Dr. G.: What are you referring to?

Jon: The electrical phenomena that characterize these Electric Wars. We were briefed at the academy, but witnessing it in person is another matter.

Dr. G.: Tell me what takes place.

Jon: Various types of dimensional apparatus are set up in a region and many electrical disturbances result. Light flashes, lightning, and the bending of space-time can be observed.

Dr. G.: What happens next?

Jon: Literally thousands of people, buildings, and other structures, are dematerialized at one time.

Dr. G.: This sounds very dangerous.

Jon: It is. My group must spend most of the time in the fifth dimension to protect ourselves. This is why many time travelers have been killed on these missions.

Dr. G.: Such as Traksa?

Jon: Yes, and many other good men have been lost due to these ridiculous wars.

Kamar, his men, and the Aethien and Ranthia emissaries were apparently successful in avoiding the fate of many of their predecessors. Kamar described many technological defenses that had to be utilized to fend off the Atlantean and Lyran controlled attacks.

Eventually, things settled down and peace was established. The Ranthia initiated their preprogramming techniques on the citizens of both continents and most of the Lyran damage was corrected.

Kamar returned home to Muvia to be assigned other missions and he will become a chrononaut with an excellent record. Jon was completely shocked and amazed at this future life progression. I too gathered much additional information as to how chrononauts functioned and the true history of our planet.

What was also fulfilling about this future life progression was the corroboration of material I received from other patients, in addition to my own communication with time travelers such as Traksa and Muat. None of this material appeared in print or was discussed by me until 1998. You can utilize the future life progression script I present in Chapter 18 to see if you will eventually come back as a chrononaut.

One final thing I noted from this and other experiences with time travelers is that our current species Homo sapiens and our primitive predecessors were the result of ETs seeding our planet and manipulating our respective DNA.

Chapter 18

Hypnosis Exercises

I do not like to tense or frustrate people by simply describing cases of past and future life experiences without teaching them how to do it themselves. Try theses scripts to review your own past/future lives. I highly recommend making tapes of these scripts. For a list of professionally recorded tapes with my voice, go to my Website (*www.drbrucegoldberg.com*) or send me a self-addressed, stamped envelope to the address provided in the About the Author section of this book.

How to Begin

I've included several exercises specifically designed to train you to experience self-hypnosis. It doesn't matter what your background is.

You can accept or reject any of the principles and concepts presented here. Empowerment is vital. I stress that in my Los Angeles hypnotherapy practice and in my personal life as well. If you become rigid and stuck in your views, you become trapped by your beliefs. You are no longer empowered because you are no longer free.

Always use your judgment and free will in trying these exercises. Use the ones you feel comfortable with and ignore the others. These exercises are all perfectly safe and have been tested for more than 25 years. You may create your own exercises from these models.

Read each exercise thoroughly to become familiar with it. Use the relaxation techniques given or use your own. You may practice alone or with others. I strongly suggest that you make tapes of these exercises. Read the scripts slowly and leave enough space on your tape to experience each part of the procedure.

Practice once or twice a day, in 15- to 20-minute sessions. In general, it is considered more effective to practice in the morning, as it may provide a relaxing start for the entire day. The more specific and realistic your schedule is, the better the chances are that you will succeed.

You should choose a part of your day when you are at your best. If you wait to practice until long after you get home from a hard day at work, you might only practice going to sleep. Self-hypnosis is most effective if practiced when you are reasonably alert. Begin by picking a good time to practice.

If you wake up alert and rested first thing in the morning, practice then, before getting out of bed. Take into account whether or not you will be disturbed by spouse, lover, kids, pets, and so forth. Choose a time when you are not likely to be interrupted. Other popular times are before lunch or dinner.

Four components of successful self-hypnosis are:

1. A quiet environment.
2. A mental device.
3. A passive attitude.
4. A comfortable position.

When you enter into a self-hypnotic trance, you will observe the following:

- A positive mood (tranquility, peace of mind).
- An experience of unity or oneness with the environment.
- An inability to describe the experience in words.

- An alteration in time/space relationships.
- An enhanced sense of reality and meaning.

If you experience difficulty with an exercise, do not become frustrated. Some techniques are quite advanced, and you may not be ready for all of them. Return to the ones you could not successfully work with at another time.

Practice these trance states when you have time and are relaxed. Be patient. It takes time to master trance states and to become accustomed to this new and wonderful world. No one way is the right way to experience a trance. Your body may feel light, or it may feel heavy; you may feel as if you are dreaming; your eyelids may flutter; or your body can become cooler or warmer. All these possible responses are perfectly safe.

Because you will at first be unfamiliar with the techniques, your initial practice sessions should run as long as you need. As you become more proficient, you will be able to shorten these sessions. Some days nothing may seem to work. Try not to become discouraged. Remember that other days will be more fruitful. Always work at your own pace and with an open mind.

Superconscious Mind Exercise

The following script will guide you to your superconscious mind (Higher Self):

Now listen very carefully. I want you to imagine a bright white light coming down from above and entering the top of your head, filling your entire body.... See it, feel it, and it becomes reality... Now imagine an aura of pure white light emanating from your heart region, again surrounding your entire body, protecting you.... See it, feel it, and it becomes reality.... Now only your Higher Self and highly evolved, loving entities who mean you well will be able to influence you during this or any other hypnotic session.... You are totally protected by this aura of pure white light.

In a few moments, I am going to count from 1 to 20. As I do so, you will feel yourself rising up to the superconscious mind level where you will be able to receive information from your Higher Self.... Number 1 rising up. Two, 3, 4, rising higher. Five, 6, 7, letting information flow. Eight, 9, 10, you are halfway there. Eleven, 12, 13, feel yourself rising even higher. Fourteen, 15, 16, almost there. Seventeen, 18, 19, number 20, you are there.... Take a moment and orient yourself to the superconscious mind level.

PLAY NEW AGE MUSIC FOR ONE MINUTE[1]

You may now ask yourself questions about any past, present, or future life issue. Or you may contact any of your guides or departed loves ones from this level. You may explore your relationship with any person. Remember, your superconscious mind level is all knowledgeable and has access to your Akashic records.

Now, slowly and carefully, state your desire for information or an experience and let this superconscious mind level work for you.

PLAY NEW AGE MUSIC FOR EIGHT MINUTES

You have done very well. Now, I want you to further open up the channels of communication by removing any obstacles and allowing yourself to receive information and experiences that will directly apply to and help better your present lifetime. Allow yourself to receive more advanced and more specific information from your Higher Self and masters and guides to raise your frequency and improve your karmic subcycle. Do this now.

PLAY NEW AGE MUSIC FOR EIGHT MINUTES

All right now.... sleep now and rest. You did very, very well.... Listen very carefully. I'm going to count forward now from 1 to 5.... When I reach the count of 5, you will be back in the present, you will be able to remember everything you experienced and reexperienced. You'll feel very relaxed, refreshed, and you'll be able to do whatever you have planned for the rest of the day or evening. You'll feel very positive about what you've just experienced and very motivated about your confidence and ability to play this tape again to experience your Higher Self.... All right now. One, very very deep; 2, you're getting a little bit lighter; 3, you're getting much much lighter; 4, very very light; 5, awaken. Wide awake and refreshed.

Past Life Regression

Use this script to perceive one or more of your own previous lifetimes:

Now listen very carefully. I want you to imagine a bright white light coming down from above and entering the top of your head, filling your entire body. See it, feel it, and it becomes reality. Now imagine an aura of pure white light emanating from your heart region, again surrounding your entire body, protecting you. See it, feel it, and it becomes reality. Now only your masters, guides, and highly evolved loving entities who mean you well will be able to influence you during this or any other hypnotic session. You are totally protected by this aura of pure white light. Now listen very carefully. In a few minutes, I'm going to be counting backwards from 20 to 1. As I count backwards from 20 to 1, you are going to perceive yourself moving through a very deep and dark tunnel. The tunnel will get lighter and lighter, and at the very end of this tunnel, there will be a door with a bright white light above it. When you walk through this door, you will be in a past life scene. You're going to reexperience one of your past lives at the age of about 15. You'll be moving to an event that will be significant in explaining who you are, where you are, and why are there. I want you to realize that if you feel uncomfortable either physically, mentally, or emotionally at any time, you can awaken yourself from this hypnotic trance by simply counting forward from 1 to 5. You will always associate my voice as a friendly voice in trance. You will be able to let your mind review back into its memory banks and follow the instructions of perceiving the scenes of your own past lives and following along as I instruct. You'll find yourself being able to get into hypnotic trances more deeply and quickly each time you practice with this tape or other methods of self-hypnosis. When you hear me say the words "sleep now and rest," I want you to immediately detach yourself from any scene you are experiencing. You will be able to wait for further instructions.

You absolutely have the power and ability to go back into a past life as your subconscious mind's memory banks remember everything you've ever experienced in all your past lives, as well as your present life. I want you to relive these past life events only as a neutral observer without feeling or emotion, just as if you were watching a television show. I want you to choose a past life now in which you've lived to at least the age of 30. I want you to pick a positive, neutral, or happy past life experience. I'm going to count backwards now from 20 to 1. As I do so, I want you to feel yourself moving into the past. You'll find yourself moving through a pitch black tunnel that will get lighter and lighter as I count backwards. When I reach the count of 1, you will have opened up a door with a bright white light above it and walked into a past life scene. You will once again become yourself at about the age of 15 in a previous lifetime. Now listen carefully—number 20, you're moving into a very deep dark tunnel surrounded by grass, trees, your favorite flowers. It is very inviting and you feel very calm and comfortable about moving into the tunnel. Nineteen, 18, you're moving backwards in time, back, back, 17, 16, 15, the tunnel is becoming lighter now. You can make out your arms and legs and you realize that you are walking through this tunnel and you're moving backwards in time. Fourteen, 13, 12, moving so far back, back,

back, 11, 10, 9, you're now so far back—you're more than halfway there. The tunnel is much lighter. You can see around you and you can now make out the door in front of you with the bright white light above it. Eight, 7, 6, you are standing in front of the door now, feeling comfortable and feeing positive and confident about your ability to move into this past life scene. Five, 4, now walk up to the door, and put your hand on the doorknob. The bright white light is so bright it's hard to look at. Three, open the door, 2, step through the door, 1, move into the past life scene. Focus carefully on what you perceive before you. Take a few minutes now, and I want you to let everything become crystal clear. The information flowing into your awareness, the scene becoming visual and visible. Just orient yourself to your new environment. Focus on it. Take a few moments and listen to my instructions. Let the impression form. First, what do you see and what are you doing? Are you male or female? Look at your feet first—what type of footwear or shoes are you wearing? Now move up the body and see exactly how you are clothed. How are you dressed? What are you doing right now? What is happening around you? Be able to describe the situation you find yourself in. Are you outdoors or indoors? Is it day or night? Is it hot or cold? What country or land do you live in or are you from? Now focus on this one carefully—what do people call you? What is the year? Take a few moments. Numbers may appear right in front of your awareness. You will be informed of exactly what year this is. Take a few more moments, and let any additional information crystalize and become clear in your awareness about the environment that you find yourself in as well as yourself. Take a few moments. Let any additional information be made clear to you.

PLAY NEW AGE MUSIC FOR THREE MINUTES

Very good now. Listen very carefully to my voice now. Sleep now and rest. Detach yourself from this scene just for a moment. I'm going to be counting forward now from 1 to 5.

When I reach the count of five, you're going to be moving forward now to a significant event that's going to occur in this lifetime, which will personally affect you. It will also most probably affect those close to you—it may involve your parents, friends, and people who are close to you in this lifetime. I want you to move forward to a significant event, but it's also going to be a positive one. It's going to be a positive event. Focus carefully now. Sleep now and rest and listen now as I count forward from 1 to 5. On the count of 5, you will be moving forward in time to a significant positive event that is going to occur to you. One, moving forward, slowly, carefully, comfortably; 2, feeling good as you move forward in time; 3, halfway there; 4, almost there; 5. Now again, focus on yourself and the environment you find yourself in. What are you doing now and why are you in this environment? Has anything changed since I last spoke with you? What is happening around you? Are there any other people around you who are important to you? If there are, are they male or female? Are they friends or relatives? How do they relate to you? Why are they important to you? Focus on your clothes now, starting with your feet first. How are you dressed? Are you dressed any differently than when I last spoke with you? Move all the way up your body and perceive how you are dressed. Then look at the people next to you. Are they dressed any differently? About how old are you now? Focus on that for a moment. A number will appear to you. Where exactly are you? Are you outdoors or indoors? Is it day or night? What season is this? What kind of occupation do you have? What do you do to pass the time? What do you do with your day? Focus on how you spend your time. Now I want you to focus on an event that's going to be happening right now that you find yourself right in the middle of. I want you to take this event right through to completion. I want you to spend a few moments and whatever this event is, I want you to carry it through to completion. This will be a positive, or happy, event only. Take a few moments and carry this event through to completion.

PLAY NEW AGE MUSIC FOR THREE MINUTES

All right now, sleep now and rest. Detach yourself from this scene that you are experiencing and listen to my voice again. You're going to be moving forward now by a period of at least three years. It can be as long as necessary, but a minimum of three years. You will not have died nor undergone any traumatic episode. It will be at least three years further in time. Now I want you to move forward to a significant event that is going to affect not only the kind of work you do, but also yourself personally. It will affect the way you relate to certain people who are close to you, and perhaps certain goals that you have. I want you to move forward to this very significant time, which is going to be positive, neutral, or happy, and it will be at least three years from now. On the count of five, move forward very carefully and comfortably. One, moving forward; 2, moving further forward; 3, half way there; 4, almost there; 5. Now perceive what is around you. What has transpired since I last saw you? Focus on yourself first. Perceive where you are, how you are dressed, what environment you are in, where you are located, if it is a different physical environment, and who are you with. Take a few moments and let this information crystalize and become clear into your awareness.

PLAY NEW AGE MUSIC FOR THREE MINUTES

All right now, sleep now and rest. Detach yourself from this scene. We're going to be moving forward again on the count of five. This time, you're going to be moving forward to a scene that is going to signify or illustrate the maximum achievements that you accomplished in this lifetime. This scene will illustrate your maximum accomplishments personally or professionally. You'll be surrounded by the people that affect you most in this lifetime. You will be achieving the maximum amount of success, goals, or whatever else you wanted to accomplish in this lifetime. Move forward to this maximum accomplishment in this lifetime, on the count of five. One, moving forward slowly, carefully, comfortably; 2, moving further forward; 3, halfway there; 4, almost there; 5. Now take a few moments and see where you find yourself. What is your environment? What has happened, and why is this time of your life so important to you? Focus on it, and see what you've accomplished. Let all the information be made clear to you.

PLAY NEW AGE MUSIC FOR THREE MINUTES

Now that you've been able to perceive this particular period of your life, I want you to be able to evaluate your life. I want you to find out what goals you were suppose to accomplish and what you actually did accomplish. What do you feel you learned from this lifetime? What do you feel you have gained from this lifetime, in your own personal goals, family life, and relationships? Let the information flow. What did you gain? Now let's focus on what you weren't able to achieve. Focus on what you felt you would have liked more time for. What do you feel you just weren't able to accomplish and why? Focus on that. Let the information flow. Now remember, in this particular lifetime, you are still alive. I want you now to focus upon your activities, whatever you're involved with in this particular scene, to evaluate why this lifetime was important to you. What necessary experience did you gain from this lifetime? Focus on this now. Let the information flow into your awareness.

PLAY NEW AGE MUSIC FOR THREE MINUTES

All right now. Sleep now and rest. You did very very well. Listen very carefully. I'm going to count forward now from 1to 5, one more time. This time, when I reach 5, you will be back in the present, you will be able to remember everything you experienced and reexperienced. You'll feel very relaxed and refreshed. You'll be able to do whatever you have planned for the rest of the day or evening. You'll feel very positive about what you've just experienced and very motivated about your confidence and ability to play this tape again to experience additional lifetimes. All right now, 1 very, very deep; 2, you're getting a little bit lighter; 3, you're getting much much lighter; 4, very very light; 5, awaken, wide awake and refreshed.

Seeing Into the Future

It is rather easy to obtain a glimpse of the future when you use time-tested self-hypnosis techniques. Try this future viewing exercise and follow it with my progression scripts:

1. Sit comfortably, apply white light protection, and breathe deeply. Visualize a symbol for the future. This may be a radio, book, or anything you like. Mentally toss this symbol out into the future, and perceive it broadcasting information back to you about your future. Turn your recorder on, and verbalize any information you acquire.
2. Ask your Higher Self to assist you in this exercise. Now, imagine that it is exactly one week from today. See and feel what you are doing. Let any images, thoughts, and feelings come into your awareness. What is different about your life at this future date? Record your impressions. Let these images dissapear.
3. Now perceive it is one month from today. Ask your Higher Self to further help you with this step. What is it exactly that you are planning, doing, and thinking? What has changed since the one week information was given to you?
4. Follow these same steps and look at three months, six months, one year, and five years into your future. Investigate any issues you consider

important in your life. Give yourself advice from the perspective of these probable futures.

5. Ask your Higher Self to comment on your advice and the accuracy of your probable futures.

Here are some questions to ask your Higher Self:

- What can I emphasize in my life during the next week (month, three months, etc.) that will facilitate my spiritual growth?
- What specific decisions and choices can I make right now to achieve my highest aspirations?
- What behaviors, thoughts, and actions can I implement to accelerate my spiritual path?
- Think of a current situation in your life and ask, "What am I learning from ________?"

Age Progression

This script guides you into the future of your present life:

Now listen very carefully. I want you to imagine a bright white light coming down from above and entering the top of your head, filling your entire body. See it, feel it, and it becomes reality. Now imagine an aura of pure white light emanating from your heart region, again surrounding your entire body, protecting you. See it, feel it, and it becomes a reality. Now only your Higher Self, masters, guides, and highly evolved loving entities who mean you well will be able to influence you during this or any other hypnotic session. You are totally protected by this aura of pure white light. Focus carefully on my voice as your subconscious mind's memory banks have memories of all past, present, and future events. This tape will help guide you into the future and dream of a future event today that will facilitate your spiritual growth. Shortly I will count forward from 1 to 20. Near the end of this count, you are going to imagine yourself moving through a tunnel. Near the end of this count, you will perceive a division in the tunnel, as the tunnel veers off to the left and to the right. The right represents the past, the left represents the future. On the count of 20, you will perceive yourself in the future. Your subconscious and higher levels have all the knowledge and information that you desire. Carefully and comfortably feel yourself moving into the future with each count from 1 to 20. Listen carefully now.

Number 1, feel yourself now moving forward to the future, into this very, very deep and dark tunnel. Two, 3, farther and farther and farther into the future. It is a little bit disorienting, but you know you're moving into the future. Four, 5, 6, 7, 8, 9, it's more stable now, and you feel comfortable. You feel almost as if you're floating, as you're rising up and into the future. Ten, 11, 12, the tunnel is now getting a little bit lighter and you can perceive light at the end—another white light just like the white light that is surrounding you. Thirteen, 14, 15, now you are almost there. Focus carefully. You can perceive a door in front of you to the left tunnel that you are in now. The door will be opened in just a few moments and you will see yourself in the future. The words "sleep now and rest" will always detach you from any scene you are experiencing and allow you to wait further instructions. Sixteen, 17, it's very bright now and you are putting your hands on the door, 18, you open the door. Nineteen, you step into this future to this future scene. Twenty, carefully focus on your surroundings, look around you, see what you perceive. Can you perceive yourself? Can you perceive other people around you? Focus on the environment. What does it look like? Carefully focus on this. Use your complete objectivity. Block out any information from the past that might have interfered with the quality of this scene. Use only what your subconscious and superconscious mind level will observe. Now take a few moments, focus carefully on the scene, find out where you are, what you are doing, and why are you there. Take a few moments; let the scene manifest itself.

PLAY NEW AGE MUSIC FOR THREE MINUTES

Now focus very carefully on what year this is. Think for a moment. Numbers will appear before your inner eyes. You will have knowledge of the year that you are in right now. Carefully focus on this year and these numbers. They will appear before you. Use this as an example of other information that you are going to obtain. I want you to perceive this scene completely, carry it through to completion. I want you to perceive exactly where you are, the names, the date, the place, and other details. I want you to carry these scenes to completion, and follow them through carefully for the next few moments. The scene will become clear and you will perceive the sequence of what exactly is happening to you.

PLAY NEW AGE MUSIC FOR THREE MINUTES

You've done very well. Now you are going to move to another event. I want you to focus on a different event in the same future time. Perceive what is going on and why this is important to you. Perceive the year, the environment, and the presence of others. Let the information flow.

PLAY NEW AGE MUSIC FOR THREE MINUTES

As you perceive the details of the next scene, focus also on your purpose. Focus on what you are learning and what you are unable to learn. Perceive any sequence of events that led up to this situation. Let the information flow surrounding this all-important future event now.

PLAY NEW AGE MUSIC FOR THREE MINUTES

You have done very well. Now I want you to rise to the superconscious mind level to evaluate this future experience and apply this knowledge to your current life and situations. One, rising up; 2, rising higher; 3, half way there; 4, almost there; 5, you are there. Let your Higher Self assist you in making the most out of this experience. Do this now.

PLAY NEW AGE MUSIC FOR THREE MINUTES

All right now. Sleep now and rest. You have done very, very well. I'm going to count forward from 1 to 5. When I reach the count of 5, you will be able to remember everything you experienced. You'll feel very relaxed, refreshed, and you'll be able to do whatever you have planned for the rest of the day or evening. You'll feel very positive about what you've just experienced and very motivated about your confidence and ability to play this tape again to experience your future frequencies. All right now. 1, very, very deep; 2, you're getting a little bit lighter; 3, you're getting much, much lighter; 4, very, very light; 5, awaken, wide awake and refreshed.

Future Life Progression

To experience your own future lifetime in reference to contact with time travelers, or just to explore the centuries to come, try this self-hypnosis exercise:

Now listen very carefully. I want you to imagine a bright white light coming down from above and entering the top of your head, filling your entire body. See it, feel it, and it becomes reality. Now imagine an aura of pure white light emanating from your heart region, again surrounding your entire body, protecting you. See it, feel it, and it becomes reality. Now only your masters, guides, and highly evolved loving entities who mean you well will be able to influence you during this or any other hypnotic session. You are totally protected by this aura of pure white light. Focus carefully on my voice as your subconscious mind's memory banks have memories of all past, present, and future lifetimes. This tape will help guide you into the future, the future of another lifetime. I am going to be counting forward from 1 to 20. As I count forward from 1 to 20, you are going to imagine yourself moving through a tunnel. Near the end of this count you will perceive the tunnel dividing off to the left and to the right.

The right represents the past, and the left represents the future. You're going to bear to the left, through the left tunnel, which will take you into the future. On the count of 20, you will perceive yourself in the future. Your subconscious and superconscious mind levels have all the knowledge and information that you desire. Carefully and comfortably feel yourself moving into the future with each count from 1 to 20. Listen carefully now. Number 1, feel yourself now moving forward to the future, into this very, very deep and dark tunnel. Two, 3, farther and farther into the future. Four, 5, 6, the tunnel is very, very dark. It is a little bit disorienting, but you know you're moving into the future. Seven, 8, 9, it's more stable now, and you feel comfortable. You feel almost as if you're floating, as you're rising up and into the future. Ten, 11, 12, the tunnel is now getting a little bit lighter and you can perceive a light at the end, another white light just like the white light that is surrounding you. Thirteen, 14, 15. Now you are almost there. Focus carefully. You can perceive a door in front of you to the left of the tunnel that you're in right now. The door will be opened in just a few moments and you will see yourself in a future life.

The words "sleep now and rest" will always detach you from any scene you are experiencing and allow you to await further instructions. Sixteen, 17, it's very bright now and you are putting your hands on the door. Eighteen, you open the door, 19, you step into this future, to this future scene. Number 20.

Carefully focus on your surroundings. Look around you. Can you perceive yourself? Can you perceive other people around you? Focus on the environment. What does it look like? Carefully focus on this. Use your complete objectivity. Block out any information from the past that might have interfered with the quality of the scene. Use only what your subconscious and superconscious mind level will observe. Now take a few moments, focus carefully on the scene, find out where you are, what you are doing, why are you there. Take a few moments, let the scene manifest itself.

PLAY NEW AGE MUSIC FOR THREE MINUTES

Now focus very carefully on what year this is. Think for a moment. Numbers will appear before your inner eyes. You will have knowledge of the year that you are in right now. Carefully focus on this year and these numbers. They will appear before you. Use this as an example of other information that you are going to obtain. I want you to perceive exactly where you are, who you are, the names, the date, the place. I want you to carry these scenes to completion, follow them through carefully for the next few moments. The scene will become clear and you will perceive the sequence of what exactly is happening to you.

PLAY NEW AGE MUSIC FOR THREE MINUTES

You've done very well. Now you are going to move to another event. I want you to focus on a different experience in the same future life. Perceive what is going on and why this is important to you. Perceive the year, the environment, the presence of others. Let the information flow.

PLAY NEW AGE MUSIC FOR THREE MINUTES

As you perceive the details of the next scene, focus also on your purpose—your purpose in this future life and how it is affecting your karmic subcycle. Focus in on what you are learning, what you are able to learn. Perceive any sequence of events that led up to this situation. If you have any contact whatsoever with time travelers, let the information flow surrounding this all important future event now.

PLAY NEW AGE MUSIC FOR THREE MINUTES

Sleep now and rest. You've done very well. Now I want you to rise to the superconscious mind level to evaluate this future life experience and apply this knowledge to your current life and situations. One, rising up; 2, rising higher; 3, halfway there; 4, almost there; number 5, you are there. Let your masters and guides assist you in making the most out of this experience. Do this now.

PLAY NEW AGE MUSIC FOR THREE MINUTES

All right now. Sleep now and rest. You did very, very well. Listen very carefully. I'm going to count backwards now from 5 to 1. This time, when I reach 1, you will be back in the present, you will be able to remember everything you experienced and reexperienced. You'll feel very relaxed refreshed, and you'll be able to do whatever you have planned for the rest of the day or evening. You'll feel very positive about what you've just experienced and very motivated about your confidence and ability to play this tape again to experience additional future life events. All right now, 5, moving back in time; 4, move farther back; 3, half way there; 2, almost there. Number 1, you are back in the present. I'm going to count forwards from 1 to 5 and when I reach the count of 5, you will be wide awake, relaxed, and refreshed. Number 1, very, very deep. Number 2, you are getting a little bit lighter. Number 3, halfway there. Number 4, very, very light. Number 5, awaken.

Accessing the Akashic Records

We all have a fifth-dimensional chart of sorts that contains the memories of each of our past, present, future, and parallel lives. This is referred to as the Akashic Records.

The experience of drawing upon the Akashic records often presents itself to your waking awareness in visual form, accompanied by the more essential sounds. Occasionally, it will be entirely auditory, as though someone were standing close behind you, telling you what has taken place, or what will take place in the future. The information you receive is actually vibratory in nature, somewhat like the impressions on a magnetic tape. The images you see or hear are all from your own mind, channeled by your Higher Self, which actually taps into your Akashic Records stored on a different dimension. Each person makes the same vibratory contact, but realizes it according to the experiences in his own image storehouse.

You can use this technique to access one of your or someone else's past/future lives. Here is a public example of how I applied this technique on network radio.

On Friday, March 24, 2000, I had the pleasure of being interviewed by Peter Weissbach, who was subhosting for Art Bell on the Premier Radio Network. Prior to the show, I discussed my Akashic Record scan technique and how it revealed Art's past life in Atlantis approximately 50000 B.C. as a geophysicist/quantum physicist named Drako.

Peter requested I repeat this technique and uncover one of his past lives. I agreed and used my Access the Akashic Records self-hypnosis tape at approximately 7 p.m. on March 24. It was very difficult to ascertain the data, but here is a summary of what I reported:

1. Peter was a member of the British House of Commons named Frederick Rash (Rashe or Rasch). These three spellings of his last name flashed before my eyes.
2. The years 1904, 1905, and 1906 also appeared.
3. Peter, as Frederick, was around 50 years old and very ill with a flu. He couldn't go to the House of Commons and was very angry at missing these sessions. He obsessed with being there, but was unable to leave his residence.
4. Strangely enough, when he finally did return to work, two of his colleagues commented on seeing him on the day he was ill and noticing him seated in the wrong chair. When they separately inquired about his health (he appeared rather pale), Rasch didn't acknowledge their presence.

My assumption was that Rash sent his astral body to the House of Commons due to his obsessive thoughts about missing these sessions. This is referred to as a bilocation.

I deduced this was not a teleportation (the *physical* body actually traveling from one location to another), because Rash did not respond to his colleagues. Teleporters easily converse with others, whereas most bilocaters do not.

Being swamped with calls, e-mails, and faxes, I didn't have a chance to research this life until Monday, March 27. I found a listing in *Whitaker's Almanac* (London) from 1905 confirming that a F. C. Rasch was indeed a member of the British House of Commons.

One of Art's listeners informed me on Monday that he read an article about Rasch in the *Whig Standard Magazine* of Kingston, Ontario, Canada (ironically, Peter is originally from Canada). He gave me the date of the publication (December 15, 1990), and I called the magazine to request a copy of the article. They faxed me a copy, and it confirmed the fact that Sir Fredrick Carne Rasch, a Unionist Member of Parliament representing the Chelmsford Division of Mid-Essex since 1900, had indeed become ill with the flu and was noticed by three members of the House of Commons (I stated two).

This case was reported originally in London's *Daily News* on May 17 and May 18, 1905. There is no way I could have known these facts. According to the *Whig Standard Report*, Rasch's astral body was not seated in his usual place and no other person (other than three colleagues) observed Rasch.

The three witnesses were Sir Gilbert Parker, Sir Arthur Hayter, and Sir Campbell-Bannerman (who was elected Prime Minister later in 1905). It isn't often that I document a case of reincarnation, but this is the first time I had one corroborated on the air. Try my "Access the Akashic Records" script and do this yourself.

1. Use any of the previous self-hypnosis or other exercises to relax and apply white light protection. Lie down or sit in an easy chair. When you are relaxed, turn your attention inward and center it on the area of the third eye. See it glow with a golden white radiance and feel it pulsate with energy. As you do this, your realization of the sounds, colors, and temperature in the room

around you should gradually fade, and as they do, the subtle psychic stirrings will become more noticeable.

2. At first, this may be only an impression of inner light, brilliantly illuminated geometrical figures, stars shooting by in ordered procession, or some other visual appearance, which will probably be meaningless. Or your first impression may be of sound, as I have previously described.
3. Focus your mind, not on the Akashic Records themselves, but on a specific historical event for your initial trials. For example, I suggest you study first the discovery of radium by Marie Curie or the signing of the Declaration of Independence in 1776.
4. Your next step is to go to that historical event and ask yourself: "What happened that afternoon?" If you have properly prepared yourself, you will find yourself drifting into a scenario-like dream.

   In the earlier stages of your development, you will not get clearly defined contacts that you can recognize, so don't expect them. Accept the dream-like sequence that passes before your consciousness as you sit in reverie. Remember what you observe and write it down as soon as possible thereafter.
5. During these practice sessions, you should "feel" this connection between your waking consciousness and the Akasha. When this has been accomplished and you can recall an incident from the past as simply as you can look up an account in the encyclopedia, you are then ready to move on to the next step.
6. Repeat the previous steps, omitting the preparation phase of reading about the historical event.

7. Check your data with specialty books written about that event in detail, not merely an encyclopedia summary.
8. After successful completion of this step, move on to your own future. Begin with a short range, say one week to a month. Log all of your observations into a journal and occasionally verify the accuracy of your prophecies.
9. With a proven track record, you are now ready to venture much farther ahead in time in your current life. Try five years, 10 years, 50 years, and so on.
10. You may move several hundred years into the future and explore future lives.
11. Lastly, tap into the general Akasha and allow your consciousness to tune into future world events, inventions, lifestyle changes, and so on.

Soul Plane Ascension

A soul plane ascension is merely an advanced superconscious mind tap. This dimension (the soul plane) is where we select our future lives.

Now listen very carefully. I want you to imagine a bright white light coming down from above and entering the top of your head, filling your entire body. See it, feel it, and it becomes reality. Now imagine an aura of pure white light emanating from your heart region, again, surrounding your entire body, protecting you. See it, feel it, and it becomes reality. Now only your Higher Self, masters, guides, and highly evolved loving entities who mean you well will be able to influence you during this or any other hypnotic session. You are totally protected by this aura of pure white light.

In a few moments, I am going to count from 1 to 20. As I do so, you will feel yourself rising up to the superconscious mind level where you will be able to receive information from your Higher Self and your masters and guides. Number 1 rising up, 2, 3, 4 rising higher, 5, 6, 7, letting information flow, 8, 9, 10, you are half way there, 11, 12, 13, feel yourself rising even higher, 14, 15, 16, almost there, 17, 18, 19, number 20, you are there. Take a moment and orient yourself to the superconscious mind level.

PLAY ASCENSION MUSIC FOR ONE MINUTE

Now from the superconscious mind level, you are going to rise up and beyond the karmic cycle and the five lower planes to the soul plane. The white light is always with you and you may be assisted by your masters and guides as you ascend to the soul plane. Number 1 rising up; 2, 3, 4 rising higher; 5, 6, 7, letting information flow; 8, 9, 10, you are halfway there; 11, 12, 13, feel yourself rising even higher; 14, 15, 16, almost there; 17, 18, 19, number 20, you are there. Take a moment and orient yourself to the soul plane.

PLAY ASCENSION MUSIC FOR ONE MINUTE

From the soul plane, you are able to perceive information from various sources and view all of your past lives, your current lifetime, and future lives, including all of your frequencies. Take a few moments now to evaluate this data and choose your next lifetime. Get a feel for the entire process.

PLAY ASCENSION MUSIC FOR SIX MINUTES

You have done very well. Now I want you to further open up the channels of communication by removing any obstacles and allow yourself to receive information and experiences that will directly apply to and help better your present lifetime. Allow yourself to receive more advanced and more specific information from the higher planes this time. Your Higher Self and masters and guides may assist you in receiving this all-important information that will help you raise your frequency and improve your karmic subcycle. Do this now.

PLAY ASCENSION MUSIC FOR EIGHT MINUTES

All right now. Sleep now and rest. You did very well. Listen very carefully. I'm going to count forward now from 1 to 5. When I reach the count of 5, you will be back in the present and on the Earth plane. You will be able to remember everything you experienced. You will feel very relaxed and refreshed, and you will be able to do whatever you have planned for the rest of the day or evening. You will feel very positive about what you've just experienced, and very motivated about your confidence and ability to play this tape again to experience the soul plane. All right now, 1, very, very deep; 2, you're getting a little bit lighter; 3, you're getting much, much lighter; 4, very, very light; 5, awaken wide awake and refreshed.

Conclusion

Death can be our best friend. It helps us to become aware of the other worlds that are denied to us on the physical plane. Death actually assists us in finding genuine happiness.

Skeptics still scoff and ridicule such notions. They declare there can be no consciousness after the physical body dies. The universe is comprised exclusively of material realities, and without the physical organism, there can be no mind, no consciousness, and certainly no life after death. Near-death experiences are but hallucinations caused by reasons that may be psychological, pharmacological, or neurological. It may be impossiblc for such a thing as objcctivc proof to cvcr actually exist in matters of the mind and spirit.

It may be argued that anyone who has not died cannot talk about death with authority, and because nobody apparently has ever returned from death (except near-death experiences), how can anybody know what death is, or what happens after it?

Tibetans will declare there is not one person, not one living being, that has not returned from death. In fact, we all have died many deaths before we came into this incarnation. What we call birth is merely the reverse side of death, like one of the two sides of a coin, or like a door that we call "entrance" from outside and "exit" from inside a room.

People in the West do not believe in rebirth because they cannot remember their past lives and deaths. Nobody remembers their birth, but the average person does not doubt their own presence in their current life. It is this dependence on the ego (conscious mind proper) and not their use of the subconscious that is the problem.

I have conducted more than 35,000 individual past life regressions and future life progressions on more than 14,000 individual patients. I can attest to the relative ease with which anyone with a little assistance from hypnosis can access their Akashic records and tap into these lifetimes.

Some of you may still have strong feelings of disbelief, skepticism, and mistrust. Others may gain additional support for their beliefs and hope for the future from reading this book. My hope is that you keep your mind open. It is not hypnotherapists who heal it is you who have the ultimate responsibility. Hypnosis allows you to expand and explore your awareness and eliminate fear, anxiety, depression, and other negative tendencies, as well as the fear of death. Hypnotherapy is neither magic nor a panacea—it is a way to help shape the future. By creating your own reality with the knowledge from your subconscious and superconscious minds, you can positively affect your present and future lives.

We sometimes forget that there is a God. God doesn't punish us—we punish ourselves. The soul always has free will. We can choose to do good or evil, right or wrong. We choose our future lives. Who would choose to kill, rape, steal, or cheat if he or she realized the karmic implications? By learning to use these principles to better ourselves, we are bettering the future for us all. The universe is connected by a linkage of the consciousness of all souls.

This entire process will end when you fulfill your karma. When you learn all the lessons you have to learn and show kindness and unselfish love to all those with whom you come into contact, the cycle will end. When it ends, you will go beyond the soul plane to the higher planes and reunite with God.

I would like to end this book with a discussion of the ascension process based on my 30 years of clinical research with hypnotherapy.

Many people ask me to help them speed up their karmic cycles so that they won't have to come back again. I can't do that. Only patients themselves can do that. They must be honest, truthful, and faithful to their own code of ethics. If they follow this simple advice, they are well on their way to the higher planes.

Our karmic cycles end when we fulfill our karma. When we learn all the lessons necessary to show kindness and unselfish love to all those with whom we come into contact, our cycles will end. When they end, we will go beyond the soul plane to the higher planes and, eventually, to God. Karma is merely a process of evolution, of achieving greater levels of enlightenment.

Our true and only purpose is to perfect our soul and ascend to the higher planes to reunite with God, or whatever you term the perfect energy that created our universe. So let us discuss this all-important concept.

What I term *ascension* has been called many things. Some describe this state as transcendence, nirvana, or bliss, while Christians label this as the attainment of grace.

Within each of us resides a type of spiritual consciousness that assists us in our path back to God, from which we came. This can only be accomplished when our karma is eliminated, and our soul reaches a state of perfection. You may be familiar with the physical realm of the universe around us, but there are other levels of which you may not be aware.

These other planes or dimensions make up our karmic cycle, including the physical world. They are both transient and illusory. It is your inner world of consciousness, or soul, that is true reality. Joy, peace, and love dominate this inter-universe, while sensations and various temptations steering us from our path of spiritual growth are emphasized in the physical realm.

These dimensions make up the lower five planes, or karmic cycle. They are, in order of decreasing density of the matter that comprises them, the physical, astral, causal, mental, etheric, and soul plane. It is on the soul plane where we will eventually ascend to the higher planes and reunite with God. Until that occurs, this realm is used to select our future incarnations.

Becoming attuned to your soul is easy when your emotions and thoughts are quieted, as in the state of hypnosis. You can now be prepared to receive that which is of God. As you receive information from your Higher Self, a manifestation of love is felt all through your very being. Now you begin to live free and in the moment. No longer are you hung up in the past, or worried about the future.

All actions will be directed toward awakening your soul from its Earth plane sleep to a far more enlightened level of consciousness. Fears, prejudices, and judgments slowly disappear from your awareness as you evolve spiritually. The resulting expansion of this awareness will allow God to reveal the truth once and for all to you. It will be like no other you have read or thought of yourself. I call this the ultimate truth, which we will discuss shortly.

By moving your consciousness into the soul and experiencing the pure wonders of the universe, your ability to learn and forgive magnifies. This greatly facilitates your soul's ability to prepare itself for its final movement—ascension to God.

Even if you believe in reincarnation and God, the personal application of this paradigm as your time on the physical plane draws to a close, is most often associated with anxiety and trepidation. Ascension removes you from the cycle of birth and death, and allows you to enter the heavenly words ("eternal now") to join God. You do have the option of remaining on these lower planes as a guide, but free of the discomforts you currently experience.

The Ultimate Truth

It must always be remembered that we exist as a microcosm in a vast macrocosm of the universe. Only by allowing a greater consciousness to penetrate our very being can we grow spiritually and rise above the illusions of the physical plane that hide the truth from us. The higher planes do not incorporate the duality and limitations that we accept in our daily lives. This pure knowledge results in the purest and most concentrated form of ecstasy that man is capable of experiencing.

Usually this process of illumination is quite gradual. Sometimes one first sees little flashes of light—they are called"stars"—when a truth is spoken or when a new idea strikes. These are gone in an instant, a fraction of a second. Later, usually when at ease with the eyes closed, a broader flash of brilliant light will appear, light very much like the brightest sunlight. This too lasts but an instant, but when it is repeated, it lingers a little longer each time. Slowly our inner vision is developed and grace or ascension is then attainable.

The divine consciousness in everything is felt and observed on these higher worlds. By seeking the truth now through very simple techniques, we can get a glimpse of this hidden unity of the God force in everything. I train all of my patients to accomplish this goal by way of hypnotic techniques I term the superconscious mind tap and soul plane ascension, which is an advanced type of superconscious mind tap.

The ultimate truth cannot be realized through philosophy, religion, willpower, or mysticism alone. It is only when we allow the perfect energy of God to manifest in us that we are placed in a position to receive our truth. Each of us will formulate a different truth based on our own experiences, level of spiritual development, and exposure to higher levels of awareness.

Enlightenment is the term we apply when we receive this truth. Fear is always at the top of the list of factors that impede spiritual growth. Almost everyone fears death, and this tendency increases as we age. Many elderly patients of mine initially describe their fear of death as entering a dark world, where there is nothing but a black void.

The "truths" of the lower realms do not apply on the higher realms. Each dimension has its own truth, which applies to it alone. These truths are always superseded by the truths of realms beyond it. Truth as we perceive it during our spiritual evolution is always relative to the ultimate truth.

To experience the truth we are seeking does not require a renunciation of our physical life as we have established it. It is only an alternation of the mind's programming and the fears and inhibitions that are consequences of society's brainwashing.

Once we maintain this connection with our Higher Self, then we can free ourselves from the tyranny of the belief that causes outside ourselves affect us. Because consciousness is spirit, the world we live in is an infinite number of consciousness. The worlds or planes beyond the physical are merely a continuation of these countless levels of consciousness.

The process of both accessing and joining our Higher Self leads to a recognition that we are never separated from the God energy. Our Higher Self is an extension of this God energy that is at our disposal for advice, comfort, and spiritual growth at any time we choose.

Psychic Empowerment

We can improve the state of consciousness we observe by entering into a level of awareness we desire and becoming one with it. This is our *psychic empowerment*, the ability to determine our own spiritual growth and perfection of our soul.

The principal of psychic empowerment can never be overemphasized. Spirit is the true underlying cause of all effects we observe. We must eliminate dependency on any person, place, thing, or paradigm that detours us from our spiritual path. Our Higher Self is the inner force that will shape and direct our lives in a manner allowing us to take charge of our world and raise our consciousness simultaneously.

The Path to Ascension

In order to place yourself on the path to attain the state of grace, there are certain things you need to do and to avoid. First, you need to give up seeking God in the manner to which you have been accustomed. It is neither necessary nor desirable to seek God actively. We are always in the presence of the God energy (Higher Self), so we are only distracting ourselves by this artificial pursuit.

The process of attaining grace involves facilitating the expression of our Higher Self through our soul. We are created in the image of God because the state of grace is our natural destiny. This process consists of us functioning as a channel for God through our Higher Self as a type of agent.

One of our purposes spiritually is to allow the grace of God the opportunity to use each one of us as a vehicle for this supreme consciousness. The reward for this is ascension, and liberation of our soul from the wheel of birth and death is karma.

Our Higher Self is composed of perfect energy. Ascension is actually the process of the merging of our subconscious mind with its Higher Self. The conscious mind dies when the physical body dies. Only the subconscious and superconscious survive physical death.

The various masters and saints have known these principles throughout history. By expanding our consciousness through altered states of consciousness (hypnosis, meditation, yoga, etc.), our questions will be answered, and our souls purified. We all have this God-given talent to transcend the material world and attain these realizations.

Notes

Introduction

1. S. Rosen. *The Reincarnation Controversy: Uncovering the Truth in the World Religions.* Badger, CA: Torchlight Pub. Inc., 1997.

Chapter 1

1. M. Bernstein. *The Search for Bridey Murphy.* New York: Doubleday & Co., 1956.

2. B. Goldberg. *Past Lives—Future Lives.* New York: Ballantine, 1988.

3. ———. *Time Travelers from Our Future: A Fifth Dimension Odyssey.* Sun Lakes, AZ: Book World, Inc. 1999.

Chapter 3

1. B. Goldberg. *Past Lives—Future Lives.* New York: Ballantine, 1988.

Chapter 4

1. B. Goldberg. *The Search for Grace: A Documented Case of Murder and Reincarnation.* Sedona, AZ: 1994.

Chapter 6

1. B. Goldberg. *Protected by the Light: The Complete Book of Psychic Self-Defense.* Tucson, AZ: Hats Off Books, 1999.

Chapter 16

1. Morris, M. S., K. S. Thorne, and U. Yurtsever. "Wormholes, Time Machines and the Weak Energy Condition." *Physical Review Letters, 61* (13) (1988): pp. 1446–1449.

2. S. Hawking. *A Brief History of Time* (New York: Bantam Books, 1988).

Chapter 17

1. Sumeria was one of the first civilizations. It was located in present day Iraq and existed from 4,000 B.C. to about 2100 B.C.

2. Lemuria or Mu is the lost continent in the Pacific Ocean equivalent to Atlantis in the Atlantic Ocean as an advanced civilization from 200,000 B.C. to 11,000 B.C.

Chapter 18

1. A selection of New Age music is available from my Website.

Bibliography

DeWitt, Bryce S. "Quantum Mechanics and Reality" *Physics Today*, September 1970, 30–35.

Dunne, J. W. *An Experiment with Time*, New York: Macmillan, 1927.

Goldberg, Bruce. *Dream Your Problems Away: Heal Yourself While You Sleep*. Franklin Lakes, N.J.: New Page Books, 2003.

———. *Past Lives—Future Lives*. New York: Ballantine Books, 1988.

———. *Soul Healing*. St. Paul, Minn.: Llewellyn Pub., 1997.

———. *Astral Voyages: Mastering the Art of Interdimensional Travel*. St. Paul, Minn.: Llewellyn Pub., 1999.

———. *Protected by the Light: The Complete Book on Psychic Self-Defense.* Tucson, Ariz: Hats Off Books, 1999.

———. *Self-Hypnosis: Easy Ways to Hypnotize Your Problems Away.* Franklin Lakes, N.J.: New Page Books, 2001.

———. *Custom Design Your Own Destiny*. Salt Lake City, Utah: Millennial Mind Pub., 2000.

———. *Peaceful Transition: The Art of Conscious Dying and the Liberation of the Soul*. St. Paul, Minn.: Llewellyn Pub., 1997.

———. *The Search for Grace: A Documented Case of Murder and Reincarnation*. Sedona, Ariz: In Print Pub., 1994.

———. *Look Younger, Live Longer Naturally: Add 25 to 50 Quality Years to Your Life.* St. Paul, Minn.: Llewellyn Pub., 1998.

———. *Time Travelers from Our Future: A Fifth Dimension Odyssey*. Sun Lakes, Ariz.: Book World, Inc., 1999.

———. *New Age Hypnosis*. St. Paul, Minn.: Llewellyn Pub., 1998.

———. *Unleash Your Psychic Powers*. New York, N.Y.: Sterling Pub. Co., Inc., 1997.

———. "Slowing down the aging process through the use of altered states of consciousness: A review of the medical literature." *Psychology—A Journal of Human Behavior*, 1995: 32(2), 19–22.

———. "Regression and Progression in Past Life Therapy." *National Guild of Hypnotists Newsletter*, 1994: Jan/Feb, 1, 10.

———. "Quantum Physics and its application to past life regression and future life progression hypnotherapy." *Journal of Regression Therapy*, 1993: 7(1), 89–93.

———. "Depression: a past life cause" *National Guild of Hypnotists Newsletter*, 1993: Oct/Nov, 7, 14.

———. "The clinical use of hypnotic regression and progression in hypnotherapy." *Psychology—A Journal of Human Behavior*, 1990: 27(1), 43–48.

———. "The treatment of cancer through hypnosis." *Psychology—A Journal of Human Behavior*, 1985: 3(4), 36–39.

———. "Hypnosis and the immune response." *International Journal of Psychosomatics*, 1985: 32 (3), 34–36.

———. "Treating dental phobias through past life therapy: a case report" *Journal of the Maryland State Dental Association*, 1984: 27(3), 137–139.

Head, J. and S. L. Cranston. *Reincarnation: The Phoenix Fire Mysteries*, New York: Julian, 1977.

Hodson, G. *Reincarnation: Fact or Fallacy*. Wheaton, Ill.: The Theosophical Publishing House, 1967.

Kaufmann, W. J. *Black Holes and Warped Space-Time*. San Francisco: Freeman, 1979.

Morris, M. S., Thorne, K. S. and Yortsever, U. "Wormholes, Time Machines and the Weak Energy Condition." *Physical Review Letters*, 1988, 61(13), 1446-1449.

Rogo, D. S. *The Search for Yesterday: A Critical Examination of the Evidence of Reincarnation*. Englewood Cliffs, NJ: Prentice Hall, 1985.

Rosen, S. *The Reincarnation Controversy*. Badger, CA: Torchlight Pub. Inc., 1997.

Sanderson, Ivan. *Uninvited Visitors: A Biologist Looks at UFOs*. New York: Cowles Educational Corp., 1967.

Talbot, M. *The Holographic Universe*. New York: Harper Collins, 1991.

Tart, C. *Altered States of Consciousness*. New York: John Wiley & Sons, 1969.

Thorne, K. S. *Black Holes and Time Warps: Einstein's Outrageous Legacy*. New York: W. W. Norton & Co., 1994.

Wambach, Helen. *Life Before Life*. New York: Boston Books, 1979.

Wolf, F. A. *Taking the Quantum Leap*. New York: Harper & Row, 1981.

———. *Parallel Universe: The Search for Other Worlds*. New York: Simon and Schuster, 1988.

Wolf, F. A. and B. Toben. *Space-Time and Beyond*. New York: Bantam Books, 1982.

Index

C

D

E

Q

R

S

About the Author

Dr. Bruce Goldberg holds a B.A. degree in biology and chemistry, is a doctor of dental surgery, and has a M.S. degree in counseling psychology. He retired from dentistry in 1989, and has concentrated on his hypnotherapy practice in Los Angeles. Dr. Goldberg was trained by the American Society of Clinical Hypnosis in his techniques and clinical applications of hypnosis.

Dr. Goldberg has been interviewed on such show as *Sally, Donahue, Oprah, Leeza, Joan Rivers, The Other Side, Regis and Kathie Lee, Tom Snyder, Jerry Springer, Jenny Jones*, and *Montel Williams*, as well as by CNN and CBS news.

Through lectures, television, radio appearances, and magazine and newspaper articles, including interviews in *Time*, the *Los Angeles Times*, and the *Washington Post*, he has conducted more than 35,000 past-life regressions and future-life progressions since 1974, helping thousands of patients empower themselves through these techniques. His cassette tapes teach people self-hypnosis and guide them into past and future lives and time travel. He gives lectures and seminars on hypnosis, regression, and progression therapy, time travel, and conscious dying; he is also a consultant to corporations, attorneys, and the local and network media.

His first edition of *The Search for Grace* was made into a television movie by CBS. His third book, the award-winning *Soul Healing*, is a classic on alternative medicine and psychic empowerment. *Past Lives—Future Lives* is Dr. Goldberg's international best-seller and is the first book written on future lives (progression hypnotherapy).

For information on self-hypnosis tapes, speaking engagements, or private sessions, Dr. Goldberg can be contacted directly by writing to:

Bruce Goldberg, D.D.S., M.S.
4300 Natoma Avenue
Woodland Hills, CA 91364
Telephone (800) KARMA-4-U or (800) 527-6248
Fax: (818) 704-9189
E-mail: karma4u@webtv.net
Website: *www.drbrucegoldberg.com*

Please include a self-addressed, stamped envelope with your letter.

Other Books by Dr. Bruce Goldberg

Past Lives—Future Lives

Soul Healing

The Search for Grace: The True Story of Murder and Reincarnation

Peaceful Transition: The Art of Conscious Dying and the Liberation of the Soul

New Age Hypnosis

Secrets of Self-Hypnosis

Unleash Your Psychic Powers

Look Younger and Live Longer: Add 25 to 50 Quality Years to Your Life Naturally

Protected by the Light: The Complete Book of Psychic Self-Defense

Time Travelers from Our Future: A Fifth Dimension Odyssey

Astral Voyages: Mastering the Art of Interdimensional Travel

Custom Design Your Own Destiny

Self-Hypnosis: Easy Ways to Hypnotize Your Problems Away

Dream Your Problems Away: Heal Yourself While You Sleep